D1706709

A WINTER'S JOURNAL

EMMANUEL BOVE

A WINTER'S JOURNAL

TRANSLATED BY NATHALIE FAVRE-GILLY

AFTERWORD BY KEITH BOTSFORD

THE MARLBORO PRESS / NORTHWESTERN

EVANSTON, ILLINOIS

The Marlboro Press/Northwestern
Northwestern University Press
Evanston, Illinois 60208-4210

Originally published in French in 1931 under the title *Journal écrit en hiver* by Émile-Paul Frères. English translation published by arrangement with Flammarion, Paris. English translation copyright © 1998 by Nathalie Favre-Gilly. Afterword copyright © 1998 by Keith Botsford. Published 1998 by The Marlboro Press/Northwestern. All rights reserved.

Printed in the United States of America

ISBN 0-8101-6046-3 (cloth)
ISBN 0-8101-6047-1 (paper)

Library of Congress Cataloging-in-Publication Data

Bove, Emmanuel, 1898–
    [Journal écrit en hiver. English]
    A winter's journal / Emmanuel Bove ; translated by Nathalie Favre-Gilly ; afterword by Keith Botsford.
        p. cm.
    ISBN 0-8101-6046-3 (cloth : alk. paper). — ISBN 0-8101-6047-1 (paper : alk. paper)
    I. Favre-Gilly, Nathalie. II. Title.
PQ2603.O87J6813 1998
843'.912—DC21   97-43700
                                                                        CIP

CONTENTS

A WINTER'S JOURNAL

Madeleine likes to pretend she's unaware that people say complimentary things about her. If you tell her that one of her friends finds her beautiful, she'll react with surprise and appear incapable of believing such a thing could be true, in spite of the fact she just heard it from someone else the day before. She has no fear her interlocutor might suspect her surprise isn't genuine, and even goes so far as to ask for details with apparently complete sincerity. It happened again today. Jacques Imbault came to see us this evening. In the course of the conversation, he told my wife that he had seen her photograph in a magazine. "I didn't know," he added ironically, "that you had been *engaged* as a model." Jacques Imbault thinks he is terribly inventive, and to ensure others realize this about himself there are certain words he uses constantly, one of which is "engage." A few days ago, for instance, I happened to meet him near the coat check at a theater. I had misplaced my check, and he noticed me lingering there waiting for all the coats to have been claimed so that I could then collect my own property. As I was waiting rather absentmindedly, as though it were my job to ensure that the service ran smoothly, he said to me with a laugh: "My word, the management has *engaged* you as a security guard!"

In spite of the fact that Madeleine had shown me the magazine only yesterday, railing against the photographers and even threatening to sue the publisher—though not, however, without betraying a certain satisfaction—she pretended to be surprised. "Do tell, Jacques, what magazine was it? We'll have to get a copy right away." Most outrageous of all was that, having asked our friend a great number of questions, she suddenly remembered everything. That sudden recovery of memory was what I found most ridiculous. Acting astonished when a friend tells you he's heard of some generous thing you did is just about excusable, but to recall a moment later that you did indeed perform such an action is intolerable. Madeleine, however, feels that once the pleasure of reviewing remarks made about her has passed, there is no reason to continue with the pretense of ignorance. She then owns up, never suspecting for a moment that her interlocutor might find this sudden about-face strange. If there is one thing my wife seems to think impossible, it is that anyone might guess what she's thinking. Blatant though her insinuations might be, it will never cross her mind that her motives might be transparent. In this respect, we are opposites. Whereas I always take great care to weigh my words carefully, lest I appear self-serving, petty, or overly vain, Madeleine thinks she conceals her hand so well that she can allow herself to make the most incredible about-face without running the slightest risk. When—after having apparently forgotten the fact—she suddenly remembered today that her photograph had indeed appeared in a weekly magazine, it never occurred to her that Jacques might think she'd remembered it all along. What I find most distressing is that when I try to correct her, when I try to show her how this sort of behavior invites irony, she becomes angry, as though all I see are her reprehensible traits. She accuses me of being jeal-

4

ous, of thinking that the world is wicked, never for a second perceiving the truth in my observations, nor the profound love which is at the heart of my desire that she not be the laughingstock of our friends. She doesn't understand I'm only trying to protect her. Instead, she thinks that I go out of my way to discover faults in her which no one else has noticed.

October 12th

As a child, I was afraid of everything, which irritated my mother, one of whose excellent principles was that one should never raise one's hand against a child. Having never struck me, she could not understand why I was so fearful. She found it all the more disagreeable because such exaggerated fearfulness could lead others to believe that she did in fact strike me. "Come now, don't act so fearful, my child. Everyone thinks that you're being tortured." But as a result of hearing myself criticized for being afraid, I came to dread being afraid, which made me doubly timid and liable to burst into tears for a mere nothing. Although I wasn't even conscious of this, deep within myself it seemed to me that tears were like a hedge that served to conceal everything. Those tears, however, were what made my mother lose her temper. Instead of being accused of being afraid of everything, I came to be criticized for crying as though I were unhappy, when in fact it was fear that left me in such a desperate state. A mere nothing made me tremble, and those mere nothings never came from the outside; they all came from within me. If I happened to knock something over, I would immediately think I'd committed some unpardonable offense. If I forgot to kiss my father, I no longer dared appear before him. At every moment it seemed to me that I had done something reprehensible for which he was going to punish me, even though I had never been punished. I was paralyzed by my fear of being punished, of being lectured. It sometimes even happened that, while playing with children of my own age, I would forget myself to the point of laughing and running about, then suddenly recall some insignificant misdemeanor, dirt on my shirt or a scrape on my leg, as a result of which I would tremble with fear that I would be punished for having dirtied myself or fallen down. As I grew older, this anxiety increased rather than disappearing.

When I reached the age of fifteen, my father decided to send me to boarding school to temper my character and prepare me to fend for myself in life. The morning came when he himself accompanied me to Oloron. Preparations had been made the day before. While my mother had rushed about, afraid she was forgetting something, a feeling of isolation had been creeping over me, for nothing breeds greater loneliness than when the people we love replace the reality of an imminent separation with obligations, preparations, and duties, however much these are dictated by love. Watching my mother come and go, I thought: "Why pay so much attention to things and so little to me?" From time to time, seeing I was doing nothing, she would reprimand me gently. She had made these same reprimands so often in the past, but always with the added threat, "You'll see how you'll change when you're at Oloron," that I was unable, that evening, to stop myself from thinking that if I was being shown any affection at all, it was only because this was my last day. There is a certain sadness, when abandoning one home for another, in watching rooms being stripped bare, furniture from different parts of the house assembled haphazardly, an object we hold dear slipped hurriedly, for want of space, into an indifferent trunk. A distressing sense of being out of one's element is born of all the commotion, of the suddenly deserted apartment with the next one yet to be occupied. But when everything is staying behind and we alone are leaving, when our possessions are being gathered from various parts of the house where, once they've been removed, their absence won't be felt, and we sense that as soon as we're far away life will go on without us just as it did in the past, that feeling of sadness is even greater. I was doing nothing, but that night, when I went to bed alone in my room—where nothing remained on the table and in the wardrobes—I felt so unhappy that I began to cry. With my head hidden beneath the sheets, I cried noiselessly, paying no attention to the tears which, in other circumstances, I would have tried to wipe away. As I abandoned myself this way, taking care only to make no noise—which was in fact a delicious stimulant—I experienced a sort of joyful despair. I was thinking about nothing at all, and when, from time to time, I felt myself beginning to calm down, I would think, "I'm going to be so unhappy," and would immediately begin sobbing again even harder. Then, suddenly, I heard the door of my room open. I opened my eyes. Through the sheets I saw a pale yellow light, and I immediately felt such a sense of shame at being discovered that I lay there as though paralyzed, as a result of which I simulated sleep without even thinking about it, with the extravagant hope that all would pass unnoticed. My body, which was betraying me by twitching convulsively beneath the covers, was soon drenched in sweat. And then I heard my father's voice above me. I can still recall how it filled me with that strange fear of being finished off one feels when one has fallen and a crowd gathers around to try and help. His voice was gentle: "You mustn't cry this way, Louis, you're a big boy now. What would your friends think, if they could see you?" As befits an excessively indulgent man, it pleased my father to appear to prefer that his child conduct himself well with his friends rather than with him.

Just then, I experienced a strange sensation which I must mention here, for it reveals something about my personality. Upon hearing his words, my blood suddenly ran cold. As a child, one of my peculiar preoccupations was to ask myself constantly how others could know what I'd been doing. I was hiding beneath the covers and yet my father knew I was crying. I was staggered by this, just as I was when, having made a detour on my way home from school, my father would tell me, without at all seeming to have made a discovery, but simply because he knew that children liked to take this route because of certain shops they passed along the way: "Louis, you know I don't like you to take that street on your way home." I would be struck dumb that he could have guessed. And I was forever being surprised by similar divinations. Although my face had been hidden from him that evening, by telling me not to cry my father had done it yet again. This was the very thing I couldn't bear. My reddened eyelids trembling in the light, my cheeks still damp, I sat up and said in one breath, "I'm not crying . . . I'm not crying . . . " "But there's nothing wrong with crying," replied my father. "You can cry. I'm not reproaching you."

All of that is over now. And yet, I'm still not a man like other men, even if I act as they do as in everyday circumstances. I no longer fear losing my freedom. In spite of this, only a few years ago, before I was married, I was still getting involved with women I scarcely knew, in the way that young men do. Despite my age, I have no prudence, no experience. I know that I seem somewhat backward, that I'm like a child, and that I'm probably accumulating the worst possible vices for my old age. Am I to blame? Should I hold someone responsible for this state, my poor father perhaps, who tried everything he could to make me into a man ready to face the world, to do battle, even going so far as to force me to spend an hour a day working with a carpenter while I was studying for my bachelor's degree?

This need to have what others have, to imitate, this willingness to assume that because someone is doing something then everyone except me is doing it: clearly these are the traits of a young man. Holidays, for example, are torture for me. I'm tempted by everything, and yet feel that I'm deprived of everything because I can only do one thing. It never occurs to me that all the people I envy, all the people I see, are in exactly the same situation I'm in and that they, too, can only do one thing at a time. As a group, they make me think they're doing everything. And it's true, they are doing everything, but only because there are thousands of them. But instead of selecting one of them and observing him alone, watching attentively to discover how similar we are, I have yet to progress past the point of watching them all.

But let's go back to what my life has been. When I look at young people today, I'm astonished at how precocious they are. Perhaps that's because I see them as a group rather than observing them individually. I'm struck by how lively they are, by how strong they seem, and above all by how orderly they appear to be. When I think back to how I was at eighteen, at twenty, and even at twenty-five, I sometimes turn bright red with shame. Occasionally I ask men my age if they remember their childhoods, their younger days, and when one of them raises a hand heavenward as though recalling how foolish he was, I feel a great sense of relief. But for every man who raises that hand to the skies, there are countless others who seem to regret the qualities they once possessed! Yes, when I look back on the young man I was, I wonder what miracle occurred which made it possible for me to possess some semblance of intelligence today, by what miracle I managed to avoid any catastrophes. At twenty, I knew nothing of life, nor was I even seeking to know anything. I was moved by the most insignificant of events. In my eyes, evil did not exist. I moved through life as though I were eternal, as though death would never find me. Defending myself against someone struck me as an extraordinarily base thing to do. This attitude stayed with me for a very long time. Arguing, haggling, doubting the pronouncements of insignificant people, these were all things I long found impossible. I was made to have no artifice, to trust in everyone. I thought neither of loving nor of being loved. I was still this way at an age when most young men already had their first mistress. Then, bit by bit, I grew tougher. If I dreamed of getting married and setting up my own household, it was more out of the need I felt to emulate my father and exercise authority over a family, as he did, than from any authentic desire of my own to do so. My vision of a family was so deeply ingrained in my mind that, for years and years, I found it impossible to believe this was a goal I could ever attain. In the models I imagined, some element I had enjoyed in my own childhood was always lacking. I would try, for example, to compare my future friends to those my parents had always had. Mine always seemed somehow less stable. Everything that belonged to me resonated with a less substantial sound than that which belonged to my parents. And what could be more typical of a young man than this unwillingness to believe in the present, this belief that the past was both better and more important, this inability to understand that my father's friend M. Guizot, for example, had not been any dearer to him than Etienne, the friend of whom I'm very fond, would be to my wife and me?

October 13th

As Madeleine complained of having a migraine after dinner, I asked whether she'd mind if I went to see André Mercier and his wife. "Go where you like, dear boy," she replied. I know it doesn't make my wife at all unhappy when I go out at night this way. To arouse her jealousy, however, I'll go so far as to pretend I'm terribly pleased to be going out, hoping to elicit at least an angry word from her, anything to show she isn't utterly indifferent to me. With time, however, she has come to believe I have no deep feelings for her, and what irritates me and makes me exaggerate my attitude all the more is that, far from holding this against me, she seems utterly resigned. But let's leave my worries aside. M. Mercier is a decent fellow, a tradesman I've grown friendly with, although I'm usually rather unsociable. It's wrong of me to admit this or boast about it, but I have very few friends, and a rather amusing situation has arisen between Mercier and myself. Although we are very solicitous with one another, whenever we meet we confess we don't trust anyone, and neither one of us ever dares ask the other whether our friendship is the exception to this rule.

I had been at the Merciers only a few minutes when Maud Bringer arrived. Ten years ago, this young woman was an absolutely delicious creature. Picture a beautiful young girl, full of freshness, imagination, and charm, moving through life without ever noticing the attention she attracted. Although compliments and tributes rained down upon her, she paid no attention to them. Oblivious to the world around her, all she did was radiate inner grace. At that time we were very much in love, and if I happened to hurt her in some way, it never even occurred to her to hold it against me. Nor did it ever cross her mind to give more of her attention to the many young people who gravitated to her. There was something deeply moving about this young girl, who could have made me the unhappiest of men at the drop of a hat, but was so unaware of her power that it was she herself, in fact, who suffered at my hands.

At the time, my jealousy was something hellish. The most insignificant of details provoked it, and although I was conscious of it, I made no attempt to control it. I reproached Maud for everything, for talking to her father, for going out with her brother, for uttering a man's first name, for knowing that my cousin had quarreled with a friend or was lucky at any game he turned his hand to, for admiring poets, or painters. I renewed my attacks constantly. I needed only hear her say that she liked something, flowers, or a town, for me to loathe it and criticize it relentlessly, for weeks on end, awaiting the deliverance that came when she yielded and ceased liking those flowers or that town. She accepted my jealousy as a proof of my love. I was terrified she would discover that I had been equally tyrannical with women who meant nothing to me. With extraordinary patience, she put up with my whims, with the most ludicrous of my desires, and when, after a fit of temper, I would remember what she'd said to placate me, I would marvel at such a surfeit of wisdom and indulgence.

Those calm interludes never lasted. If anything at all was troubling me, I vented my frustrations on her. Bit by bit, my demands became such that I wonder today how she ever accepted them. One day, I begged her not to kiss her father ever again. I don't recall the theatrics I employed to make her understand just how unbearable I found it that a man, be it her own father, should press his lips against her cheek. "But that's impossible!" she replied. Of course I knew my request was impossible, in spite of which I persisted in my demand, even swearing I would never see her again if she didn't obey. I was constantly resorting to blackmail. If she refused to yield, even on a trifling point, I would immediately threaten to leave for God knows what distant country. She would grow pale, and I could feel she was grappling with a terrible dilemma. Nonetheless, I would be prevented from reassuring her by the wickedness within me, by that harshness I have been unable to eradicate completely. With deliberate cruelty, I would refuse to give in. She would start to cry, and it was only after she'd calmed down that I would beg for her forgiveness.

The next day, however, I wouldn't be able to stop myself from repeating the whole scene all over again. After a delicious hour spent in her company, I would abruptly remember that she had refused to agree to ask her father not to kiss her anymore. A sort of blind rage would rise within me. Once again I would harass her mercilessly, until she broke down and cried.

Several months before meeting Maud Bringer, I had flirted with one of her friends, Simone Charavel, who was the sister of one of my friends. Unlike Maud, she was flirtatious and knowing. At sixteen, she was already inventing excuses to meet boys after school. Although the feelings I had for her were nowhere near as deep as those I later had for Maud, I tormented her in the same way. I cared less for her, and yet I suffered more. She would laugh at my pretentiousness. One day I told her, "You'll see the power I'm going to have over you, Simone: the day will come when I'll even forbid you to kiss your father." She burst out laughing. As I had so little hold over her, I began to lose interest. That was when I met Maud.

One day, after an incredibly violent quarrel, Maud failed to appear. All at once my boldness vanished. I was afraid of losing her, of having gone too far. I called her on the phone, using some vague pretext. I got her mother, who was short with me.

I spent the entire day keeping watch in front of her house. She never came out. I was panic-stricken, I had only one desire: to see her. I called again. This time, her brother answered. He informed me quite kindly that Maud was unwell and would not be out for three or four days. This reassured me, and I rushed home with the hope that she had sent me a note. But there was nothing. I spent the next few days in a highly anxious state. Despite feeling awkward at finding myself in the presence of a family I had so often maligned, I could no longer hold off from going to see her. After having made me wait a long time, she finally appeared. Her face was changed, thinner. She looked at me sadly and then, as I was saying nothing, she said, "Later on, when both you and I are free, we can see each other again. That will be much better for you, Louis, and for me." I was thunderstruck. In hushed tones, I begged her to forgive me. I had no idea what to do to win her back. But patient as she had been, her mind was now firmly made up. I hadn't seen her since that day. All I'd been able to learn about her was that she'd married.

When she suddenly appeared at the Merciers, I was deeply moved. She was no different from the young girl I had known. Upon seeing me, she showed no sign of turmoil. But somewhat later, seeing I was alone in a corner, she drew near. After having exchanged a few banalities, she asked me whether I remembered our past friendship. Then, trembling slightly, she added, "You mustn't think, Louis, that I still hold it against you. On the contrary, I have been reproaching myself, I was unfair to you." As she uttered these words, a painful sensation came over me. She spoke with feeling, as though still suffused with the past, but as I listened to her I was surprised to realize that her voice stirred no regrets in me. She was addressing the young man I had been, as if there were no distance separating me from him. It seemed to me that she could just as easily have spoken those same words a week after her monumental decision. She had preserved everything intact within herself. Her marriage had not erased anything. And what may be even sadder still is that she now thought she had been unfair, and was guilty at the idea that she had made me suffer, whereas I, who was the real guilty party, had forgotten everything.

October 16th

We had dinner at a restaurant. There was a time, several years ago, when Madeleine always felt a need to try and help those serving whenever she was being waited on. But she was so embarrassed when a well-schooled waiter refused to be assisted, and she blushed so furiously, that ever since she has remained utterly impassive when in the presence of any servant. Ever since that rebuke, she even seems to think it a form of distinction never to assist a waiter in any way, and indeed to hinder him in his work. I could, in fact, list thousands of similar details. They are the result of her upbringing. For example, she likes to give outlandish tips to people who are unaccustomed to receiving any at all, and whom I always fear will refuse her. She also has a tendency to address people by their profession. When we traveled to Nice, she said, "Conductor, save us two seats." It is quite possible that conductors don't take offense, but I am terribly embarrassed by this. Fortunately, she is always somewhat more restrained when indoors. In the street, however, it isn't unusual for her to approach a police officer and say, "Could you tell me, constable, where to find X street . . . ?" This trait of hers brings back memories of our stay in Nice.

Every "health resort" has its facade and its back streets,

though the latter are far more visible than in a big city. Behind the row of hotels looking out over the sea, there will always be a rue des Belges, a rue des Serbes. It's here, in the wings, that the less well-heeled winter visitors take up residence. I would have preferred a good hotel in the city center, but Madeleine insisted we choose one of these rooming houses. When she married, it never occurred to her that her life was going to change, and she wanted the two of us to live just as she would have done had she come to Nice alone. What Madeleine liked were places where, by the affluence she displayed, it would be understood that she had come because she wanted the family-like atmosphere, and that although she belonged to "society" she preferred the peace of an out-of-the-way place to the bustle of a grand hotel. She seemed terribly amused by the lodgers' habits. She would let out astonished cries whenever a ritual differed from what she was accustomed to, as though in her mind the only difference between a boardinghouse and a grand hotel was not the luxury and exquisiteness of the service but the tranquillity, and that these new habits were in no way worse than her own, but merely different. And yet one could see, if only by her astonishment, that she did find them worse. She graciously obeyed the strict regulations, barely letting it show that she knew things were done differently elsewhere. The other lodgers all seemed taken in by this. They came to believe that we were intelligent and, leaving aside all financial considerations, that we preferred the lunches and dinners provided by Mlle Davis to those of the large hotels. Mlle Davis herself, in fact, kept this belief alive, never failing to recount how, the year before, a certain prince had left the Hotel des Anglais in disgust and come to take up residence at her establishment. To hear her tell it, all of her clients had, at some point, been far worse off elsewhere. After many a disappointment, they had finally found Mlle Davis.

I don't know why I've just remembered Madeleine used to tell me at that time that, if ever we had a child, we should buy it furniture, a bathtub, a bicycle, all made to his size. She greatly relished the idea that children should inhabit a world scaled down to their proportions. Needless to say, I found this ridiculous. I remember, too, the walks we used to take along the seafront. Madeleine, who has no insight and thinks the man standing before her is the noblest man on earth when in fact he is a scoundrel, would suddenly think herself equipped with superior powers of deduction when deciding the extent to which depravity played a part in the matter of bathers disrobing. "You need only observe men," she would say, "as they parade about in their swimming trunks, wipe their legs a dozen times, touch their clothes without putting them on, to see with what regret they finally decide to get dressed." If, by pure chance, it happened that an indecent sight appeared before her eyes, she would invariably think it was deliberate. If, for example, she'd opened the wrong door and entered a room to find a man there, the thought would immediately cross her mind that, by failing to close his door properly, the man had been hoping someone would open it. I can still recall Madeleine's amazement when I pointed out a female bather to her. "You see," I told her, after having asked her to analyze what was and wasn't beautiful about the stranger, "you see, her elbows are sharply pointed, which is very ugly, but look at her feet, how lovely they are. Just like in Greek statues, the second toe is longer than the big toe." Madeleine was long astonished by this, for in her mind, to be beautiful, toes needed to be aligned in perfectly descending order of size.

October 18th

Last night, I made the mistake of taking Madeleine to the home of Désiré Durand, a friend, or rather an acquaintance, whose invitations one never refuses because it's so obvious he's included you to help make up a crowd. Going to this businessman's home is like going to an entertaining performance.

He greeted my wife and I immediately upon our arrival at the rue Pierre-Levée, and received us with such a show of spontaneity and familiarity that, as soon as I was alone with Madeleine, I gave her an ironic smile. Her face was stony, however, and she didn't seem to know what to make of my smile. "I don't understand," she said, "how you can accept such an invitation. You must not have much respect for me." Whenever Madeleine finds herself somewhere where people are enjoying themselves, she is immediately unhappy. The happiness of others offends her. She accuses the women of flirting, of drawing attention to themselves, of speaking ill of one another, and the men of being superficial, of thinking they are irresistible, of boasting about their good fortune. She doesn't say a word. She had dressed to go out as though she was going to be the only beautiful woman present, almost as if she would be the only female guest at a gentleman's luncheon; that is to say, with refinement and simplicity. She had pinned two large carnations to her bodice, but upon seeing the couples dancing and laughing when she arrived, she removed them and held them in her hand. Knowing as she did that she inevitably attracted attention, she was suffering from having made no apparent impression, in spite of being convinced, from certain signs that women alone are capable of discerning, that everyone had, in fact, noticed her. The truth of it is that she would have been deeply disappointed if I'd turned down the invitation. She had wanted to come, but had become withdrawn as soon as we'd arrived. Nonetheless, I did everything in my power to ensure she spent a pleasant evening, introducing her quite automatically into any conversation. She would say a word or two, then fall silent. Undeterred, I would immediately ask her a question, trying to draw her out so that she would be happy. Nothing gives me greater pleasure, in these situations, than the popularity she is capable of attaining, not because it feeds my own vanity, but rather because she is transformed when she pleases those around her. It pained me if a guest happened to treat her coldly. I would then be as nice as possible to her so that, seeing I loved Madeleine, he would be friendlier to her. Nonetheless, her face would remain stony. Whenever I sensed she was taking pleasure in someone's company, I would move away and, while pretending to be terribly interested in what the first person I met happened to be saying, I would watch her from a distance, anxiously scrutinizing her face for a smile, which would have filled me with happiness. If her interlocutor tried to break away, however, she merely stood there silently, pretending not to have noticed a thing. She is one of those women who never detains anyone, yet who is offended if she is left alone. I returned to her side. During the few moments we were alone together, a painful embarrassment overcame me.

Guests continued to arrive, barely able to move now in the crowded front hall and drawing room. Without saying a word to me, Madeleine suddenly moved into a corner of the room from where, facing the rest of the guests, she assumed the attitude of a superior being observing the miserable revels of humanity. I followed her. I put on a good-natured air, so that her attitude would not be misinterpreted. "This is pathetic," said Madeleine. "But what's pathetic?" I asked. "What does it matter to you if these people are like this? You have to accept them for what they are. It's of no importance whatsoever." Madeleine remained silent. Just then, I saw that Durand was motioning for me to join him from across the room. I wanted Madeleine to come with me, but she refused. I couldn't make up my mind, uncertain about whether or not I should leave her. "I'll be right back," I said automatically, "I don't want to be rude. But come with me." "I really don't want to." Madeleine had put on a martyred look. She added, "But if you want to go, don't let me stop you. Enjoy yourself. Don't worry about me." I moved away. "Ah! Dear friend, there you are at last," said Durand. "It just so happens that I wanted to introduce you to Madame Barrère, who has heard a great deal about you, and to Madame Chaumier." Without wanting to show it, the industrialist was behaving protectively toward me, like someone trying to make himself indispensable to the very person he is trying to cultivate. For example, it wasn't Ceccaldi who had obliged him by winning his court case for him, but rather he who had obliged Ceccaldi by allowing him to represent him.

There comes a point when wealth so overshadows all other qualities that, for some, a doctor becomes merely an anonymous little man whose knowledge is limited to giving advice and suggestions. In a sense, Durand had introduced me to these two women as the friend of someone to whom he was obliged. He finally wandered off with one of the two, leaving me alone with Mme Barrère. She was very pretty and seemed to take an immediate liking to me. Just then, I saw my wife looking at me with such a distressed air that I was thunderstruck. I left Mme Barrère abruptly and returned to Madeleine, who said only, "Let's go home. I need to talk to you." In the taxi taking us home, she didn't say a word. When I tried to kiss her hands, she drew away with such a disgusted air that I was dumbstruck. "What's wrong with you?" I asked, knowing full well that this was all due to my having talked with Mme Barrère. She didn't answer. She was suffering deeply. So this was the man to whom she had sacrificed her youth! Everything was slipping away from her. No one understood her. Her irritation with the party and the minor role she had played there had filled her with profound loathing for me. Suddenly she said: "I don't want to go home. It's too early." "But what do you want to do?" "I want to have fun. I'm no worse than all those women who spend their lives flirting. I want to enjoy myself. I'm still attractive, you'll see for yourself . . . " We went to a nightclub. As it was still early, the place wasn't very full; at eleven o'clock in the evening, the room looked somehow matutinal. "You order . . . ," said Madeleine. The kindness of the waiters, the busboys, the maitres d'hôtel, the admiring glances of a few of the patrons, had restored her, and she could feel her good humor returning. She drew deep, hungry breaths. As for me, however, I watched her anxiously. I knew from experience that this gaiety was artificial and concealed something. When Madeleine gets angry, she always starts by pretending not to care about anything other than some vague notion of freedom. It was as if she wanted me to know that she had a life of her own, and that if I was just like other men, well then, she was just like other women. But if you pay attention to her and are particularly considerate, she will forget all her grievances, at least for a time.

Late-night diners were beginning to arrive, and almost every man among them looked over at her. "You see," she said, "things aren't the same everywhere." With deliberate irritation, she clamored for cigarettes. She was happy. And yet, deep within her, I sensed an unspoken anger with me. "What if I asked you to leave me here alone?" she asked abruptly. I suppose I must have looked alarmed. "No, don't be afraid, you can stay. You're not bothering me. That woman can wait." She said this in an ironically sincere tone, as though the only thing in the world she wanted was for me to be happy with Mme Barrère. She was becoming increasingly tense. Instinctively, I knew not to contradict her, and so I let her continue with the hope that she would calm herself of her own accord. The orchestra played uninterruptedly, and a few drunken patrons had begun throwing paper streamers at one another. All at once, she turned to me and said, "You know, I'm still pretty. You'll realize it soon enough." Having said this, she got up abruptly. "The fact is, I've had enough. I'm going to my father's. That way you can do what you like, all on your own." In vain, I tried to calm her. As soon as the cold air struck her out in the street, she began to cry, then to whimper. The fact is that jealousy plays no part in these hysterical states she gets herself into. Madeleine feels no jealousy where I'm concerned. No, it was her pride that had been sorely tested during the party we'd been to. She took her revenge on me for the indifference with which she thought she'd been treated.

October 19th

I called Madeleine's father first thing this morning. He'd been about to call and ask me to come and see him. I feel something akin to respect for M. Curti. He has truly borne misfortune philosophically. He would never have behaved like his friend Diéghera, who, sensing his business was on the brink of failing, tried every possible measure to save it, as though his own life had been at stake, even going so far as to plead tearfully with strangers and ask them to intervene on his behalf, although doing so would have been detrimental to their own interests. Mind you, Diéghera himself would never have lifted a finger to help someone. His fear of going bankrupt was such that he lost all his dignity.

In fact, this Diéghera was a curious sort of chap. It sometimes happened that he offended his closest friends, and when their quarrels grew to unexpected proportions, there was no limit to what he would do to gain forgiveness. He would cover himself with apologies out of all proportion to the wrong he had committed, yet an hour later he would feel no qualms about behaving rudely toward the very person to whom he had just apologized so theatrically. A mere trifle would cause him to act like a man sentenced to death, who, led to the site of his execution, pleads with the executioner, his lawyer, the priest, and the onlookers to save him. Imagine, then, how he behaved when he went bankrupt. Well, M. Curti behaved entirely differently. He accepted his ruin like a disease, never for a moment thinking of blaming someone for what had happened to him. Just as, after a separation, we suddenly think of the man or woman we have left, it seemed to him he was a victim of his own imagination, that nothing at all had happened, that things could not go on this way, that, by some means he could not predict, everything would return to the way it had been. But when, after reflecting for a time, he took stock of how things really were, he was filled with a painful sense of his own impotence. Everything was well and truly finished.

It often happens that Curti is brought together with men who are as powerful as he himself once was. He will never allude, then, to anything that might reveal his former position, and this in spite of his wife, Jeanne, whom he married much later, and who, unlike him, wanted everyone to know what her husband had been, even going so far as to allow a certain aura of confusion to hover over the past so that people might be led to think that it was not just Curti who had lost everything, but she too. Certain women feel quite at ease in the midst of this sort of confusion, which allows them to imagine that the riches a man possessed before they knew him had been stolen from them. For example, in spite of everything, Curti had managed to preserve a few vestiges of his former opulence, among which were several paintings of no commercial value. To Jeanne, these were sacred. But it happened that one day Curti promised one of the paintings to Diéghera, who liked it so much that each time he came to see his friend, before anything else, he would ask permission to go admire it. Jeanne was present when the gift was made. She hadn't said a word, and had even offered to wrap the painting. But as soon as Diéghera was gone, she flew into a violent rage. "How dare you!" she cried. "It's bad enough that you've deprived me of so many beautiful things; now you feel compelled to give away the miserable remains! You insist upon flaunting your generosity, to my detriment!" For as a sort of affectation, Curti—who was never particularly generous before—has now become extraordinarily munificent. He is incapable of refusing anyone anything. Compared to what he once had, his possessions are now so insignificant that it gives him pleasure not to be attached to any of them, to create the impression that he is even more generous than he appears, that he shares what he owns because what he has left no longer means anything. He always seems to be saying that worldly possessions are illusory, and this is partly sincere, for if his fortune was returned to him by some feat of magic, he would doubtless preserve the detached attitude he acquired when deprived of it. In fact, one of the consequences of his bankruptcy has been to teach him that he never knew the value of money. All of his indulgence is based upon that knowledge.

On his face, one reads that his bad luck was not such a cruel blow after all, since it allowed him to acquire a knowledge of life he would never have had without it. He takes great care now not to allow anything to reveal his former familiarity with wealth, and even strives to be ever more humble in his manner, to the great despair of his wife. Thus, when he says good-bye, if I ask him whether he would like me to send for a car, he replies that he would rather take the tramway, that he is used to it, that it bothers him to change his habits. Jeanne interpreted this as a ridiculous need for humiliation, and had soon decided it was in fact a manifestation of his desire to belittle her. She reproached him for having given gifts to his mistresses in years gone by. One of her more peculiar traits was that while she never reproached her husband for his past mistresses, she did resent the money he'd spent on them. Of modest origins herself, she was one of those women who are convinced that lavish gifts are a sure sign of love. A sort of fury would well up inside her whenever she thought of the women who had known Curti in his better days. When it happened that her husband would inadvertently speak of his youth, of the holidays he'd spent with his family in Florence, a mute rage would take hold of her, and she would cry out abruptly: "I want to go to Florence too; I don't see why I shouldn't go." "We'll go," Curti would answer. "We'll go, well then! Let's go. I've had enough of all these promises. Let's go, let's go . . . " Her husband would always calm her with his patience. He never lost his temper. He occasionally yielded, and the two of them would actually set off for Florence. It would take too long to elaborate on those trips; what has to be said is that they were difficult. Curti would reproduce for his wife, but with vastly reduced means, what he had done in bygone days in grand style. While Jeanne persisted in trying to ascertain whether this was indeed the hotel her husband had once stayed in, he would try to make her understand how unimportant this was.

Curti is more himself when circumstances bring him together with someone who, like himself, has been a victim of fate. As with people who are engrossed by similar pursuits, the two men will speak to another with exaggerated politeness, taking care not to stray from that point at which it is pleasant to be entirely in agreement. Curti holds forth on the events which brought about his downfall, on the rules governing his existence he has since set, speaking in that sort of professional tone it is startling to hear, for example, in a doctor whom one is accustomed to frequenting socially and whom one then overhears one day delivering a medical opinion. That is when one understands that Curti hasn't forgotten, that deep within him lies a zone in which all of the past has remained intact. The abrupt seriousness which emanates from him allows one to glimpse, with some astonishment, that he harbors resentments, that he has enemies, that he suffers in a way which is peculiar to him, and which he never discusses. Jeanne was always delighted if she happened to be present at one of these conversations, for as with most women, she believed that if you want to, you will recover what you have lost. She would set out to make the two men accomplices, victims whose position would be strengthened if they would only join forces, and who should, without further ado, move heaven and earth to try and recover fortunes that no longer existed. In her mind, nothing was ever lost forever.

I said earlier that I feel something like respect for Curti. This is true. When I'm with him, I sometimes even feel the way young people do when speaking to celebrities. And yet it's slightly different, in the sense that there is no shyness on my part, but rather a need to agree with and approve of everything he says, while manifesting a degree of independence in my opinions when questions of taste arise. The reason for my admiration lies in the great dignity Curti has shown in the face of adversity, in his modesty, his humility, and in the fact that he never speaks about his past glory. I have to add that my admiration includes a budding desire that Curti should perceive how greatly I admire his discretion.

When I arrived, I was afraid he was going to be angry and reproach me in some way. Instead of the severe look I was expecting, however, he smiled at me as soon as were alone together and said, "This has to be patched up. It's so childish to quarrel over such trifles." I felt awkward, the way you do when your interlocutor, out of tactfulness, appears unaware of the reason for something you have done, thus making it impossible to explain yourself. Curti spoke kindly, as though he had no idea why his daughter was angry with his son-in-law, and yet he had to know, since he'd sent for me. I was intimidated and didn't dare bring up Madeleine's outburst the night before, about which her father seemed to know nothing. And yet, I couldn't stop myself from saying, in that tone one adopts in man-to-man conversations, "But Madeleine is so sensitive, so fanciful, that she imagines things which don't exist." Curti took no account of this view. It was obvious that he thought his daughter was perfect, and not wishing to know the truth, he preferred not to understand. "Such ridiculous incidents," he continued, "cannot be allowed to come between you this way." Curti never sides with anyone, which is often the case with people who have passionate feelings and don't want to be disappointed. He grew increasingly friendly with me, to avoid learning anything which would have wounded him. Just then, Madeleine appeared. She had recovered, and looked rested. Seeing her, her father said, "There you are, that's good. You must be reasonable, Madeleine. You can't let yourself get carried away by such childish nonsense." By saying this, he was imperceptibly finding fault with the person he loved, the person he felt sure of, in order to avoid having to learn anything from me, his son-in-law, whose friendship he was both trying to win and pretending to consider meant more to him than the love of his daughter. As I smiled at her, Madeleine looked at me in that manner peculiar to people who are being reconciled with someone they don't love. "It was nothing," she said, "I was simply overwrought. Things always look better in the morning." "That makes me happy," said Curti, "but promise me, Madeleine, you won't do this again." In reality, Madeleine was indifferent. Once her anger had dissipated, sleep had eradicated everything. She was now just as she had been yesterday morning, albeit slightly embarrassed by her behavior.

When we got home, I was particularly attentive to Madeleine, but she pretended not to notice. As soon as we'd arrived, she felt compelled to make some disagreeable remarks to the maid, to show that her absence hadn't undermined her authority in any way. She grew ever more irritable. She had obeyed her father so as not to cause him any pain, but was furious at the thought I might think she'd come back home because of me.

October 20th

I asked myself whether a life devoid of any affection, of any goal, a life one fills with a thousand trifles intended to relieve its monotony, populated with human beings one seeks out in order not to be alone and whom one flees to avoid being bored by them, whether such a life isn't ridiculous, whether anything whatsoever wouldn't be preferable. I wondered about this while out walking this morning; the weather was superb. There was not a cloud in the sky. Summer seemed to be coming back. The sun gave off a gentle warmth. The tips of bare branches undulated softly in the blue light, and I, with no love, no woman I could talk to about how beautiful I found this morning, I felt old. Rather than letting my being be filled with happiness, I thought of myself. To console myself, I went so far as to imagine that I was perhaps the only man so alone and unhappy. And yet there is in me, as in everyone, a great desire to be loved. However, and this is what most saddens me, there is also a profound inability to please another, to be loved. I am made to live alone, but I cannot be alone. I need faces around me, friends. I have noticed that I am always happy in the minutes just prior to the moment when I am due to meet one of my friends. I feel, then, that I am like other men, and my despair lifts. An appointment with the most insignificant of acquaintances will light up my day as though that person were one of my dearest friends. As soon as we have exchanged polite greetings, however, I'll suddenly feel myself falling into a yawning abyss as I become obsessed with a single thought: getting away. And yet the mere thought of being alone again fills me with such horror that I haven't the strength to leave. People may bore me, I may find them ridiculous for one reason or another, but if they happen to leave me earlier than I'd planned, I suffer intensely. I then try every possible means to stay with them, even at the risk of seeming tactless. I offer to accompany them, to wait for them. I ask them if I'm really not intruding. And when they finally get rid of me, claiming they don't want to force such a thankless task on me, I sometimes catch myself letting out a cry of joy at being faced with the fait accompli.

October 23rd

I again saw the banker whose unfortunate advice made me lose over a hundred thousand francs. Spigelman's manners are charming. Whereas before our relationship was confined exclusively to business matters, there is now a real bond of friendship between us. Can this change be explained by his feeling that he is at least partly responsible for my losses? I don't think so. What he likes about me is my disdain for money. It may seem strange that a man whose life revolves around business would like someone to whom business means nothing. And yet that's how it is. For him, I am a likable figure from another world. His attitude toward me is always vaguely superior, even when he launches into extraordinarily polite attentions, for he likes to humble himself—not in the manner of an inferior or a petitioner, but rather with the air of a man who is yielding to the capricious or foolish behavior of others. My father used to have the same expression when he forgave me for one of my temper tantrums. It is an expression, however, that can be profoundly irritating if all one said was that a minister's speech was particularly fine. Nonetheless, he is fond of me. But when, for example, he does something especially kind for me, he always feels compelled to say that he did it for me, that normally he would never do such a thing, thereby seeking—very naively—to lend his gesture extra value. I think the reason he likes me is that he thinks I'm very wealthy and don't let it show. In different circumstances, I would find such a situation awkward. It is always disagreeable to feel that we would be a disappointment to someone if they knew the truth about us. But with him I have no scruples, nor am I worried in the least about having won his friendship by dint of advantages I don't possess. Every time he comes to see me, his first words are: "So, Monsieur

Grandeville, have you been happy with the stock market?" "But I stopped taking any interest in it long ago." "Quite right, Monsieur Grandeville, that is the best way to succeed in business." I sense that he is dying to know the name of my stockbroker—who doesn't exist.

Yesterday, he came by to ask me—though this was presented as a piece of advice—to reopen an account with his bank. And yet he should understand that, where money is concerned, one easily becomes superstitious. There are people who find it impossible to stay on in a city where they have been unhappy. The great number of cities makes it easy enough for them to settle elsewhere. To my mind, the same holds true of bankers. This is something of which he is totally unaware. I tried to make him understand this, for I find it amusing to tease him a bit, but in vain. He enumerated a great many reasons, and always managed to find another whenever I told him my answer was still no. Nuances of any sort escape him completely.

As he was about to leave, Madeleine arrived. She addressed him with that tone she uses with people who are neither attractive, young, nor excessively rich, saying, "Good evening, Monsieur Spigelman," as though she were speaking right through the person standing before her and addressing some distant soul who was aware she knew how difficult it is for two beings to understand one another. Spigelman took her hand and smiled, revealing a gap-toothed mouth that gave his face a quality of immeasurable kindness, and motioning to me with his chin, he said to her, "He's a good fellow . . . he's the best of husbands." For I forgot to mention Spigelman's little oddity, which is a fatherly affection for the intimate life of couples, and unbounded joy when he succeeds in orchestrating marriages, principally between men and women who are separated by extremes, be they of age, character, or social standing. In these circumstances, he becomes genuinely good-natured, and his air of superiority is transformed into one of mischief.

October 24th

It seems to me that the peace I'm searching for is exceedingly difficult to find. What am I to make of this desire I have to lead a quiet life, when my emotions are so easily aroused? I have retreated from the world, but what sort of retreat is it if a mere trifle can fluster me? Not participating in life is no guarantee of happiness. I continue to endure vexations. People interest me more now than they did in the days when I was out and about a great deal. The older I get, the more vulnerable to wickedness I become. Early in my life, I felt untainted. And in fact I lived well beyond intrigues, ambitions, and human frailty. But now here I am, in the boredom of my monotonous life, lacking the courage to live, yet still taking part in all of this small-mindedness, though without enjoying any of the satisfactions life usually affords. I am like some old codger in his well-worn lair, my indirect suffering greater than any I ever experienced directly. What's left for me, if isolation doesn't bring me the peace I seek? I distanced myself from everyone, because I thought my resolution to live apart from them would last forever; it was, I thought, the greatest of all resolutions, of the sort one makes only once in a lifetime. Today, however, I realize that this sacred resolution of mine has gone the way of all the others. My life will have been a series of abdications. Now that there is nothing left for me to abandon, I have reached a pinnacle of sorts, from which I may well derive the most happiness: that point at which one realizes that desire is an endless chain. Retreat is a vanity like any other. One begins by judging one's peers from a great height, then from slightly lower, then from even lower still. Little by little, they creep into one's existence, not as adversaries or friends the way they once did, but by dint of minor incidents. Idleness makes these minor incidents assume the gravity important events once had. We suddenly notice that we're not living at all the way we'd hoped, but instead just as we did before.

October 28th

Early on, I used to imply that my passion for Madeleine was a thing of such beauty that the gods themselves smiled upon it. For example, if we'd planned to meet in the evening and the day had been a stormy one, thus making Madeleine fear she would have to go out in the rain, I would say, "No, no, it won't rain; it can't rain, because we're going out." Ever since one of my predictions turned out to be incorrect, however, I now take great care to avoid alluding to this celestial protection.

The other day, when discussing Curti, I forgot to mention one of his more charming traits, which Madeleine told me about. In the course of the walks he used to take with his daughter, it sometimes happened that, out of thoughtlessness, she would say something that hurt her father. He would let the remark pass, but the next day, or sometimes even several days later, he would repeat it as though it were coming from him, making his daughter laugh when she remembered what she'd said. There are, in fact, a great many things I've neglected to say about Curti which keep coming to mind, in particular this manner he has of becoming engrossed in trivial occupations, in the unimportant details of life. He is prodigiously attached to his habits, and nothing irks him more than the failure to observe one of these. As is often the case with people who find themselves relegated to a minor role after having led an eventful life, he derives great pleasure from dawdling, from tracking prognostications and checking on their accuracy the next day, reading weather forecasts, catalogues, interrogating servants to learn all of the reasons which caused an object to be moved to a new place.

I've also noticed how aggrieved he becomes when something happens that focuses attention on the world he was once a part of. He is distressed when things that were once second nature to him are discussed by his entourage or in the newspapers without his opinion being solicited. Without saying a word, he'll observe those around him taking sides, with that disagreeable sensation which comes when you are better qualified than anyone to render an opinion, yet no one ever asks you to do so. That said, it sometimes happens that he does speak up, but before long he'll realize that twenty years have gone by, and that in spite of his efforts to appear well informed, there are strangers who know more than he does.

Although he was once extremely quick to take offense, it now seems to him that nothing is worth the slightest show of anger. He is like those men who find the slightest criticism from a friend intolerable, yet remain silent when taken to task in public, as though they were weary of having answered too often and are saying: "I'm above this." And nothing, in effect, touches him anymore. All the same, he takes great pains to avoid letting others mistake his indifference for pride. His greatest fear is that he might offend someone. He always agrees with the person he is speaking to, and doesn't get flustered, even when he isn't treated with the respect that is his due. When his wife used to insist he take her to visit people from his past, he would refuse, pointing out their vanity, their stupidity; already, his judgments showed no indulgence for the very society which, in casting him off, had created this severity in him.

Since the death of his wife and the marriage of his daughter, Curti has lived alone. His favorite evenings are the ones he spends at home with a musician friend who comes to play him his favorite pieces. He will give instructions to the effect that he is not at home to anyone and, locked away with the musician, will listen with rapt attention, never asking for another piece when the musician stops playing. His love of music is such that he would never dare ask for more, for fear of appearing profane and ignorant of the fact that inspiration is a fleeting thing. If it happens that he comes across a musician who takes his silence for incomprehension and stops playing, Curti will begin conversing casually in spite of his disappointment, without seeming to regret a thing.

He always looks mournful, and things that make others laugh barely bring a spark of life to his face. It is curious to see how taken aback he is when someone who has suffered a stroke of bad luck seems to be taking misfortune in stride rather than being devastated by it. Such optimists leave him perplexed. I would like to relate an anecdote my wife told me which I think sheds some light on the man's character. One day, one of his friends said to him: "If you're not doing anything this evening, I'll come by and get you and we'll go to the theater." Curti, who wasn't free, had been forced to decline, but his refusal had left him feeling somehow dissatisfied with himself. The desires of others, no matter how insignificant, are like an obligation for Curti. No sooner was he back home than he set about finding ways he might be forgiven for his refusal, in spite of the fact it had been received with these words: "It doesn't matter in the slightest. I only thought of you on the odd chance you might be free. In fact, even if you'd been able to come, I think I might have been forced to cancel at the last minute." The next day, he decided to call his friend and extend an invitation of his own. But he didn't call. He was prevented from so doing lest he learn his friend had in fact gone to the theater without him. Had that been the case, his original distress would have given way to another, the one we feel when we realize that people have substituted others in the plans they had originally intended for us.

When still a wealthy man, Curti came to the rescue of many a friend, and he instinctively turned to those people when he lost the better part of his fortune. They avoided him, however. As a young man, Curti had entertained vague notions of becoming a great orator. Ever since, he has used the phrase "a natural speaker," which, even today, comes up constantly in his conversations. The ingratitude of the people he once helped likewise left him using the following expression: "He refused to shake his hand." Although one doesn't need to go bankrupt to observe what little value men accord gratitude, it so happens that it was precisely the bankruptcy that taught Madeleine's father everything. As a result, his opinions of the world are both worse and not as bad as they might be; worse, because he accuses the world of being responsible, at least indirectly, for his downfall, and not as bad because had the downfall never occurred, nothing would ever have made him speak ill of others.

November 4th

I can't remember when I've ever felt so weary, sad, and defeated. It was a frightening sensation. I hate to talk about myself, but when I think of all the people I see every day, it does me good to forget them and turn my thoughts inward. In these moments of depression, I think no one loves me, that I'm a poor soul incapable of desiring anything, of attempting anything. It seems the entire world has joined forces against me. It's dreadful to live like this, never being loved, always giving everything and devoting oneself but never getting anything in return. I'll make the greatest sacrifices for Madeleine, yet she isn't happy. I feel I'm isolated, a victim, and that if I fell seriously ill I would be alone. Friends would come to see me, but what for? Because they have to stir themselves, because you need to go somewhere to avoid being bored, and rather than going elsewhere they would come to see me, which would not be uninteresting since I would be on the verge of expiring. I would prefer to have no one around me, to be surrounded with silence, if only I could be certain that, somewhere, there is a soul I love who loves me, a being for whom I am everything. As night fell, I sat down in my study and wept. I wept, I don't know why. There is nothing particularly awful about my life. I never had unfulfillable ambitions. I'm losing money, but that doesn't bother me. It hasn't changed my life. I'm not particularly bored. Why, then, did I weep? There are, in fact, entertainments that do distract me. Last night I went to the theater, and afterward Madeleine and I went out for a late supper. I was lighthearted; I wasn't thinking about anything. So! The man who is currently feeling so overwhelmed is a normal man after all. I am neither neurotic nor sentimental. I am nothing in particular. How can it be, then, that I'm such a wreck? Had someone come in unexpectedly while I was crying, I would have straightened up as though nothing were wrong, and with suitable lightheartedness would have done whatever it was they suggested, as though I'd never been unhappy. And yet none of this is an act. I am not mistaken. I weep. I suffer, have no way of helping myself, and so I live like everyone else. I am incapable of imagining another sort of life. More than anything, that is what astonishes me: that I can be crying one minute and yet be no different from any passerby the next. I have the same occupations as everyone around me, I go to the theater, I enjoy myself, yet deep within me there is always some unhappiness, some dissatisfaction. I love Madeleine, she makes me jealous, I feel my life would be over if she were to disappear, and yet, at the same time, there is something else in me. As soon as I'm alone, that "something else" stirs, obliterates all the rest, and I suffer. I can't be alone, but I hate company. I love Madeleine and at the same time I don't love her. Not a day goes by when I don't approach a friend to speak to him and then suddenly flee. What terrifies me is that I'm constantly unhappy, and yet always act like a happy man. I never embrace happiness entirely. Deep within myself, I scorn happiness. Now that I am somewhat older, it's true that I've begun accepting it as it comes, without dwelling too much upon the fact that this happiness isn't real. Nonetheless, at every step, at every event, a voice wells up within me; it tells me everything that happens to me is due to mere circumstance. I may love Madeleine deeply, but she's still just a woman I happened to meet. I'll never meet the one I love, because it's impossible I'll ever find her among so many people, or she may not have been born yet, or she may have died hundreds of years ago. Every action, every passion, is shadowed by a feeling that I am marooned in the midst of a meaningless world, and that everything that happens to me is but a miserable approximation of the life I should have lived. Even as I think this, I realize how ridiculous it is: things are no better elsewhere, either in the past or in the future. I have no reason to bear anyone a grudge. That is what's distressing. Happiness is impossible, and when I cry as I did yesterday, it isn't because I can't achieve happiness or because happiness is impossible, but because I'm unhappy with what I have, because I don't know which way to turn to avoid all these people, and suffer from belonging to a class which may be no worse than any other—indeed, I know it's no worse—but which disgusts me all the same. There is nothing to be done, therefore, nothing, nothing, Therein lies the heart of the problem. It's knowing that I will never be any happier than I am now, nor any unhappier, and that everything which might happen to me is going to seem devoid of any interest. And yet I continue to live, I take an interest in life, I love, and sometimes I'm happy.

November 10th

Although Madeleine usually likes having her coffee and sitting by the fire after dinner, tonight she suddenly grew melancholy, as if every aspect of her life were in vain and had no reason to be. She looked at me. I was just then searching for a newspaper out of a pile, and thinking that what we're looking for is always the last thing we find. Madeleine got up and went to her room. My mood at that particular moment was such that I didn't take offense. She was most chagrined by this, for it's just when she thinks she wants to be alone that she most wants me to put aside what I'm doing and speak affectionately to her. "He thinks only of himself. He would even rather read than be with me." Whenever she's on edge, she thinks that others would rather do anything than keep her company. That is how she feeds her melancholy. She draws the energy she needs for her unhappiness from the feeling that people around her don't understand her. She would like others to feel sad when she does, and be happy when she is happy, again at *exactly the same moment.* It doesn't occur to her that I could reproach her for being equally inadaptable. Once she's in her room, she breaks into tears. After a few minutes, she pulls herself together and returns to me, her face freshly made up. She thinks it a sign of her singularity to hide her worries from the world: not as those do who conceal them with the intention that they nonetheless be inferred, but instead concealing them entirely. Playing at concealing her feelings intoxicates her. Keeping her unhappiness to herself and misleading whoever she is with makes her feel so noble and grand that she becomes deeply happy. "Did you find your newspaper?" she asked me upon returning. "Yes. But are you sure you don't mind if I read?" My question caught Madeleine off guard, for a lack of interest can suddenly make her attitude seem slightly ridiculous. If one is tender with her just when she thinks she is utterly alone with herself, she is embarrassed. Therefore, to ensure she is left alone, she will resist the very tenderness whose absence first gave rise to her attitude. She refuses to acknowledge it. Were one to utter the very words she so desperately hoped to hear, she would do all she could to deform their meaning. She would make herself disagreeable, accuse me of sentimentality. What was lacking a moment ago has now become superfluous.

Toward nine o'clock, the maid announced François Joly. He is one of the few men I respect. He must be in his fifties, and there is nothing attractive about his appearance. His honesty and rectitude have prevented him from being successful in life. You may recall that in 1912 a woman named Jeanne Hurtu gained notoriety as a result of a series of reckless speculations, the last of which landed her in court. This woman, of modest origins, was reputed to be a genius at business. As a way of demonstrating her good faith, she had taken it into her head not to choose a celebrated lawyer, and the instructing magistrate therefore appointed a public defender to her case. Fate designated Joly. The trial ended with Mme Hurtu's conviction: she, her lover, and her parents had all instructed Joly to mount the most minimal defense, for her innocence was meant to be self-evident without recourse to any vulgar strategies. As a consequence, Joly had merely limited himself to refuting a few inaccuracies. When it came to her appeal, however, she chose a different, and highly reputed, lawyer. This time, she was acquitted. Thanks to this affair, Joly became the laughingstock of his colleagues, and his career was seriously compromised. Far from complaining, however, he adopted a dignified attitude. He and an associate set up a practice, taking on only minor cases. Joly is something of a misanthrope. He believes everything is corrupt, with the rather odd exception of his clients' cases, which he handles with quiet professionalism. He lives alone in a gloomy apartment in the rue de Lille; alongside him, I seem an ambitious bon vivant. Apart from his legal briefs, all he cares about is friendship. For him, friendship is neither an accident nor a fortunate coincidence. He takes his time in choosing a friend, and when he speaks to him, he is obviously doing so in anticipation of the happiness that may follow. As a result, his friends are quite genuinely devoted to him, and don't hesitate to do him any favor at all. No one abuses his kindness, but this kindness is also a trifle sad, as feelings can be when they are neither very deep nor very pure. His professions of friendship are always marked by some detail which warns you that, basically, they are not terribly substantial.

Joly had come to ask me if I didn't happen to know a good cardiologist, for his mother had been suffering with heart problems for the past several weeks, and her close friends and family were worried. Although he had just come from seeing his great friend Sarbelos, he hadn't mentioned a word about this illness to him. He had refrained from doing so so that he could ask me for a recommendation first, thinking thereby that I would hear him out seriously, for, in spite of everything, he thinks my life is somewhat frivolous. Joly wants to turn people into what he thinks they ought to be, and he seemed to think I would be impressed by the importance of his request. In other circumstances I would have shown real compassion, but for some reason I replied, "I'll be happy to," as if he'd invited me to a masked ball. As I was leafing through an address book, Madeleine struck up a conversation with our visitor. "Why don't you come to see us more often? It's always such a pleasure to see you. You should come and have lunch with us some day. We should decide on a date right away, otherwise we'll never do it." Madeleine was being friendlier than usual to Joly. She knows the esteem I have for him, and I sensed that her show of exaggerated friendliness was intended to be disagreeable to me, for she cannot accept that I have feelings for anyone but her. No sooner does she divine that I like or respect someone than she immediately appropriates those feelings as though they were her own and exaggerates them. Whatever the circumstances, she can't tolerate interest in anyone else but herself. She turns it into caricature. Though she has every reason to be friendly, she takes her revenge by exaggerating that friendliness, and does this with transparent innocence, so that if you were to challenge her, she would say with apparent sincerity, "But I don't understand you anymore! You tell me he's your friend. It's altogether natural that I be nice to him!" She's been behaving this way since before we were married. Despite having no real feelings for the person with whom she was behaving so affectionately, it would amuse her to put on this act, simply because I happened to be fond of him. She carried on this way for the rest of Joly's visit, and as he believed everything she was telling him, he no longer knew how to appear worthy of such friendliness. Once he'd gone, however, I found it impossible to keep from reproaching Madeleine. Perhaps because of the strange mood she was in that evening, rather than playing the innocent and saying what she usually does in such circumstances, Madeleine declared that she'd made a conquest of my friend to teach me a lesson, to show me what I was like, and that none of this had been her doing: she'd merely been imitating me.

November 12th

Although he is always afraid of intruding, Joly telephoned to tell me that his mother had been very pleased with my cardiologist. I found this somewhat disagreeable. I reproached Madeleine for having tried to seduce such a perfect human being and toyed with his feelings, even going so far as to say that I would never have thought her capable of such behavior. She didn't flinch. She heard me out, and when I was finished merely shrugged her shoulders with a smile, implying I didn't know my friends, and that while men might well be models of rectitude, this wouldn't stop them from taking advantage of an "opportunity" if it arose. Her shrug and smile wounded me. It irritates me to see Joly put in such an awkward position, and at the same time I can't hold it against my wife. My only fear is that by some extraordinary stroke of fate, Madeleine will prove to be right. Whereas before I would gladly have seen Joly every day, I now find myself apprehensive at the thought he might come by. My own rectitude makes me abhor a situation in which a man and his wife are accomplices, where she has made him aware that a friend is courting her and yet he says nothing to the friend, allowing the latter to think he knows nothing. These are the depths into which I sink as a result of the trouble Madeleine creates. My love for her is so great, however, that it gradually became apparent to me that she might be blameless. The only aim of her friendliness had been to please me; at heart, the fault lay with me.

November 13th

Joly came to see me this evening, much like the last time. Before he was shown in, Madeleine said triumphantly, "See what they're like, your friends. If that's what you call a friend, well then! You're easy to please." "He's only here to thank us," I said, without much conviction. "He already rang; surely he isn't going to go on thanking you forever. It's up to you to make him see that he's behaving badly." In her thirst for power, this was all Madeleine wanted. Just then Joly came in. His face was pale and he seemed flustered. He'd come to ask whether my doctor really was a top man, for he'd become pessimistic about his mother's illness. Something strange occurred then. After having taken so long to admit there might be some truth in Madeleine's insinuations, I now thought I detected a certain awkward love for my wife in my friend's words. She, however, had changed her tone completely and was speaking to Joly with genuine kindness, much as she'd done on his previous visit, but with heartfelt sincerity now. One of Madeleine's peculiarities is that she is totally independent in her feelings. If she changes her mind about someone, she'll immediately forget everything she said before. Seeing Joly so despondent, she'd abandoned her seductive manner and, and without taking into account the confusion this created, was now showing herself in a new and quite unexpected light. Like those people who walk at a brisk clip and are startled to see their companion lagging behind, she failed to understand that no one was following her. If it happens that someone then says to her, "But that's not what you thought a little while ago!" she'll get terribly angry, as though she'd been publicly accused of being a liar.

After Joly left, ushered out with the sweet words of my wife, who'd suddenly discovered he was a man of great compassion, I looked at her tenderly. I was astonished by the way she could be so natural, so attuned to life, so sincere about what she thought. I wanted to tell her I loved her. But I sensed this would displease her, for she didn't want to appear to agree with me now, and believe as I did in my friend's virtues. "I'd rather be alone," she said. "François isn't terribly engaging, but I felt sorry for him just now when he was talking about his mother."

November 14th

Raoul Sospel, Curti's sole friend, has an only child, Roger, who is the same age as Madeleine. It was for that reason, I think, that the two men became friends. Different as they are, they had in common the fact that each adored his child. Roger is a tall young man, hindered by excessive modesty and shyness. He has an extraordinary mix of purity and dissatisfaction with himself, of sincere verbal generosity coupled with an inability to see things through, a tendency to display the sort of dedication and sacrifice which almost always accompanies base sentiments. Impulsive and violent, he wants to please, only to offend as soon as he has succeeded. He can be arrogant when in the company of his more feeble, poor, and defenseless friends, which seems calculated to show how little importance he accords to everything he's been taught.

Madeleine has told me in the past that she was once deeply

fond of this young man. I therefore found it very difficult to control myself when she announced she'd seen him today. Before we were married, they used to see a great deal of one another. Although there has never been anything more than a long-standing friendship between them, the idea of it has always made me uncomfortable. Many are the times I could have lost my temper on the subject of that young man, if I hadn't restrained myself! I can imagine the scenes.

I'm certain that when Madeleine saw him again it must have dawned on her that she could love him. He must suddenly have looked different to her. I imagine it was about six o'clock in the evening. In the fading light, Roger was also looking at her with newfound interest. Madeleine must have been surprised that she could have so completely forgotten a man she'd known so well. She scrutinized his face. Although he was truly a man now, she felt as comfortable by his side as if he'd been a member of her family. He had changed and yet he was the same. Roger, too, felt a similar sense of surprise, but rather than finding the strength and maturity Madeleine had perceived in him, what he saw was weakness and submission, coupled with a critical air against which, subconsciously, he defended himself. Unconcerned with my existence, the pair of them were like two completely new people who know and appreciate one another; they were now gazing into each others' eyes as though they'd never met, so powerful was the attraction between them. Whereas in the past Roger was never particularly thoughtful or considerate, he took extra care to be so today, because he wanted the change in him to be readily apparent. Madeleine accepted his gallantries as she would those of a stranger. She was moved by the fact that, beneath this new outward appearance, they shared a past, and everything they knew about one another.

When she came home, I noticed immediately that she was flustered. I pretended not to be aware of anything and said, "I've been waiting an hour for you, I didn't want to leave the house without having seen you. The thing is, I've got to go dine with Sabasse. I'll be back at half past nine. Listen, my darling, I'll eat almost nothing and we'll dine together when I return." Madeleine was only too pleased to be able to hold something against me. "Go, have your dinner with Sabasse, if that's what you want," she said. I decided to stay. After a moment, she picked up the phone and called her father, asking in a mechanical voice, "Has he gone?" "Who?" I asked. "Roger." "Ahh, so you saw him this afternoon," I added distractedly, as though I had forgotten that Madeleine must have met M. Sospel and Roger at her father's home. "You know perfectly well I did," she answered. I fell silent. Apparently the person at the other end of the line had said the young man was gone, for she replaced the receiver looking rather pleased. When away from those we love, there is something pleasant about hearing that they have resumed the normal course of their lives, that they are now slowly walking home and smoking a cigarette. For the next few minutes she was lost in thought, probably about what she'd just said, searching for a reason to see Roger again without making this obvious. "You know," she said, "we're going to have to invite him." Madeleine has such a fear of lying that it would never occur to her to see Roger in any way other than one she could admit to me. "He'll be able to go out with me," she went on, "since you never want to." As I'm often busy, she was sure I would accept. "But then again," she went on, "I don't know if he'd find that much fun." As I looked at Madeleine, I realized she was embarrassed at the idea Roger might think she was dominated by her husband. Lately, I've noticed her ill humor intensifies if she feels trapped in any way. "I need only ring him, after all," she must have thought, "and ask him to come fetch me here when no one is at home, and take me somewhere I could never go alone." Having formulated this plan, she was now waiting to announce it to me as though it were the most natural thing in the world. Her scruples at initiating the contact with the young man had already vanished. The truth is Madeleine has a strange personality. Whereas she would rather die than appear obviously enamored of someone, she is capable of actively pursuing a man after only a few hours, without any discretion. I was annoyed. "I don't see why you're calling your father," I said. "What difference does it make to you if Roger has left or not?" "Would you rather I called him directly, perhaps?" "Do you have something in particular you need to tell him?" "No." "If you're so desperate to see him, then ask him to come here, or if you want to go out with him, ask Marguerite to go with you." I could see Madeleine wasn't at all happy with this last suggestion. Although in other circumstances she wouldn't even have bothered to reply, she now agreed with me. As soon as she senses she is wrong, she becomes conciliatory. She was soon on the telephone to her friend, but deliberately avoided discussing Roger. I asked her why. "Ah, you're right!" she said. "I forgot. And yet I meant to. Sospel is so anxious for me to look after his son a bit." After my initial wave of astonishment had subsided, her words made me terribly happy. I understood that I'd been a victim of my imagination, and that Madeleine's interest in Roger was not what I'd thought. Knowing the influence my wife had once had over his son, Sospel had asked her to take him under her wing, introduce him to some friends, which was quite natural given the fact that Roger had been away from Paris for the last four years. Everything has an explanation. And yet, in spite of my relief, I couldn't stop myself from thinking about how very strange Madeleine was. To arouse my jealousy, instead of telling me the truth from the outset, she had deliberately concealed it from me in a very curious manner, pretending to be obedient, as though I'd caught her doing something wrong.

November 16th

Last night, Madeleine and I went to visit friends, where I knew we'd be seeing an art collector. On our way there, I said to her, "If Catifait [that is the collector's name] is there, you're going to have some fun. I've never met a more ridiculous or pretentious man." That was the impression he made on me when I was first introduced to him. This evening, however, Catifait was charming, and as the hours slipped by I saw everything I'd said about him melt away in the face of reality. Instead, he was extraordinarily kind, charmingly modest, and talked about his collections with regret that his passion deprived others of the same pleasure. As he described his rare pieces, one sensed not pride but rather embarrassment that he alone possessed such marvels. I've recounted this trivial incident to illustrate Madeleine's unpredictability. She's spent her life reproaching me for my bitterness, claiming I don't love anyone and envy everyone around me. Yet in the present situation, when she could easily have attacked me, she never breathed a word of my hasty judgment. After we'd left our friends, she told me she found Catifait charming, and seemed to have forgotten all about my earlier opinions. The fact is Madeleine has a very commendable quality: she pays no attention to things one says lightly. Whereas I will persist in drawing the worst possible conclusions from something unfortunate I've said, she won't even mention it: her indulgence for the dreadful emptiness of words is boundless. She doesn't listen to words. If I happen to insult her in some way, she'll pretend not to have heard me if she is well-disposed and answer instead as if I'd paid her a compliment. It's not that she's grown accustomed to the deplorable disorder of my conversation, but simply that she judges me by her own standards rather than in light of what I actually said. It may well be that one of the traits I find most objectionable in myself is my tendency to get carried away, my haste in passing judgment and deciding to like or dislike someone, only to change my mind immediately afterward and say the opposite. That's the sort of man I am, lacking clarity and greatness, unable to draw on a past filled with improbabilities, mistakes, and incoherent acts. The past horrifies me. How I long to have willpower, to be able to defend my opinions and remain in agreement with myself. I would like each of my actions, each of my words, to be the building blocks of an edifice I erect as the years go by. Instead, everything is vague, everything tends to make me regret something, everything is wicked when it should be good. When calling up some experience from my past to help me resolve a current problem, I sense there are a thousand other experiences which would lead me to the opposite conclusion, particularly when the matter in question is something I long for with all my heart.

November 18th

This afternoon, Madeleine dragged me off to Marguerite's. I tried to refuse, but she was so insistent, claiming her friend had called to invite the two of us to tea and would be terribly disappointed if I didn't come, that I went along in the end. She didn't mention Roger, but I was certain she'd made arrangements behind my back for him to be there. If it seems surprising that Madeleine was so insistent I come along, the reason is she's incapable of lying. Whenever she feels she's at fault, she forgets about her own pleasure. Meeting Roger without me, with the knowledge that she'd planned it, would become hateful to her when the time came to go through with it. She can make elaborate plans to be free at a certain hour, but when that hour strikes it will seem to her that the entire world is going to know the truth. Her fear of being caught in a lie is probably so great that she'd rather renounce the pleasure she'd orchestrated with such care.

To our great surprise, when we arrived at Marguerite's we found she was alone. "I'm feeling so unwell," she said, "that I canceled everyone but the two of you. I did so want to see you." As often happens with people whose lives revolve around social engagements, this woman retreats into a shell on a daily basis, more so even than people who scorn society. Whether caused by inattention or hypersensitivity, she is easily, and frequently, upset. Something strange then happens, and has been happening almost every day for years now: she withdraws from the world, saddened and discouraged, until something happens to draw her back out again. She is filled with a deep sense of peace during the hour she spends scorning society's intrigues and pettiness, dreaming of simple pleasures and criticizing her own ambition to play a role and be influential. But these reflections of hers are like a doctor's advice to a man who eats too much. She views them as something external, a warning rather than a cry from her own conscience. Comfort soon returns, that same comfort the man who was frightened by his doctor's advice finds as he gradually forgets that advice and resumes living as he did before. It soon became apparent Marguerite was feeling low because of an unkind comment made about her which a friend had then repeated to her as though it were a pleasant remark. That friend had pretended to be astonished at her surprise and assured her she must be misinterpreting the remark, so that she was left feeling disappointed both in the person who'd first said it and the one who'd repeated it to her. Madeleine could see there was something unusual in her friend's expression.

After they'd exchanged a few banalities to which Marguerite replied as though nothing were amiss, Madeleine couldn't help but ask about Roger. "You should invite him, Marguerite, with a few friends. That boy needs companionship. Promise me you'll look after him as soon as you're feeling better. He's very fond of you, you know." Madeleine's words had a terrible effect on Marguerite. She had just been thinking that she would never invite anyone again, that she'd had enough of society, that she could very well live alone . . . and now she was being asked to do this favor. She hesitated for a moment. "There's no hurry about it," said Madeleine, who'd noticed her friend was put out. Just then, the two women caught each other's eye. As though a spell had been lifted, Marguerite suddenly came back to life. She now looked like those people who bear no grudge and, after having been insulted, carry on as though nothing had happened. "But naturally," she replied, "if that's what you want. I'll invite some friends too; it will be more fun that way." I guessed that Marguerite had understood my wife was hoping to meet Roger at her home, and in a show of that feminine wickedness Madeleine so despises, had taken up her cause. The abruptness of her manner, however, was clearly intended to bring this to my attention and create an incident between my wife and me as soon as we were alone.

Madeleine was unable to conceal her discontent when we left. "Women are Machiavellian," she said. I pretended to be astonished. "But Marguerite is so sweet." "Oh! You think so!" "What I mean is, there's nothing wicked about her." Madeleine is so oblivious that she expected me to be angry with her friend without knowing why. She wanted me to agree with her, and yet the underlying reason for her anger was that I'd been made a party to her innermost thoughts. She was still brooding a few minutes later. "So, you think it's proper to drag people out, supposedly for a tea party, and then tell them that everyone's invitation has been canceled because of a supposed migraine." "Come now, it's not that serious," I replied. "She did it on purpose," added Madeleine. I realized then that Madeleine suspected her friend had never had a headache at all, and had only canceled the invitations to prevent Madeleine from seeing Roger. In a further refinement of cruelty, she had then let her come to savor her disappointment.

November 19th

"Louis," Madeleine said in a playful tone of voice, "something amusing just happened. You know I saw Roger four days ago at his father's. He so wanted to see me again that I promised I would call him. He's such an old friend, what else could I do? I called him a little while ago and asked if he would take me to the Louvre. He used to paint, and it's so interesting to be with someone who can explain the beauty of the art." To emphasize the technical and self-serving side of her phone call, she then added: "After all, one has to put this young man to some sort of use." I said nothing. This time, I didn't want my jealousy to be as apparent as it usually was. "And when will he come?" I asked with studied indifference. "Tomorrow, after lunch. I thought it best to go on a day when you were busy. That way he won't be stealing me away from you." "But it just so happens that I'm not going out tomorrow," I replied automatically. "I thought tomorrow was the day you were going to see Sabasse." "Ah, that's true, I'd forgotten. You're quite right. Go along to the Louvre. That's fine," I added, suddenly afraid Madeleine would sense my jealousy. I felt tense, my jealousy rising, and this condition was made worse by being unable to rail against such a trivial matter. If Madeleine looked at a man in the street, I would suffer in silence rather than make the slightest remark to her. I find all my reasons for being jealous ridiculous. And yet this time, the fact of having made a date with Roger struck me as something serious. Like all men who lack self-confidence, however, I couldn't be sure if it was serious. This visit to the Louvre was perhaps as insignificant as my wife was leading me to believe. What would she have thought of me if, in my error, I'd made some remark to her? She would have been justified in being unhappy, in complaining about me, and that I don't want, even if it means I must suffer. I smiled and changed the subject. Madeleine was relieved. In her own mind, to ease her conscience, she really had called Roger because she wanted to go to the Louvre. After a moment, however, I couldn't help but ask, "Do you really think such a visit will interest you?" Madeleine looked at me with astonishment. "I never claimed it would be interesting for me. I'm doing it to make Roger happy." "Ah! Fine," I answered distractedly. Madeleine could see I was irritated by her plans, but she pretended not to notice. Any scruples and regrets she has are always before the fact. As soon as she is with the person she is going to hurt by admitting to something, she is transformed and becomes amazingly agile. What always helps her in such situations is letting herself be extraordinarily influenced by the person she is with; thanks to a sort of forgetfulness about her actions, she truly believes she has done nothing wrong. As we were talking just now, she had genuinely lost sight of the rea-

son for her phone call and saw only a date made for the purpose, as she claims, of going to the Louvre. Had I lost my temper rather than reacting with such equanimity, she would have
been angry with me for misunderstanding her and ascribing
evil intentions to such a harmless act. She is so convinced of
her own innocence that she didn't even try to be friendlier than
usual so I would forgive her. In fact, she was so sure of being in
the right that she was acting genuinely irritated and complaining about the many things which social obligations force one to
do in life. None of this was intended to reassure me or allay my
fears; she was doing it for herself, as though to convince herself
there really was no harm in what she was planning.

November 21st

After lunch, Madeleine couldn't conceal her anxiety. Roger was
due at any moment. Because his visit was no secret to me, she
felt no awkwardness about it, and yet I detected something like
apprehension in her face. The truth might well be invisible
now, but there was always the chance it would burst out one
day. The day might come when, at the very moment Roger
entered her house, his presence alone would suffice to reveal
everything she'd done to see him again. The thought that this
might occur in the home she shared with me was distressing to
her. She briefly considered going downstairs and pretending—
for the sake of Roger whom she would arrange to meet on the
way—that she had thought he wouldn't come, so that in the
evening she could say to me: "I got so bored waiting for him that
I left, and bumped into him just as I was leaving the building."
To keep from lying, she has this curious habit of feeling obliged
to do in reality what she later plans to say she did. The thought
of being cornered, her back to the wall, makes her prudent.

Just then the maid announced Roger had arrived.

Madeleine's scruples suddenly vanished. Not for a moment had she thought of asking me why I wasn't going out. Before having Roger shown in, she arranged herself in a flattering pose, sitting down and leafing through a fashion magazine with a distracted air. When he appeared, she greeted him with a phrase she knew people found charming: "You've become the very model of punctuality, Roger." She looked up only after having finished speaking, and was struck by how much more independent he seemed. Without knowing why, she wanted to be like a sister, or a mother, to the young man. She felt powerless to resist this new urge. Although she'd been dreaming of a lover when alone, now that he was standing before her she suddenly felt completely different, and had lost all desire to flirt with him. She was stripped of all sentimentality, as if time had moved forward only for her, while Roger remained the young man from her past. Madeleine was rather pleased by this development, for it made everything she had done harmless and everything she had said true, albeit after the fact and in spite of herself. It was clear to me that she was no longer attracted to him in any way. "You'll have coffee," she said, apparently in no hurry to go out. She was suddenly proud to be receiving him as a married woman, to be seen running a household. The hasty, anxious greeting she had prepared was replaced by something unexpected. This often happens with my wife. If she meets someone she knows in the lobby at the theater, for example, the play she has so been looking forward to will suddenly cease to exist for her. Roger seemed rather embarrassed, and looked over at me constantly. He found Madeleine charming, but didn't want this to be obvious; some men are like this, as are most women. Out of pride, or vanity, they don't want to reveal their desire. They conceal their feelings entirely, having never grown out of youth's natural modesty. They cannot bring

themselves to declare their love, and if you try to make it easier for them, they deny everything. Nonetheless, he was here,
and that was what now made him feel awkward, the way a
woman would who goes to meet a man without any plausible
reason. In a surly tone, he said, "I came on time, because the
museums close at four." "If we want to see something, we
ought to leave right away," added Roger, who suddenly found
the offer of a cup of coffee disagreeable, because the intimacy
it involved was not being sought by him but by another.
Madeleine, increasingly a changed person, said, "The fact is I
no longer want to go to the Louvre, not in the least." Obeying
some mysterious force, she was greatly enjoying acting capricious with Roger, as if to show that years of marriage had not
in any way altered her impulsive nature. The truth was that she
really had lost all desire to go out and that, incredible as this
may seem, she was proud of showing me how she treated the
young man. "But then why did you ask me to come meet you
to go the Louvre?" he asked her curtly, his manner deliberately showing me that my presence didn't disturb him in the least.
"Because at the time, that was what I wanted. Aren't we
allowed to want to do things, Roger? If I asked you to come
back tomorrow, I hope that you would come . . . " Now that
she no longer felt attracted to Roger, Madeleine was so self-
assured that she was having fun toying with him. Just as a very
young child will hesitate to touch a strange toy, then grow
bolder as he sees it won't hurt him, until finally he throws it to
the ground, tramples it, and breaks it in an obscure desire to
take revenge on something of which he had mistakenly been
afraid, Madeleine was deriving great pleasure from toying with
Roger, certain she wouldn't suffer when forced to admit that
her power had been illusory. At the same time, it seemed to her
that women were always happy when they behaved this way. As

she mistreated Roger, she was imagining she would be able to exercise power this way throughout her life. Like people who find themselves, thanks to happy accidents of fate, living a life they dreamed of but never thought possible, she was getting slightly drunk on her own words, and on the part she was play-ing. Roger, who hadn't spent much time with her, must have been thinking this was the sort of person she'd become. A mute dislike of Madeleine was beginning to gain in him. Like most young men, he expected women to treat him with the same kindness a good friend would show. He found Madeleine's new attitude disconcerting. But while he reflected that this couldn't last much longer, that she really was being too nasty, Madeleine continued. As the maid was putting lumps of sugar into the coffee cups, Madeleine said with deliberate irony, as if suggesting sweet things were for children, "Plenty of sugar for Monsieur." "No! Not at all," said Roger quickly, "I don't take sugar." "Fine. Fine, then, Roger. We won't give you any sugar. That way you'll be happy. I'm not difficult." Roger's anger was increasingly apparent. Madeleine was beginning to annoy him.

Throughout this exchange, I hadn't moved a muscle, pre-tending to read. What else could I do? It would have made Madeleine furious if I'd joined the conversation; besides, I would have been unable to hold my tongue. I love Madeleine so much that I sat there in silence watching her little produc-tion. As far as she was concerned, I could hold nothing against her which took place in my presence. She was doing nothing wrong. She always seems to be saying that these diversions have nothing to do with love; were I to forbid her from seeing Roger, she would pretend to think I'd gone mad.

As soon as Roger had gone, Madeleine returned to the magazine she'd picked up an hour earlier as a mere prop, as if he'd really interrupted her in her reading. She was thinking of nothing and seemed truly engrossed by the clothes. She even began to hum. All of a sudden, however, she put down the magazine and fell silent. "What happened?" she asked. She looked at the time. It was three. Less than an hour ago, she'd thought she wouldn't be home before six. Yet here she was, looking at a clock that marked three o'clock, humming to herself and reading a ridiculous magazine. "But what happened?" she repeated. "I must be going mad." She rang for the maid. "Is it really three o'clock?" she asked again. "This can't be, I'm dreaming." She picked up the magazine again, looked at the cover, then resumed her humming. "I was reading this magazine!" she said to me. "Yes, I was reading this magazine. Really now, this is hardly to be believed!" This monologue went on for several minutes. In truth, it occupied only the surface of her consciousness. She reminded me of an actor speaking his lines while thinking about something else entirely, though the difference was she wasn't thinking about anything. She hadn't learned the lines she was reciting. I realized abruptly that she was now aware of her surroundings and was thinking of Roger. She regretted not having gone out with him. "It's stupid, really," she must have been thinking, "that I was so diplomatic, and this is the result, whereas I would have been so happy to go out with him." "What if I called him," she said to me. "What I did wasn't very nice." "Come now," I said, "leave the poor fellow alone." It was clear that her only desire now was to see Roger again. "He won't be back home yet, certainly not," she went on, speaking to herself and paying no attention to what I'd said. Had Madeleine known where to find him, I'm sure she would have gone out immediately. She wouldn't have thought herself ridiculous or flighty for doing so. She is one of those women whose pride, however great, never stops them from chasing after a man. They think it the right thing to do to ensure the man they love, if left on his own, doesn't fall in love with another woman. The prospect of such an outcome must have been unbearable for her and made their separation even more distressing. She grew increasingly restless. She got ready to go out. But at the last minute, she was unable to stop herself from picking up the phone and calling Roger, without bothering to justify this. She needed him so desperately that as soon as he was on the line, she put on a soft voice to beg his forgiveness, and above all ensure he came right back, "Roger, be a dear. Come and get me, quickly. We still have enough time to see the primitives." But Roger, who'd been deeply disappointed, failed to understand what lay behind Madeleine's supplicating tone. Unable to see her face, he must have thought she was still playing capricious, willful games. "It's too late," I heard, "and besides, it wouldn't be any fun. Another time, if you like." "You must, Roger, I'm begging you. Do it to make me happy. There's time enough." It was three-thirty. Like many women, Madeleine never believes that closing times are real. If the two of us have errands to do together, for instance, she often arrives so late that I have to run, that she has to rush like mad, in spite of which we'll arrive in front of a shop with its shutters pulled down. "I promise you there's still time, Roger. You can't refuse me this pleasure." I suspect he still thought she was putting on an act, and rather than seeing her as she was, desperate and on the verge of tears, he imagined she was reclining lazily, testing her powers of seduction. Seeing that nothing was going to make him change his mind, and to make everything she'd just said palatable to me, before hanging up Madeleine added, "You're right. We'll do it another time."

No sooner had she put the phone down than Madeleine was overcome by an urgent desire to go out, to leave the apartment. She was afraid that if she stayed, someone, I don't know who, might come and bore her. Her cheeks were aflame. She needed air, motion. She was suffering because of what had just happened, yet never for a moment did it occur to her that she was to blame. No matter what happens to her, she never thinks she is even partly responsible. Just as a bitter man who's committed a wrong will never blame himself, so it never occurs to her to tax herself with the slightest criticism. She is who she is. The stirrings of her conscience may make her uncomfortable, but they are never of an intensity sufficient to make her feel guilty. For Madeleine, feeling guilty would be a form of self-betrayal.

November 25th

Something unexpected happened today, and I have to admit that I was rather pleased by it. Roger vanished. He left a letter on his father's desk, in which he stated his intention to "make the most of life so that, having exhausted all possible pleasures, [he] could commit suicide with no regrets." Although nothing about my attitude hinted at my satisfaction, Madeleine guessed it. I've often noticed that circumstances which make others suffer sometimes make us happy in spite of ourselves. There is nothing to be done about it: we're happy. But I've also noticed that the people who sense that happiness could just as easily be feeling it themselves. If not, how do they perceive it at all, since, as I just remarked, we conceal it so carefully that it's virtually impossible to detect. "Aren't you ashamed," asked Madeleine, "to be happy about such a tragedy?" "But I'm not happy," I replied. "You don't understand, do you," she continued, "that he means to kill himself. It means nothing to you, you have a heart of stone." "That's just a young man talking."

Madeleine was panic-stricken. More than anything else had done, that letter showed me just how much Roger meant to her. In the face of a potential drama, she'd stopped bothering to hide her feelings, especially as subconsciously, she wanted to punish me for any advantages the situation might bring me. All my life I've yearned to be a man, and yet I have to admit that I've constantly found myself in the disagreeable position of being one of those people who profits from others' misfortunes. When I observe myself, I find I have their deceitful air, their doggedness, their tendency to retreat in the face of adversity, which, in the ensuing calm, is always succeeded by the need to take charge.

November 26th

I saw Curti again. He is changing before my eyes. I suddenly feel he's growing old. As naturally as could be, he told me about something that happened yesterday, never realizing what the episode revealed about him. He had gone to see some friends, and while there a Spaniard by the name of Guerrera, who hadn't heard Curti's name properly when they were introduced, insinuated that the Curti family made a rather bad impression in Madrid during the Gomez affair. Curti demanded an apology, which the Spaniard delivered with much gesticulating, declaring that he'd been deeply mistaken, and even swearing, with unbelievable thoughtlessness, that he'd said more than he'd intended to. He now wanted only to make amends to the man he'd offended, inviting him to Spain, swearing he couldn't leave him with such a bad impression, asking if he could see him again, perhaps spend the rest of the evening with him, and even declaring that he wasn't sorry about his faux pas since it had allowed him to further his acquaintance with the most marvelous man he'd ever met. Years ago, Curti would certainly have forgiven the fellow's blunder, but he now refused his apologies and coldly left. The illness ravaging him is not the only explanation for this change in him. From what Madeleine told me, an apparently insignificant incident touched off a revolt which, unbeknownst to him, had been brewing in him for thirty years, concealed by his deeply accepting, fatalistic nature. A few days ago, he read in the paper that while exploring in central Africa, one of his former friends, André Michaud, discovered the remains of an expedition that was lost in 1850. This relatively trivial news item led to the following scene. At a small party, he showed someone the clipping and said, "I used to know Michaud quite well. He was a strange, rather reckless fellow." Among the guests present was a man named Léger, who happened to be a recent friend of Michaud's and began talking about him. Curti was then completely overshadowed in the eyes of everyone present. His descriptions of Michaud were contradicted by Léger. More than ever before, he felt then just how dead his past was, and how little the things he had to say interested the people around him. They were all paying rapt attention to Léger, who'd had business dealings with Michaud a year ago.

November 29th

Although this rarely happens to me, today I felt the need to unburden myself and confide in a friend. Because Curti seemed so low the day before yesterday, so near my own state of mind, I turned to him. This is a man who's lost everything, who's suffered more than anyone from the world's ungratefulness and indifference, a man who conceals tremendous bitterness beneath a cheerful demeanor. And yet this man, with whom I feel a spiritual kinship which ought to make him my friend, failed to understand my sadness. I told him what I thought was wrong with the world. No voice came back to echo my feelings. To be consoled, above all one needs to be understood. But consolation without that deep-seated under-standing, wrong-footed consolation which we must redirect ourselves, what an ineffectual thing! I realized just how great the gulf between us was when he told me, "You're young, you can expect a great deal from life" (whereas I expect nothing from life, and have never for a second thought my age had any part to play in my unhappiness).

One might think that Madeleine is the reason I'm suffering so much. Not in the least. And if I'm so reticent to discuss my feelings, it's because revealing them at all horrifies me. There is nothing more craven than using one's general unhappiness to exaggerate the unhappiness caused by a particular situation. I think I understand now that Curti's apparent lack of sympathy for my troubles must have stemmed from his belief that they were caused by his daughter. Even if I'd understood this soon-er, however, I wouldn't have tried to dissuade him, for I have no doubt he would have interpreted my explanations as a sign of my indifference toward Madeleine. Only in ourselves can we find consolation. I've now reached the point where I dread each day. As I move forward, I become increasingly afraid of the unknown, as though it were drawing ever closer with the pas-sage of time, rather than staying at a safe distance as it used to.

December 3rd

The Comte de Belange telephoned to say that he would like to see us. I was surprised when Madeleine asked him to come by the same evening, for I had thought her totally preoccupied with Roger's fate. At six o'clock, she began considering what she would wear. When she is going to see people from her past, she likes to look her best, as though to show them that their absence hasn't stopped her from remaining beautiful, quite the opposite, and maybe even to make them regret they didn't come see her sooner. Her most pressing problems disappear when the time comes for her to get ready. The care Madeleine lavishes on her appearance is so important to her that it would never occur to her to sacrifice it to some private grief. Just as a worried man will meet a friend and cheerfully make plans for a pleasant evening he knows he won't enjoy, so Madeleine, when distressed, keeps up the appearance of being a happy woman with outsiders. She rang for the maid and gave an order in her customary tone of voice. Beauty is her defense. She suffers less when she is powdered, elegant, adorned, as if being well turned out somehow raises her above everyday concerns. In a sense, the care she takes with her appearance is a mechanism of self-defense.

We became acquainted with Belange during our stay in Nice, or rather that is when Madeleine called him to my attention; it seems she already knew him, though I'm not sure how. We were sitting at the terrace of a tearoom when she suddenly said to me, "In a minute or so, look off to my right. You'll see an elderly gentleman. He's the Comte de Belange. We traveled down to Nice from Paris together. But don't look now." I thought Madeleine seemed flustered. Her voice had sounded different as she'd said those few phrases. To avoid annoying me, she'd probably thought she wouldn't mention she knew this man, but it often happens we're incapable of hiding things we've done—even bad ones—when they may prove interesting. She therefore hadn't been able to resist pointing him out to me, not unlike a woman who, although madly in love,

nonetheless tells her jealous fiancé that she was once on intimate terms with one of his friends. In retaliation, I looked over
immediately where she'd indicated, like those men who humil-
iate their wives by being rude, insolent, and making themselves
look ridiculous, so obsessed with a need to take revenge that
they never stop to consider the person they're offending may in
fact be perfectly charming. "That gentleman?" I asked in a
loud voice, nodding in his direction. Madeleine had nowhere
to hide. The blood rushed to her head. "If you keep this up,
I'm warning you I'll leave and you'll never see me again." I realized then that in her eyes the Comte was some sort of paragon.
Madeleine likes to think she's alone in understanding superior
beings. Just then, whether by chance or because he'd overheard
our conversation, the count turned toward us. He saw my wife,
but didn't appear to recognize her. Although she should have
been hurt by such a slight, she smiled at him, making herself
seem like a woman of easy virtue who is inviting conversation,
offering herself, a particularly distressing sight in a woman who
is normally so reserved. None of this escaped the count, who
had probably recognized her. He is a gallant man, accustomed
to women, a man who sizes people up surreptitiously, but
accurately. Being solicited like this is exactly what he waits for
before making a move. He'll pretend to know nothing about
his feminine admirers, and treat the lowliest of them as if they
were members of the aristocracy. He knows how to pretend he
feels no desire for a woman. The day we arrived in Nice, he
said good-bye to Madeleine straightforwardly, made no
inquiries about seeing her again, was indifferent, elegant, and
apparently hoped for nothing further. Today, therefore, he wasn't
at all embarrassed by my presence. He smiled at Madeleine as
though she were alone, a smile without the slightest innuendo,
intended merely to express his pleasure at meeting someone he

knows. Despite his innocuous air, I was furious, for I understood the count's game all too well. Seeing Madeleine was with
a man, he averted his gaze immediately, out of discretion.
Madeleine was filled with renewed admiration. "He's from a
generation," she whispered to me, "that really worshipped
women." She then took great care to avoid looking in the
count's direction. Whenever Madeleine recognizes and greets
an acquaintance, even very affectionately, she makes it a point
not to catch his eye again, thinking it more distinguished to
make no further contact. I glared at him at every opportunity,
however, making Madeleine remark, "You're so ill-mannered!
Don't you know that it's rude to stare at people that way?" Her
notions of manners are as vague as some people's notions of the
law. Rules of etiquette were something written down, she knew
neither where nor by whom, but they were written. She
believed that her tactfulness came from her knowledge of these
rules rather than from any innate quality. Things one has been
taught have always been more important to her than what her
own delicacy suggests. A polite man was one who did things
that might seem impolite but were, in fact, done only in proper society. She therefore applied herself to looking anywhere
but at the count. He wasn't fooled by this in the least, and after
having shot her a few furtive glances, cunningly adopted the
same attitude, being in no hurry to achieve a result. He finally
rose to leave, and passed our table. As he did, Madeleine raised
her head and looked him straight in the eye. This act so
unnerved her that she was forced to conceal her disarray
behind yet another smile, realizing as she did that her smile
could be construed as an advance, which made her blush.
Perhaps what most bothers Madeleine is the idea that a man,
though outwardly polite, could think she wants him to speak
to her. The count took the liberty of addressing her: "You're

enjoying Nice. It's a beautiful city, Madame, isn't it?" Madeleine was disconcerted. She replied in monosyllables. Then, because the count seemed so harmless, so pleasant, she introduced us. "Won't you join us?" she added. "I wouldn't want to disturb you," said Belange as he drew up a chair. Then, turning to me, he asked with a broad, friendly smile, "Perhaps Monsieur just arrived?" He knows how to appear interested in everyone, even if his interlocutor is a boor. Were he with a group of friends and one of them told a bad joke, he would laugh as heartily as if it had been a good one, and so in this situation he applied himself to falling in step with a disgruntled husband. "You've come from Paris, no doubt?" he went on. I sometimes behave like those ridiculous people who, when asked a simple question, give all sorts of intimate details in their reply, even when they barely know the person they're speaking to. No sooner has a question been asked of me than I feel compelled, perhaps out of generosity, to explain why I left, to say that it's because my ailing mother once spent a holiday in Nice and was very taken with the area. That evening, however, I answered in monosyllables, to show Madeleine how unhappy she had made me. Belange was well aware of my ill humor, but he craftily pretended not to notice it, knowing there is no better way of pleasing women than by appearing not to notice the things they hope to keep hidden. Madeleine answered for me: "Yes, of course, my husband has come from Paris." At last the count rose. He sensed that he had seduced Madeleine and exasperated me. With the same cheerful air, as though he had no idea in the world what had been going on, he left us.

When Belange arrived last night, Madeleine greeted him with a great show of friendliness, even though she was suffering terribly. Roger's flight hadn't affected the way she thinks of the count. It would never have occurred to her to receive him the way she would receive just anyone. She is like those people who keep quiet about problems caused by someone they admire, but go on at great length about those caused by people they don't care about. The count existed on a plane high above anything which might happen to her.

December 5th

Belange's visit makes me think back to something which happened just before we left Nice: a scene as ridiculous as the one in the tearoom. Madeleine and I were strolling along the jetty when we happened to meet the count. She hadn't forgotten him. She'd thought about him every time she'd gone out, and prepared what she would say if they happened to meet. When he saw us, the count approached and very simply, as though addressing an old lady—in other words, without appearing to want to linger—asked, "Don't you find this weather delicious?" He said this without saying hello, without risking any of the formalities of good manners. "Delicious indeed, Monsieur," said Madeleine, gazing out at the blue sea, which was dotted here and there with sailboats. Belange continued, "It makes you want to be out at sea, to be even closer to nature." "It's so beautiful," replied Madeleine in an unnatural tone of voice. Although she constantly talked about beauty, and could be ecstatic about flowers, gardens, or villas, the truth is she is totally insensitive to beauty. Her contemplation was part of a pretty young woman's necessary paraphernalia. You should see the contempt with which she treats people who are insensitive to art, or to the sky's pastel shades. Her only real interest, however, is in what tourists have already discovered, in places to which organized excursions travel; the more difficult and expensive it is to get to a place, the more wonderfully wild and grandiose she finds it. Though she longs to be refined, she has this idea that true beauty must be untamed. As the Count walked with us, he apologized for joining us by saying, "Since you're on your way to the casino, I'll make a little detour." Madeleine was delighted. Had Belange thought it expedient, he might have told another woman that he thought the scenery looked too much like a stage set, as if this were an original thought rather than something he'd heard a hundred times, therefore finding her amusement at his remark quite appropriate. With us, however, he gushed with admiration, although he still wanted to slip in "stage set." He had innumerable similar expressions which amused him and with which he adorned his conversation, for example, that a villa looked "like a Swiss chalet," or a small square on the Place Masséna "like the Tuileries in miniature." Finally he said, "Don't you find that this area looks like a stage set, though of course much prettier and more realistic?" Madeleine agreed by nodding politely. She was totally impervious to wit, and didn't understand the meaning of words when they were used out of context. Saying that the scenery looked like a stage set struck her on the one hand as elegant, yet also, although she couldn't explain why, as terribly superficial. If there is one thing she can't abide, it's superficiality. The count suddenly seemed alien to her, and in spite of herself she became mistrustful. For once, Belange failed to notice. At the end of the jetty, Madeleine said she would like to sit down (she had said so at the very start). The count brought chairs. Madeleine looked at him but didn't sit down, her pout indicating that the chair she was to sit on wasn't quite level. He immediately set it right. To show that he hadn't forgotten he'd said he would make only a slight detour, he remained standing, not wanting to appear he thought himself entitled to sit down just because he'd walked this short way with us. It was then Madeleine felt she hadn't quite risen to the occasion. Like the time the maitre d' had refused her help, a sensation she finds more depressing than any other overcame her: offering something which is refused. It hadn't occurred to her as she sat down that the count might not follow suit. She nearly got up again, but thinking this would look ridiculous, she forced a smile and said: "But do sit down, Monsieur," a remark Belange took as a sign that she'd failed to notice his tactfulness. He must have thought that, in future, he wouldn't need to take quite so many precautions. This made him bolder. In the early stages of any liaison, the count will be exquisitely delicate. But he doesn't remain so. Delicacy is only useful if is noticed. With someone crude, he will eventually become crude himself. Like many women, Madeleine believes in the honors men pay her. She wanted to be worthy of his tributes. He was sitting near her and talking to her quietly about her voice, praising it, and the unexpected and rare nature of this praise seemed to add to his distinction. This was already a higher plane: the discussion had moved beyond lovely hair to warm voice. Although Madeleine never flirts, and doesn't even know how to, she was beginning to put on airs, so that the count wouldn't think badly of her or regret having spent this time with her. After a few minutes, he asked her which hotel we were in. This was the question she'd been dreading. She answered "a small hotel," because she hated noise and had come to rest and be alone. All of a sudden she broke off speaking and blushed. I looked at her, astonished. She lowered her head. I then saw Mme Laferrière walking in our direction, though she hadn't seen us. She was one of Mlle Davis's lodgers, a former dancer with whom we'd talked a few times. Mme Laferrière was still quite flirtatious. It was said that she'd had her hour of glory in postwar Parisian society. Throughout the day she wore enormous jewels and makeup like an actress. She enjoyed making friends with younger women, so she could feel sorry for them. She seemed to understand all their problems, because she'd had similar ones herself. She put on airs like a dowager, talking constantly about how her apartment was too big for her, about the charitable organizations she belonged to, about servants. While she'd been befriending Madeleine, she'd also been interviewing all of the staff at the rooming house, and had even offered some of them jobs. She was advancing toward us with small, measured steps, accompanied by another lodger, Joseph Courbet. We'd met him, too. He was a man of Mme Laferrière's age, who respected her deeply. He had worked in a bank on the boulevard des Italiens all his life and then retired to Grenoble. His only pleasure in life was spending three months in Nice every year, which he'd convinced himself was good for his health. Since retiring from the bank, he'd begun to discover life. He now liked to repeat that had he known what he knew now, he wouldn't have wasted his life as he'd done, but gone around the world instead. Having lived in the shadows for thirty years, he now took great pleasure in rediscovering the time he'd lost by listening to the tales of people like Mme Laferrière, who'd lived a freer life. He listened with delight as she told him about the receptions and society events she'd attended, belatedly taking instruction in how he should have lived his life, which was a compensation of sorts.

The two approached slowly, saying nothing as they walked. Now and then, Mme Laferrière would point to the upper floors of a hotel with her cane. She had stayed in all of them, and enjoyed resurrecting a long-dead past, both for herself and for Courbet. Madeleine was pale, horrified at the thought that the two old people might stop to talk to us, as Mme Laferrière would have thought nothing of addressing the count like an old friend. They were drawing ever nearer. The count sat silently, his legs crossed. Although he'd said very little, he was now staring out to sea with the air of a man worn out by a long conversation who is taking a moment's rest before starting in on a fresh topic. He hoped by this to make my wife trust him. He wanted to show he wasn't one of those men who latches onto his prey by talking uninterruptedly, but rather a dreamer who falls silent when he has nothing to say. The old people were getting closer. Madeleine lowered her head further. Just as they passed us, however, Belange asked her a question. Madeleine had the very distinct impression just then that if she failed to answer, it would seem strange not just to Mme Laferrière and Courbet, who would conclude she didn't want to see them, but also to the count, which was more serious. Madeleine gets worried and embarrassed when she is ashamed of knowing certain people. Then all at once she'll think it's silly to be so concerned with what others think, pull herself together, and become lively and confident, as though she'd never had a moment's hesitation. As the old people passed in front of her, she looked at them without appearing to recognize them, and burst out laughing at something the count said. Mme Laferrière and her friend had continued along their way. When I looked in their direction a few seconds later, I saw the old woman pointing us out to her companion with the tip of her cane.

December 7th

I grew very worried today when I heard that Chambige had been implicated in a speculation scandal. I once browsed through a book that listed the themes with which every good playwright should be familiar. One in particular struck me: a man commits an offense when young, which is witnessed by someone. He now loves a woman. Happiness awaits. He has carved out an agreeable life for himself, until the witness to his past reappears. He demands money, threatening to reveal all he knows. Once paid, he seems appeased. But just when the guilty man begins to let down his guard, thinking he's been forgotten, the blackmailer reappears. He grows increasingly demanding. In the eyes of some people, I am that blackmailer. For example, ten years ago Paul D. came to see me in a frantic state, saying he'd contracted a dreadful disease from a woman. I reasoned with him. He talked of killing himself. I took him to see a doctor, a friend of mine. He was cured, and only needs an additional course of treatment at regular intervals to ensure the disease doesn't recur. I know he never told his wife. He's taken extraordinary care to conceal it from her. This man certainly can't be happy. Sometimes I run into him and his wife. He is a sorry sight. He lives with the constant fear that she will learn of the disease and leave him in disgust. As he adores her, that thought terrifies him. I know another secret, also about a married man. Caught in a police raid on an hotel, he was discovered in circumstances upon which I would rather not elaborate. After having taken down his name, the police let him go. Mortified, he confessed everything to me, asking whether he would be found out, and whether it was true, as he'd heard, that his family would be notified. I reassured him by saying that only the families of "repeat offenders" were notified, a fact I invented on the spot to reassure him. As it is, his wife was never notified. Years have gone by, and I'm the only person who knows about his unfortunate adventure. When I meet either of these two men, they are extraordinarily amiable to me. We never discussed what happened. I suspect they think I've forgotten everything. Occasionally, I've been invited to their homes, and spent entire evenings with their wives. There is always something distressing about those evenings, even frightening, especially when the wives imply, with little giggles, that they know their husbands far better than I do. Needless to say, I would rather die than betray their confidence.

To my knowledge, only one man holds that sort of power over me. I have no fear that he'll try to blackmail me, but what I fear is that he has told others what I did, and that one day one of them might tell Madeleine. This is what happened. When I was twenty, my greatest ambition was to influence other people, to dominate them in the course of endless conversations, to control the weak and make them obey my every whim. At the time, I was in love with a young woman. At one time or another, we have all persuaded a friend to do us a favor knowing it would later prove damaging to him. Although my only income was the modest allowance my father sent me, for months on end I begged Lucienne to leave her family and move in with me. I hinted at a fabulous life. The more she refused, the more I insisted, even going so far as to threaten, as I'd done with Maud in the past, to break off with her if she didn't agree. When she finally yielded, I was taken aback. It wasn't long before our financial troubles were such that I had to insist she return to her family or ask her father for a stipend. She refused. In retaliation, I made life impossible for her, threatened to lock her out at night, and behaved so cruelly that today I'm ashamed. Terrified, she finally left one day and never came back. Despite all my searching, I never found her. Had she committed suicide? Left the country with the first man she met? I had no idea. But then one morning, her father came to see me. He was none other than Chambige. I don't know how he'd discovered where I lived, but he found me. He asked me where Lucienne was. That was when the affair turned sour. I grew frightened and lied to him rather than telling the truth. I told him that Lucienne had come with me of her own free will, but that, because she was a creature of luxury, she'd quickly tired of the life I made her lead and abandoned me for a very rich gentleman. I'll never forget the contemptuous look her father gave me. He pulled a sheet of paper from his pocket and read it aloud to me. It was a letter from Lucienne in which she told him everything: my cruelty, how I'd made her suffer, and asked him to forgive her for the pain she'd caused him. The letter was infinitely distressing. Though he was still furious, Chambige began to weep. I briefly thought we would come to blows, for he had drawn close, grabbed my shoulder, and was shaking me. I didn't defend myself, because of my respect for his age but also because I felt so guilty. He was in despair. His daughter's coming to live with me was nothing compared to what had just happened. His inability to exact any sort of revenge was driving him mad. He finally left, saying, "I'm keeping this letter, you cad. It will haunt you for the rest of your days. Life is long, and mark my words, you're going to regret what you did, for I will take my revenge. Everyone will know what you did. No woman will want you, do you hear me, when they learn what you did to an innocent young creature, for you've killed my poor child, I'm certain of that. You're an assassin, you've killed her."

I have to say that, as badly as I treated Lucienne, I did love her with all my heart. I thought of her constantly when she wasn't with me, and was racked with jealousy. But as soon as she would return, something strange would happen to me: I would feel compelled to torment her. It was beyond my control; after reducing her to tears, I wasn't even capable of behaving nobly and comforting her. There was something monstrous in my heart at the time, something extraordinarily unyielding. In fact, I recall an incident that demonstrates how unfeeling I was, at least in appearance. While at school, I struck a friend so awkwardly one day that he fell and hurt himself quite seriously. Taken to the headmaster's office (I was then fourteen), I was duly accused and offered the chance to apologize for what I'd done, in which case the matter would be dropped. That I would not do. Three teachers, the headmaster, and a woman who'd joined them spent an hour badgering me to make me say I was sorry, but I maintained a stony silence. Exasperated, they locked me in a little courtyard. As soon as I was alone I burst into tears, but not in any ordinary way. For the next three hours, I did nothing but cry, my body racked with spasms, impervious to everything around me, and when I finally stopped, I could no longer stand on my own two feet. I fell to the ground and had to be carried home like a dying man. In a sense, that was my revenge, for I remember that in spite of the condition I was in, I could detect the teachers' unease. I spent the next four days at home in bed, and only returned to school two weeks later. With such a harsh, headstrong nature, it's easy to see how trivial the things I forced Lucienne to endure must have seemed to me, and what reserves I could draw on to keep from revealing what I really felt for her. Lucienne was very sensitive. She'd grown increasingly worried and fearful since leaving her family. She almost never spoke; she'd become spineless, as though she had no will of her own. I constantly reproached her for cringing, but my reproaches only made things worse. She was like a whipped dog. She no longer dared to speak or act, terrified I would lose my temper, when in fact if I lost my temper at all it was because she did nothing. The more I bullied her, the more I terrified her, the more satisfied I felt. I wanted to make a slave of her, a being who no longer had any personality. And yet she rebelled one day, just before leaving me. It would be impossible to relate how shocked, and then how furious, this made me. For a moment I was pale and stunned. Then I started to insult her. Her impassive demeanor so infuriated me that my shouting grew increasingly violent. I found myself digging my fingers into the palms of my hands with all my might to control my urge to strike her. I was livid with rage, unable to find words more insulting and hurtful than those I'd already used, which only made me angrier. She remained imperturbable. Suddenly, rather than bursting into tears, she had a fit of nerves. Cruel as it is to say this, I cannot describe my relief at that moment. Seeing that pitiful body racked with convulsions, I felt as though a warm shower was rushing over me, soothing my own nerves. Everything around me took on a new clarity. I was alive again. I stopped talking and, with no tenderness whatsoever, like a stranger, I put her on the bed and began massaging her temples with cool water. I was calm and detached, but above all preoccupied with stopping my ministrations before she realized I was administering them. Such was that miserable love. And yet, I don't think I'm wicked. All of that was pride, the harshness of a young man. I loved her, and to prove this, I merely want to cite one fact. It sometimes happened that Lucienne spoke entire sentences as she slept. She dreamed a great deal every night, and remembered all her dreams the next morning. One night I was awake and heard her say in her sleep: "No, no, you're not nice. I can assure you, sir, that I'll care for him. And in fact he knows me better than you [she was talking about a black cat]. You'll never have the patience to raise him. They need to be given their milk regularly, otherwise they die. Let me have him, I beg you. If you take him, he's going to be very unhappy. He loves me so. No . . . no . . . I beg you . . . leave him . . . " I understood she was dreaming that a stranger wanted to take a cat she imagined she owned and that she was suffering at the idea of this separation, probably just as she imagined her own father—and this was no doubt the source of her dream—was suffering. She began whimpering softly, as though in pain. I took pity on her then, and got up noiselessly. It so happened that there was a cat in the hotel we were living in at the time. I put on my overcoat and started down the darkened staircase in search of the cat. Naturally, I couldn't find him. I went up to the sixth floor and peered into all the corners, lighting my way with matches. Then I went back down to the ground floor. Although everyone was in bed, I noticed a faint light coming through the door of the office. The maid who was on night duty opened the door. The cat was with her. I took him, went back up to our room, quietly closed the door and went back to bed. Lucienne was sleeping peacefully. I woke her gently and showed her the cat, which was purring. She didn't understand at first, but then, as she remembered her dream, her face lit up with a ray of pure joy, which filled me with happiness. This may seem a ridiculous anecdote, but it seems to me that it was truly out of love that I got up in the middle of the night and went to look for a cat in our hotel.

The hours after Chambige left were terrible ones. Long afterward, I felt my happiness was in the hands of this man, and that he could shatter it whenever he wanted. It was only several years later that I learned, quite by accident, that Lucienne was now happily married. Our relationship remains a painful memory. Although this all happened fifteen years ago and has long since been forgotten, I felt as worried today as I did in those early days. Reading the newspaper this morning, I learned that Chambige was about to be arrested. My peace of mind evaporated. I'm afraid he's going to appear at my door, not wanting to be alone in his fall from grace, and tell Madeleine everything, make a scandal, even tell the judge, to show how fine a nature he has, and how kind he was to the man who caused him such heartache.

I think of my wife. This morning I found her even more beautiful and desirable than ever. I don't know if you've ever felt disgusted with yourself when, alone in bearing a shameful secret, burdened with vice and ugliness, you suddenly find yourself face to face with the pure, intact person who shares your life. How fine that person seems, then, and how unworthy we feel! What a tremendously powerful feeling of regret we have for the harm we've done her! We swear never to do it again, and if, by the grace of God, we've managed to avoid the consequences of our actions, what happiness we feel as we embrace our loved one! But then the happiness fades, boredom sets in, and we need something new. Being a man is so dangerous! We are so sincere in regretting our lost happiness, when we're miserable! And yet we compromise it so carelessly, so thoughtlessly! If I could make a vow, it would be to have enough self-control never to risk anything again, to succumb to no temptation, to remain worthy of the woman I love. Even as I make that heartfelt vow, I reflect that Chambige is still alive and that later today, or perhaps tomorrow, he will reveal everything.

December 8th

My resolve abandoned me, and for once I rebelled. I was beginning to lose patience. Madeleine was heaping more ridicule on me by the day. There was no reason for this to stop. Perhaps I acted in a fit of temper. I don't know. I don't want to know. Here is what happened. When I came home late this afternoon, I went into our bedroom. Almost immediately, I noticed a bouquet of magnificent orchids on the mantelpiece. Their presence didn't surprise me; what drew my attention was the basket decorated with ribbons they were in. Suspecting something was so far from my thoughts that I forgot about them for the next few minutes. I sat down. It was only out of idleness that I looked at the basket again. A seed of doubt planted itself in my mind. I drove it out, for it seemed utterly impossible that those flowers would be in this room if they were in any way compromising. The more I looked at them, however, the more it seemed they came from another world. Gradually, they began to symbolize lust and falsehood in my eyes. I couldn't take my eyes off them. "It simply can't be that she bought those flowers!" I thought. I am no stranger to this reflection. It is common among husbands whose wives regularly turn up wearing dresses and jewels they can't afford. "But if she hadn't bought them herself, she wouldn't have dared put them in our room," I added, to reassure myself. I got up and tried to find the florist's name. Picking up a crumpled piece of cellophane, I smoothed it out. The basket came from Jolibois. Without planning my movements, because I was preoccupied, I moved it, placing it squarely in the middle of the room, and then, mimicking what I'd done so often as a child when I was jealous of a gift a cousin had received, I put it on a chair in front of the door, so that Madeleine would knock it over when she came in. I had just sat down again when I heard the sound of voices in the hall. I leaped up. To prevent my wife from noticing what I'd just done, and above all to avoid making her angry, I ran to the basket. I was just about to replace it on the mantelpiece when Madeleine came in, surprising me in the ridiculous posture of a visitor caught touching something that doesn't belong to him, which increased my ill humor. As soon as the door was closed, I asked her curtly, "What are these flowers called?" "They're orchids." "Were they given to you?" "No." Did you buy them?" "No." "Well, where did they come from then?" "What does it matter to you?" "I really think I have the right to know where these flowers came from." "What about me, don't I have the right to have the flowers I like anymore?" Madeleine asked this with the utmost sincerity. I was beginning to get irritated. "I'm asking you to tell me where these flowers came from." "It doesn't concern you." This is a phrase I'm accustomed to hearing from Madeleine. She feels very strongly that she owes no one an explanation regarding objects which incarnate pleasure, or beauty, anything which is a part of her ideal, and gets irritated if I dare to question her. One would have thought that by wanting to know where the flowers came from, I was trying to penetrate the innermost reaches of her soul. The flowers were presumed to be so foreign to me that she'd left them in our room without even thinking I might ask where they were from. She had even displayed them ostentatiously on the mantelpiece, but my repeated questions suddenly made her aware of her folly. "I want you to tell me who gave you these flowers," I said, angrily this time. Madeleine lost her composure. She regretted her flippancy; fear was gaining her. All the same, she hadn't resolved to give me a straight answer. I found something beautiful in this determination to reveal nothing. My wife could have confessed, and although I always pretend not to believe complicated explanations and accounts that require the narrator to travel far back in time to make his story plausible, she would eventually have convinced me. The fact is she didn't want to. She could said any name, but how would she then have explained the reasons for such a tribute? And if this tribute from an infatuated man was as harmless as all that, how would she have managed to defend herself, when she never reacts to any injustice? If accused of stealing an apple as a child, she would have denied it, because she'd picked it up off the grass and therefore hadn't stolen it. But if finally forced to admit that she'd eaten the apple, it would never have occurred to her to exculpate herself by telling the truth, which was that she'd found it. Her denials about the orchids were just as vehement, and all the more obstinate because she sensed appearances were against her. A sort of pride, however, prevented her from coming to her rescue with explanations. "Are you going to tell me who gave you those flowers?" "No, no, absolutely not . . . " When being questioned by a man, she is so oblivious to his state of mind that even when his voice begins to betray his impatience, she replies as curtly as she did to his first question, even raising her voice if he raises his, while not varying her replies in the slightest, and this until she bursts into tears. "If you don't tell me, I'll ask the florist," I said, staying calm while reserving myself the trump card of naming Jolibois. The threat made a deep impression on Madeleine. If there is one thing she finds distasteful, it is checking where someone has been, not because she finds such verifications shameful, but rather because they compromise her pride with the people one interrogates. She likes to leave a good impression everywhere, and often wonders what people say about her after she's gone. In her eyes, going back to question a tradesman would be humiliating. She probably admired the man who'd sent the flowers for his gesture, and was horrified at the idea it might lead to her husband going to interrogate the florist. She began to tremble. "You won't go to the florist," she said, "you wouldn't do anything so wicked; if you do, you'll never see me again." She still had no intention of explaining anything, for she had done nothing wrong. But she was behaving exactly as if guilty of some wrongdoing. That was when I failed to be generous, and decided instead to be cruel. I knew perfectly well that Madeleine was virtuous, but as appearances were against her, I quite automatically chose to take only those appearances into account. I was playing—with a touch of sincerity, I might add—the role of the husband who's sure of his facts and finally has proof of his wife's infidelity. I'd been casting about for such a pretext for some time now. Subconsciously, I'd been waiting for a reason to lose my temper. Even as my blood began to boil, I sensed I'd been given a unique opportunity to have the upper hand, because something had happened which, though my conscience might excuse it, was no less serious for my choosing to ignore it. "If you don't tell me right now who gave you these flowers, I'm going to Jolibois." This time the effect was considerable. Madeleine no longer had the energy to conceal the truth. Nonetheless, she hesitated a few seconds. Finally she murmured, "Belange." She looked at me, crushed, then burst into tears. "Ah! Yes! Now I understand everything. I understand why you go out. I understand why you never have any time to spend at home with me." I was now acting only out of jealousy, whose violence I stoked with my bitterness. "Women like those sorts of gentlemen. It's only natural. They have such refined souls, they understand your sensitivities so well." Like a man coming back to life, my words flowed freely now. Events had proved me right. I'd always known this would happen spontaneously, that the day would come when the truth burst out into the open and confronted Madeleine. That day had come. I could walk away without hesitation or suffering, since she was the one who'd behaved badly. I could leave her, swearing I never would have gone if she hadn't been unfaithful to me. Yes, I could swear this, and even believe it in perfect good faith. I was almost sincere. I went so far as to inject a tender note into the words I spoke. "Since you wanted it this way, since you preferred a stranger's love to mine, have it your way! You'll be happy, that's all I want." Unbelievable as this may seem—though the remark was no more vile than the others— I even added: "Later, you'll regret it. You'll see that you'll regret choosing another man over me." In spite of everything, my voice betrayed some emotion. The truth lay close to the surface, and if I didn't get carried away, it was because I sensed I would regret it later. Later, but not now. Today, there were these flowers. They were here. A man had given them to Madeleine. Madeleine had accepted them.

As I spoke, Madeleine looked at me anxiously. Despite her anguish, she never thought of trying to exculpate herself. When I've made scenes in the past that were more violent though the offenses were less serious, she's accepted my insults as though she really deserved them, with tears in her eyes. She would listen without hearing what I was saying, aware only that I was filled with rage, and that she was the cause of this rage. I began pacing up and down, no longer talking to Madeleine but to myself. "Well naturally she has a lover, a very sensitive lover, that's what she's wanted all her life. At heart, she's happy. Why would I stop her from being happy? I have no right to do that. She doesn't love me." From time to time I would interrupt myself to address her sharply, "Isn't that right, you don't love me?" And still she said nothing, as though it were true she didn't love me.

When I realized abruptly that I was repeating myself, and that my anger might be starting to ebb, I said, "Since that's the way it is, it would be best if I left." I took out a suitcase and threw some shirts into it. Seeing it my hands, Madeleine suddenly grew frightened. But she didn't move. Something in her prevents her from acting until the last possible moment. I walked toward the door. It was only then that Madeleine, who had been watching without saying a word, threw herself at me like a madwoman, sobbing. This wasn't the woman who'd heard me out, but a different, shaken, woman who seemed to be saying, "Enough of this wickedness. You know I'm incapable of betraying you." She even seemed to be smiling behind the tears, as though to show me how ridiculous this was and say: "Just look at me, will you! Can a wife like me possibly be unworthy of her husband?" I had before me a creature terrified by the consequences of her actions. It was impossible not to realize this. I sensed then how fragile the evidence was on which I'd rested my case, and how harsh my words had been. I had gone too far. Making no further attempts to mask my voice and give myself the airs of an offended man, I tried to disengage myself, saying, "Let go of me. You can see I have to go." It was obvious it no longer made any difference what tone of voice I adopted; it was the real me Madeleine now clung to. But she didn't let go. She babbled aimlessly, though without making any attempt to justify herself, still convinced I had nothing to reproach her for. I managed to open the door. Madeleine's choking sobs made me realize she was no longer herself, but a creature in pain. This changed the nature of my effort to leave her: I'd become like a priest trying to take his leave of a condemned man. I was suffering tremendously, though no longer because of Madeleine. Her tears and distress had stripped her of her personality. I felt myself relenting, and said, "But I'm not leaving. I'm going to go spend a few days in

Versailles. I'll be back. I do know that you're honest, and that those flowers mean nothing." For a moment, I nearly went back into the bedroom, then caught myself. "You have to make a start," I thought to myself. "After that, she'll be much nicer to you. The worst of it is over now." Once again I tried to disengage myself, and to my surprise suddenly found I was free; nothing was holding me back. Madeleine stood before me, unrecognizable. I smiled. "The fact is, I had to go to Versailles today anyway; I hadn't told you yet because I didn't want to hurt you." Meanwhile, I was enraged that she wasn't trying to stop me anymore, that she was setting me free. I wanted to scream my contempt at her, but was crushed by this unexpected freedom, by her renunciation. "Can't you see that I'm leaving?" I asked angrily. Madeleine didn't reply. She seemed indifferent to anything I might do. I was slowly overcome with a deep disgust with myself.

When we succeed for months on end in adhering to the course we've set ourself, when an iron will keeps us from wavering for an entire year and we've already started thinking we're improved, transformed, and then, in a moment of anger, we become worse than ever, the most painful feeling overwhelms us, as though we were a laborer who, after a lifetime of hard work, sees the fruit of his efforts swept away in a night. We find ourselves back where we started. Today I reverted to being the man I used to be. What was it that made me a happy man yesterday? It was that each passing day distanced me that much more from the man I'd been, that time strengthened my will and made it increasingly unlikely I would fail. Now, however, it's going to be so hard for me to control myself! Whenever the temptation arises, I'll behave as I did today. I'll say to myself, "What's the use?" since yesterday, or the day before yesterday, or a week ago, I wasn't able to curb my emotions. I threw my suitcase off to one side and knelt down in front of Madeleine like a father in front of his child, begging her to forgive me. She was unmoved, however.

December 9th

I spent a miserable night. After dinner last night, Madeleine suddenly put her coat on and coldly announced, "I'm going to sleep at my father's." I tried to hold her back without being overly insistent, for fear of bringing on a fit of nerves. She left and I stayed here alone.

After reading for an hour, I wandered through the empty apartment. Everything reminded me of Madeleine. At times she appeared before me, as though she'd never left. Then she would suddenly disappear like a ghost, and everything would be empty again. The space between the pieces of furniture seemed unusually vast. The objects she normally uses were more immobile. Everything seemed frozen. The lamps had lost a measure of their brilliance, and when I left one room to walk through several others before finally coming back to my starting point, I felt painfully alone, much the way I feel when I return home in the evening to find the house is empty. The idea of going to join Madeleine at her father's came to me after I'd already undressed. When I lived alone, it often happened that this urge to go out came over me after I'd readied myself for bed and laid out the evening newspapers I always read before falling asleep. At heart, I've never been a homebody. Wherever I've lived, it's always been temporary. The night holds no terrors for me; I face it as naturally as the day. Tonight, however, I told myself no, and was further inclined to stay in by the thought of how tedious it would be to get dressed again. In addition, fear of seeing people again—night people, who are so little aware of others—and unease at the thought of being out in public made me hesitate further. I went to bed, turned on the little bedside lamp, and began to think. I was calm. I was thinking of the fevered pitch at which everything had happened during the day. I was entirely myself now, with no witnesses, no excitement. All at once, it struck me that rather than going to her father's, Madeleine had taken the train. I pictured myself talking to her as she stepped into the railway carriage. "Madeleine, my darling Madeleine, you're quite mad to go off this way. You mustn't. Haven't you thought about the pain you're causing me?" In spite of this, she left. Then I went to meet her, in a hotel room in Brussels. "Will you never realize, my darling, how unreasonable you are? Does your husband have no part to play in your life? You treat him as though he were an absolute stranger." And then, still in my imagination, I met her one evening. "You see how useless it is to hide. You belong to me, and wherever you go, God will always put you on my path."

Even though these imaginary situations differed, I spoke in the same flat, toneless voice, which made it clear there was no way of escaping me. Suddenly, I imagined Madeleine had returned. I heard the key in the lock. She approached our bed: "My darling, why did you frighten me this way? Since we have to live together, try to be patient." I listened to myself speak without quite realizing I was addressing someone who wasn't there. All at once, however, I understood I was hallucinating and that I was merrily allowing the vaguely rational ideas passing through my mind to take on a life of their own. To cut them short, I got up, turned on all the lights, and began wandering through the apartment, running my fingers along the furniture, walls, vases, and radiators as I passed, perhaps to reassure myself that nothing had changed. But everything that played a part in making my home so dear to me had vanished, as though I were now in a prison cell. Something then happened I find hard to believe. Although every fiber of my being was suffering, I suddenly became obsessed with assuring myself that the comforts of home still surrounded me. I went into the bathroom, mechanically lifted Madeleine's perfume to my nostrils, touched the hot water pipes with a distracted finger. Returning to my room, I sat on the bed to test the springs. I wanted to breathe new life into a gentleness I never thought about, and which I now feared I had lost. Hard as I tried, that gentleness had vanished. All the familiar objects were in place, but they lacked any warmth. Nothing had changed, and yet nothing existed anymore. I made an effort to forget everything and reclaim my surroundings, if only for a moment, even if it meant suffering afterward, but my efforts were in vain. I went back to bed after having carefully closed every door so that I would be in the smallest possible space. Putting a mirror within arm's reach, I spread some newspapers out on the bed. Madeleine's absence now seemed less distressing to me. I felt as though I were living in a space designed for a single person. For a brief moment, I felt better, but then suddenly the solitude surrounding me grew enormous. "If I get up again," I thought, grappling with the urge to get out of bed yet again, "it will serve no purpose, and I'll be back in bed immediately." I stayed in bed, filled with that strange, disagreeable sensation born of not doing what we want because it's pointless. Without thinking, yielding to a need more urgent than the rational thought that had ordered me to stay in bed, I leaped up. In spite of my momentum, I remained immobile for a second at the foot of the bed. Remembering all the doors I'd closed, it occurred to me that if I now opened them, I would have to reclose them all immediately afterward. Without thinking any further, I got back into bed. For a long time, I struggled to convince myself that any movement would be in vain. Then I sprang out of bed like a madman, ran to open a door, went into the living room, where I turned on the lights, then on to the dining room, and from there to the next room. This wasn't because I needed freedom, or air, but rather to destroy everything I'd so carefully prepared. When I was as far as I could be from the bedroom in which I'd organized my night's peace and oblivion, I collapsed into an armchair and squeezed both hands against my temples, trying to cry. No tears came. As though incubating an illness, I felt hot, dry, tense, and unable to cry. Taking my lower lip between my fingers, I pulled it as hard as I could while turning it outward, trying to inflict pain. I was absolutely unrecognizable. At the peak of this crisis, I suddenly imagined Madeleine had come in. "It's over for me . . . I'm dying slowly . . . ," I shouted. And then I was filled with tremendous happiness. Madeleine was here. What did my tears matter! Everything was for the best. I was coming out of a bad dream. But the approaching peace stopped just short of me. It had struck me that I was exaggerating my suffering, and that it was only to embellish it that I was doing battle with a ghost. I got up out of my armchair. It wasn't yet midnight. "I have to go to sleep right away," I thought, "otherwise my curiosity will keep growing, and I'll be up all night." So far, everything was normal. I never went to bed any earlier. But I'd reached the limit. If I exceeded it without falling asleep, I would be making an exception. I have reached an age at which we try to control our unhappiness and, above all, not disturb our habits, that age at which we've been deeply marked by life and dread exceptions of any kind, fearful of the excesses we remember from our youth. And yet I indulged in no excesses; but it's often the case that people who fear things the most are the very ones who've suffered from them the least. I returned to my room, closed the doors, and went to bed, telling myself sternly: "I must go to sleep. I must forget everything until tomorrow. I must go to sleep." I turned off the light, closed my eyes, and made a great effort to think of nothing as I tried to fall asleep. The struggle for sleep is a terrifying thing. One has no grip. The mere desire to fall asleep keeps you awake. I was thinking of nothing, and yet, unbeknownst to me, my desire to fall asleep was keeping me awake. I turned this way and that repeatedly. From time to time, through the darkness, I heard the ringing of a distant clock. Everything was dark. My willpower was gone. And yet I wasn't asleep. How much time passed this way? I don't know. I completely lost all sense of time. I was as if asleep, and yet sufficiently aware to know that I was, in fact, awake. After endlessly tossing every which way in the bed, my drowsiness grew more pronounced. This filled me with a minute sense of joy. I was on the verge of drifting away when, imperceptibly, I had the sensation my brain was growing bigger and bigger, that my body was turning to lead, that my entire being was being inflated, and that the bigger it became, the less able I was to move about in order to resume my normal appearance. Nausea made me want to sit up, and yet I couldn't. Waking up earlier than usual is one of the symptoms doctors look for in patients suffering from systemic poisoning. At dawn, mysteriously warned that an illness is invading, we awaken to chase it away. I had been warned. I sensed I needed to regain consciousness, and yet it felt as if I were glued to my bed. I suddenly had the impression that all the doors were opening at once, even the front door (so it, too, had ceased defending me), that the apartment was brightly lit and Madeleine was advancing toward me. I was fighting for breath as I watched her approach. She drew closer, not even bothering to walk on tiptoe. I shrieked and sat bolt upright. My eyes were open. I looked for Madeleine everywhere, thinking she was hiding. For a moment, I was sure she was next to me. Then suddenly I saw nothing, as though a hand had been lowered over my eyes. Groping in the dark, I tried to turn on the light, but my hand was moving so quickly that I failed to find the switch. Although I was wide awake now, I had the impression the apartment was brightly lit, only to fall back into darkness a moment later. I finally switched on the light and looked at my watch. It was two in the morning. Still groggy, I leaned mechanically across the empty half of the bed in hopes that Madeleine would be there. There was, of course, no one. To reason with myself, I resumed speaking aloud, just as I'd spoken to Madeleine a little while ago: "You must go to sleep. Things will sort themselves out. Madeleine will be back tomorrow morning." I turned the light off, then fell asleep reflecting, rather strangely, that I had just had a real hallucination.

December 10th

Madeleine came home this morning, which surprised me. Although she'd left over something much more trivial the last time, I'd had to go get her. Today, however, whereas I'd been entirely in the wrong, she came back on her own. When she appeared, I felt slightly awkward. At first I pretended nothing had happened, asking her if she'd slept well and chatting about this and that. She made no reply, however. I then said, "I hope you weren't too hurt by my behavior." She gave me a withering look, as though it were fatuous of me to imagine I could upset her. I briefly considered telling her about the awful night I'd spent without her, but it was so obvious she would never believe me that I thought better of it.

Now that I've calmed down, I'm amazed at how fearless I was. What amazes me is that, just like Maud, it never occurred to Madeleine to be arrogant in the face of my outburst. What would I have done then? I'm amazed I resorted to such violent tactics, thinking rather dimly that this was war. I'm even more amazed Madeleine didn't choose to raise her voice over mine, lose her temper, threaten me. What's surprising in great fits of temper is the potential we have suddenly to become as gentle as lambs, which a single word can unlock. If, while in the blackest rage, we happen to think of that weakness, that gateway to serenity, it's always startling to realize our adversary doesn't think we even possess such a potential.

I was terribly depressed all morning. Although I had expected Madeleine to react to aggression with even greater aggression, she'd behaved instead like a poor, defenseless child. There is nothing more distressing than crushing someone's pride. When, wounded by their indifference, we get carried away, a voice cries out to us, warning that our reserves aren't going to be enough. Then, in the heat of anger, we acquire the strength we were lacking. But when we suddenly realize that our opponent has capitulated and collapsed miserably, we suddenly find ourselves alone with our disproportionate effort, as though we'd used a powerful catapult to launch ourselves across a tiny stream. We feel cruel, wicked, harsh, and ashamed of dominating the situation so totally. Pride won't allow us to ask for forgiveness; we're left perched atop positions we did everything to capture and which are now meaningless. Only then do we begin to realize how inhuman we were. Madeleine hasn't spoken to me yet. I watched her getting dressed this morning as though nothing had happened, and yet something in her face revealed she'd pulled herself together. Not once did she look at me. I felt so strong yesterday, but today, in her presence, it seems to me I'm weak. There is no sensation more unbearable than seeing loved ones resume life as normal after we've tormented them, secretly fortified by decisions they won't abandon, and which we can only guess at. We worry. We don't dare speak first, afraid of being told something terrible. Instead, we anxiously observe them preparing with a determined air for a new life we know nothing about. Watching Madeleine come and go as though she were alone in the house, I prayed with all my might for a visitor. We need others at times like this, because what we most want is to see the beloved face grow animated and relaxed, even for an outsider. And yet I betrayed none of these emotions. I realized how unfair it had been to inflict such a scene on Madeleine for some flowers an old man had given her, which, as she'd pointed out, should have made me proud. But I hadn't the courage to admit I'd been wrong, especially as I sensed my wife wouldn't accept my apologies. Had I begged her to forgive me, she would have reacted with scorn, for although she isn't vindictive, she does feel very strongly that an offense is irreparable. I dreaded hearing her say, "It's all over between us," and therefore watched her with a wariness I made no attempt to conceal, all the more so as she was paying so little attention to me. Although I hadn't the courage to speak to her, I could have broken down and cried in front of her without feeling ashamed. I finally dared ask why she was dressing with such care. She didn't reply. I went into my study for a moment, then came out again and, with studied indifference, asked, "Have you given the kitchen orders today?" I thought that, in spite of everything, this was the sort of question she would respond to. Her answer was not at all what I'd expected, however: "If you're having lunch here, you can give the orders yourself." She resumed her preparations. I fell silent and went back to my study. Just before noon, the maid came to tell me M. Spigelman was here to see me. I went to greet him happily. If I'd had to choose the one friend whose company I most valued just then, my preference would have been for Spigelman. I knew how indulgent, how concili- atory he was. I was never embarrassed to show myself as I real- ly was with him, concealing neither my jealousies nor my fears. "Well then, how are you?" he asked immediately. "You were wrong not to follow my advice. Those shares I told you about went up, and they're still going up." M. Spigelman said this kindly, the way you might tell a friend you had a pleasant time without him. "And how is Madeleine?" he went on. "You have a treasure in that woman." With a gesture, I indicated things weren't going well at all. "Now what have you done to her?" he asked genially, as though this were merely a lover's spat. I sensed from his question that he was willing to consider any possibility, but not a separation, not deep-seated hatred. Although he lives alone and has no close relations, M. Spigelman deeply loves and respects family life. It is the only thing he gets sentimental about, the only fine thing in the world. It would never have occurred to him that something serious could come between Madeleine and me. "I'll patch things up," he said with a smile. I understood then that my happiness at seeing him was unfounded. "I suspect," he went on, "you've quarreled over something childish again, a hat." Although he is cunning and shrewd when discussing money, this man is like a child on the subject of love. I suddenly felt ashamed of what had gone on between Madeleine and me the night before. Had he witnessed the scene, he would have been terrified by it, he would have wondered if he wasn't dreaming. For some time now, I'd sensed he silently disapproved of my not having a child. For him, a household was made of two peo- ple who loved one another, who were united and never argued. "Where is Madeleine?" he asked me. "I don't know," I answered, afraid he would see her. "She's probably off in a corner, crying," he went on. "She's must be waiting for you to come and ask her forgiveness. I won't leave until you do." Poor innocent Spigelman! You would have been horrified if you'd understood the seriousness of what happened, realized there is no remedy for what separates Madeleine and me! All I could think of now was concealing the truth from him, changing the subject, diverting his attention from the two of us. "Listen, Spigelman, I'm delighted you dropped by, because it just so happens I was going to ask you to buy me some shares of that stock you recommended." The banker looked at me with a semitriumphant air. "It's too late now, too late. You should have told me a month ago. There's nothing interesting at the moment. How can you be so indecisive?" That last question left me reeling. It's true that I don't know what I want, and always choose the wrong moment to act. I make a terrible scene with Madeleine when she's done nothing wrong, but when she makes it clear I'm playing second fiddle to Roger, I say nothing. Although I felt miserable, I didn't have a chance to reflect on what a pathetic creature I was, because Spigelman said, "Come on, Louis, take me to your wife. We must be indulgent with one another." I was increasingly tense, and explained to Spigelman that my wife was perfectly fine but couldn't join us because she was resting. "I'm just an old man," he said. "I won't tire her. As a matter of fact, I'm certain you're in the wrong here, Louis. You never know what you want. Today you want to buy shares even though the market is bad, but when I encouraged you to buy, you wouldn't hear of it. You're capricious." As he spoke these words, he moved toward the door I'd come through a moment earlier. "May I?" he asked me. All I could do was nod my head in a sign of acquiescence. As soon as he'd left the room, an oppressive anxiety overcame me. I knew Madeleine well enough to know that she would lose her temper with a man foolish enough to meddle in her affairs and give her advice. In fact, Spigelman had barely left me when I heard my wife saying harshly, "Monsieur, it's not worth wasting your breath. My husband is a brute. Every woman he's ever been involved with has suffered. With me, however, it's over. I hate him." A few seconds later, I saw Spigelman reappear, his face completely altered. He was crushed. The smiling, self-confident, peacemaker's air he'd had a moment earlier had disappeared. He seemed not to understand anything anymore, aghast at having glimpsed an abyss whose existence he had never suspected. He came over to me and said very gravely, "But after all, she's your wife, isn't she?" I lowered my head. Suddenly the door flew open and a radiant Madeleine cried out in a shrill voice, "Louis, I forbid you to continue talking about me. Wait until I'm gone, which will be very soon now." Then, speaking to the banker, she said, "As for you, Monsieur, I don't understand why you listen to him." Upon that she left, slamming the sitting-room door behind her. Madeleine's rages are chilling, and they last for hours. They are never caused by a word, or an act, but always by something that happened earlier, sometimes as long as a week ago. It isn't just one door she slams, then, but all of them, and for days on end. During those periods of frigid bitterness, she reveals a trait that distresses me even more than her anger: a sort of vulgarity. You sense she could slap you, and although she never uses crude language, could very politely call you a cheapskate, a hoodlum, a brute. I looked at Spigelman. His face told me that I had become a stranger in his eyes, and that he was wondering how he could ever have entrusted me with his friendship, especially as he holds marriage sacred above all things. Just as he loathes people who try to put on airs, he can't abide families where there is no harmony, couples who argue constantly. He was now thinking he'd been wrong about me. His eyes never left me, and looked like those of a father whose child has been found guilty of a crime. Something extraordinary happened then. Little by little, his features hardened. Though nothing he said was uttered in a disagreeable tone of voice, as he prepared to go he began talking about this and that, without making the slightest allusion to Madeleine. When I asked him not to make too much of what had just happened, assuring him this was merely one of those occasional disagreements between two people who love one another, thereby trying to imply that the next time he saw us this would all be forgotten, he said, "But of course, we all know how these things are. We've all had our little problems." He must have realized I thought he was lying, for he then felt compelled to add, "I've had worse happen to me." Having recovered from his shock, he was now trying, as any friend would have done, to make me think that he was just like me, but I didn't believe him. As I walked him to the front door, he said, "Dear Louis, you ought to come and see me about those stocks of yours: I may be able to do something for you. You never know, with the stock market. An opportunity will doubtless come up quite soon." After he'd left, I tried in vain to understand why he had urged me to come see him. Was it that he didn't want to lose a client, even if he'd given up on our friendship? Or had he suddenly had some inkling that such a violent scene must have been caused by financial problems and now wanted, as a mark of his friendship, to reconcile me with Madeleine by helping me play the market successfully? Had he spoken merely in order to say something, with no ulterior motive, just to break the silence? I wondered. After having examined what he'd said from every possible angle, I lost interest and grew despondent. It seemed to me that, through my own fault, I was losing all my friends, that Madeleine would never forgive me, that I was already abandoned. I didn't know what to do. Spigelman's last words kept coming back to me. It suddenly seemed strange to me that while still my friend, the banker had discouraged me from buying any shares, only to give contrary advice at the very moment when he no longer had any affection for me. This about-face surely proved that, not satisfied with abandoning me, he now wanted to injure me further by making me lose money. I decided to go out for a change of scene, to forget everything that had happened and try to pull myself together. My disgust with myself only intensified when I'd stepped out the door, however. Losing a friend, even one who means very little to us, is never easy. As I walked the crowded streets, I thought about my past, about myself, who I was. Though I can't explain why, it occurred to me that I often find myself regretting the opportunities I had as a young man to indulge in vices which, unfortunately, I didn't possess at the time. As we grow older, the complications involved in satisfying our desires make us regret our youth all the more. I sometimes find myself prey to such regrets, which is awful. With a mentality like that, anything is possible, and it's ridiculous of me to then be surprised that a man like Spigelman would shun me. Everyone should shun me, and leave me to my fate. I'm astonished that people have any regard for me at all, and wonder how it is that anyone can take my life seriously. I would have found it perfectly logical if all my friends abandoned me, and was stunned to realize that the repercussions of my behavior affected my entourage. Madeleine was suffering because of me. How was this possible?

December 11th

Madeleine hasn't been the same since Roger disappeared, and since the scene I made. She seems unconnected to anything. When I speak to her, she barely answers. I don't know then if I should insist or say nothing more.

I saw in this morning's paper that Marcel Perceval had been named governor of a French colony. I was utterly indifferent to the news—although when you know the man there's cause for astonishment—and wouldn't bother to mention it at all if my old friend Loustalot hadn't come to see me. Upon hearing the news, this miserable fellow thought it marvelous that his closest friend had been honored with such a distinction, as a result of which he felt indirectly honored himself. He couldn't deny himself the pleasure of announcing it to me, in hushed tones, as though it were a secret. Everything this unhappy man ever dreamed of is being achieved by someone else, who happens to be his best friend. He was calm, almost lifeless, in the face of this wounding reality. A mute rage, born of impotence, was visible in his eyes.

Envy and ambition are eating away at him. He dreams of an event that will elevate him above his fellow men overnight. Such an event has never occurred, however, and as it never will, he has grown bitter. In his eyes, success is never merited. It's nearly impossible to convey what a schemer he is. He feels no qualms about writing to an influential friend quite out of the blue and, after having asked how he is, requesting some favor. He needs to know immediately whether you consider him a friend; he is so desperate for success that his greatest fear is wasting his time, being amiable for nothing. Whenever he sees a familiar face, all he cares about is whether the person can be useful to him in some way. But as he doesn't know exactly what he wants, the conversation inevitably dies away without his having known what to solicit. Then, as an afterthought, he will ask, "Do you have anything for me?" Asking such a question seems so natural to him that he blurts it right out, without even bothering to disguise it. Even when he meets a friend who's already done him a favor, he'll find it impossible not to petition him again.

It's not difficult to imagine how much envy Perceval's good fortune must have generated in such a mind. He was pale as we spoke. Even as he detailed his warm feelings for the governor, he was doing his best to downplay the latter's merits. Lighting a cigarette, I said to Loustalot by way of consolation, "It'll be your turn soon, you'll see." "I'd rather it were yours!" replied the unhappy man, who thought he'd detected a similar note of envy in my voice, and who, though indulgent with himself, forgave nothing in others. "How did he react to the news?" I asked, so that he wouldn't think I'd been made speechless with envy. "Very well. He didn't even seem to grasp the significance of the thing. In any case, I can tell you he's not a man to forget his friends now that he's made a success of himself. I believe he's capable of doing more for them than his peace of mind and security would suggest he should. You realize, of course, that the success of a good government official lies in his ability to resist solicitations." I have to admit that this pompous declaration filled me with a most unpleasant sensation, for when some of my friends do succeed, like Perceval, it seems to me that they behave just as I would have done in their place. I couldn't keep from saying, "Success only turns the heads of men who overestimate their worth."

Needless to say, Loustalot found it necessary to demonstrate, with the help of the pretext I'd supplied, that he was a closer friend of Perceval's than I was. "I see that you really don't know Perceval at all. I don't know anyone who would do what he's doing. He's not waiting for people to approach him. Why, you may be his new cabinet minister at this very moment, and not even know it." Such a supposition exasperated me. "But I have no such desire." "Don't say that. You would be delighted." I was indignant. Only a child would have believed it possible to be extended such an unwarranted mark of consideration. Although Loustalot was making me a part of Perceval's destiny, the truth was that he wanted only one thing: to be the governor's sole friend. His jealousy extended even to me, in spite of the fact that I had just made it perfectly clear I sought no privileged status. Perhaps my disinterestedness was what worried him the most, for he was so afraid of being forgotten that he hadn't the strength to be disinterested himself. At the same time, he was keenly aware of how appealing an attitude like mine could be. But how could he be sure it didn't conceal scheming maneuvers of my own? If instead I'd told him that I was hoping to be named head of Perceval's cabinet, a position to which he doubtless also aspired, he would have been relieved. At the moment, he wanted to be alone in knowing Perceval. Had that been the case, I'm sure he would have accepted no favors. He would simply have shown his idol that he shouldn't trouble himself, that petitioners, even those who seemed to have something to offer, should be brushed aside. He thought himself made to play the part of a woman protecting her influential and besotted lover from anything which might diminish his love for her, or tempt him to follow a different path. It was obvious that Loustalot's greatest ambition now was to become Perceval's only advisor, to protect him from pitfalls which he alone would be able to foresee. It was equally obvious that what he most wanted was to have a long meeting with Perceval. From what he just told me, however, it appears that he hasn't seen the latter in a week. He rushed there this morning, but the busy governor wasn't able to receive him. Ever since, Loustalot has been like a man on a bed of hot coals. I suspect he will neither eat nor sleep until he has managed to reestablish that connection. Few sensations are as upsetting as being kept at a distance from important events in which you could have been participating had you only risen an hour earlier that morning. When lady luck has smiled at you, however briefly, the mere fact of having been seen by her makes misfortune seem less brutal, and makes the happiness she brings others seem more bearable.

Just then, for a reason I can't remember, Madeleine came into my study. I told her the news without the slightest hesitation, having often observed the remarkable trait women have of never envying a man's success. She was, in fact, totally indifferent to the information. It never even occurred to her to be disappointed that I had been awarded no such distinction. Something in the way she looked at me, however, made me sense she thought me unworthy of such an honor. To please my wife, Loustalot thought it seemly to repeat his earlier remark that I might at this very moment be the head of Perceval's cabinet. Madeleine said nothing in reply, as though the possibility were too remote to merit her consideration. I was enraged that she could treat me with such scorn. Because Loustalot was there, I contained myself, but all I now wanted was for him to leave. At the risk of seeming rude, I suddenly said that I had business to attend to. From Loustalot's expression, I understood he thought I was angry with him for having brought me the news of Perceval's success.

Left alone with Madeleine, I found I didn't know how to

begin my attack. I was irritated. Although I didn't want to admit it, Perceval's good fortune had put me in a foul humor. Without any warning, I began berating her. "Deep down," I said to her, "you admire Perceval. You think he's a remarkable man. Money and honors are the only things that matter to you. Yesterday it was Belange, today it's Perceval, and tomorrow? Who will it be then?" When I'm angry, not only do I lose my self-control, the urge to show myself in the worst possible light also comes over me. I soon find myself saying things I would never dream of saying when in a normal frame of mind. "Oh, I understand. If you don't love me, it's because I never did anything to make myself important. What you want from a man is that some part of his distinction reflect on you." I was suffocating. Madeleine was unmoved by what I said, however. No matter how justified your reproaches might be, she is one of those women who always thinks you're being unfair. She sees only herself. And because no reproaches are ever entirely accurate, not only does she fail to grasp what led you to make them, she immediately points out their inaccuracies. A single point of error in any criticism suffices to convince her she is right. As I spoke, however, I wasn't lingering over such reflections. My anger was growing, fueled by a vague impression I had that Madeleine would have loved me if I'd been more like one of those fatuous creatures I so despise. "That's the way life is, isn't it," I said, "women admire imbeciles, but when a man is deeply in love with a woman he cherishes, when he lives simply, and only, for her, he is considered ridiculous. Fine, then! Madeleine, I'm telling you here and now that this is all going to change. You're at my mercy now. I'm all you have. You're going to have to do what I want; otherwise, if you lose me, what will become of you?" Although I said this in the heat of anger, I noticed that, unlike the day when I'd made a scene about the orchids, Madeleine seemed sure of herself, and apparently afraid of nothing. I would have had to raise my voice further to upset her, and that was something I didn't have the heart to do. In spite of this I went on, increasing the intensity of my tirade to see if I wasn't closer to my goal than I thought, but to no avail. Finally, disgusted with myself and hoping this last word would accomplish more than the entire scene which had preceded it, I exclaimed as harshly as I could, "You might as well leave!" As simply as could be, she left the room. I realized then that she could have walked out earlier if she'd wanted to, instead of which she'd been submissive and heard me out. An abrupt change took place in me. My anger vanished. I ran after her to beg her forgiveness. But as I was doing everything in my power to convince her of my affection, she interrupted me and said coldly, "Enough of these charades." The silence of the past few days had slowly been building this abscess. What I'd vaguely been dreading had come to pass. No matter what I said now, she was going to look at me like a stranger. She had thought long and hard, and had decided that I—who adore her—was putting on an act. Never again would my words make her suffer, never again would she be angry with me. I was a man who was incapable of being sincere, and so she had cut me out of her world. I was so overwhelmed that it didn't occur to me to justify myself. A deeply tragic thought had struck me: everything was over between us. I couldn't even defend myself anymore, because once Madeleine thinks she is right, she is unassailable. I could have spoken the most touching words, the most deeply sincere, fallen to my knees and wept; now that she was convinced of my duplicity, she would never have believed me. I felt powerless. The most dazzling proof of my love would have left her indifferent, since she no longer believed in that love. Nonetheless I stayed with her a moment longer, with the wild hope that, seeing my distress, she might change. It was only when she picked up a magazine and began leafing through it that I left, without saying a word. My attitude must have seemed exactly that of someone playing a part. I had arrived in tears, full of warm feelings, and was now leaving after just one remark she'd made. She must have taken this as a confirmation of her judgment.

December 15th

Friends came to see us. I don't know why, but Madeleine didn't want Mme Borel to notice we were quarreling. It seems hard to believe she would have any such scruples, given the scene she made when M. Spigelman was here. As soon as M. and Mme Borel were shown in, however, Madeleine began addressing me amiably, as though we'd never had any disagreement. Having thought about it, I believe I understand why. Madeleine feels a sense of feminine pride when with her friend. The latter probably told her that all men are wicked and think only of themselves, that they are egotists, and Madeleine must have disagreed with her, not out of love for me, but rather because she has such high expectations. As a result, she doubtless finds it abhorrent to be near this woman now, after having contradicted her.

Were Madeleine suddenly to develop a loathing for one of her friends, then meet another friend to whom she'd previously spoken of the first in glowing terms, she would, while with the second woman, forget her feelings about the first. This isn't because she fears the loss of a relation will lessen others' opinion of her, but rather because she finds it unpleasant that people know what she is feeling, whether or not this detracts from her image. I was so clearly out of sorts that I heard Jacques Borel ask his wife what was going on. He is terribly proud of being married at long last, and needs to invest the condition with such importance that he's acquired the habit of asking his wife to apprise him of everything, as though it were impossible for him to understand anyone else's explanations. This peculiar zeal reminds me of people introduced to a social circle they have long heard about and which they know in theory, but whose reality is a mystery to them, or of army recruits who are astonished to discover that the officers aren't more stern, but who retain the attitudes they'd prepared when expecting to face harsh discipline. But just as the last thing those soldiers would say is "It's not as bad as I'd expected!" Borel had no intention of telling his wife that our marriage was not all he'd thought. "What's the matter with you?" Madeleine asked, noticing my sullen expression. I couldn't help but wonder what would happen if I revealed what was wrong. I think that Madeleine would have lost her self-control. Refusing to play along with her is the one thing she can't abide. One must yield to her desires. Although she was being pleasant with me, I knew it was only temporary. And yet, she expected me to play along with this act, even though she must have realized I knew it was just that: an act. And I'm supposedly the actor here! It would have been futile, however, to try to make her understand how capricious her behavior was. Things had to be this way at this particular moment in time, and nothing we'd said earlier was allowed to alter the equation. It took every ounce of self-control I had not to lose my temper on the spot, in front of everyone. I have become prey to a sort of nervous excitability, which terrifies me. I can no longer control myself. Whereas in the past I could tolerate anything, for some time now I've felt the need to show that I exist, that I'm a living being, that I have a personality. Basically, this is due to the fact that losing my temper is all I'm good for, that I'll never be able to control myself, and above all that I allowed myself to get carried away once before. What held me back before was my fear of shocking Madeleine, of allowing her a glimpse of an abyss whose existence she'd never even suspected. Those scruples are meaningless now that she's seen me raging out of control, which, by the way, failed to make the impression on her I'd expected. It was as if she'd always known the essence of my nature, even though I carefully concealed it, to the point of pretending to be indifferent when she claimed to be in love with Roger. I was made even angrier by the fact that the Borels seemed intent on making it obvious they'd come to see Madeleine and not me. Without taking any real notice of me, my wife smiled at me pleasantly from time to time. Finally, I couldn't control myself any longer. "I've had enough," I said violently. "Why don't you stop passing yourself off as an angel in front of your friends!" "But what's wrong, my darling?" she asked, sincerely interested. Her question infuriated me. "Enough!" I shouted. I then had the leisure of observing my wife. Her face registered no spite, no anger. I had expected cries, tears, but she merely seemed surprised. Rather than getting angry, she was treating my outburst as though she loved me. She looked at me sadly, and for a moment I even thought her eyes were filming over. I understood my words had hurt her, probably because of the Borels, for she wanted them to believe we were a happy couple. In fact, I had been mistaken in judging the reason for Madeleine's kindness. It wasn't at all that, in the presence of a woman who'd pointed out the ridiculous nature of dependence, she felt ashamed of belonging to a man. The reality was that she was repelled by Mme Borel's theories; at heart, she derived a great sense of comfort from appearing to be a cherished slave, from feeling dominated, advised, guided, from sensing she was exactly the woman I so wanted her to be. "It hurts me, Louis, when you're so unkind to me. It isn't nice." I hadn't the courage to go on. It was beginning to seem to me that such complex emotions could never be resolved. I craved light, air, a deep and simple love, and instead of that I was struggling in such a maze of emotions that there were moments when I believed that the mere fact I thought anything at all meant it was untrue. I no longer knew, or understood, anything. Ah, if Madeleine had only wanted! If she'd only wanted to love me with all her heart as I love her, if she'd only wanted to understand that life isn't very long, and that when circumstances bring two people together who aren't so very different, it's better to accept that fate than make a spectacle of oneself. Borel was listening to what we were saying. He was all but offering to act as mediator. Having spent part of his life listening to others recount their romantic entanglements without ever having any of his own, he was curious rather than genuinely moved.

Finally the Borels left. I remained silent. I have no idea what I was waiting for. Madeleine, too, was silent. She came and went in the apartment as though I didn't exist. I found her indifference reassuring. It may be sad to say this, but I preferred that to another argument. At dinner, Madeleine had nothing more to say about her friends. Her face had resumed the expression she wore before their visit.

December 17th

I inflicted another scene on Madeleine, one so violent that for a moment I thought she was going to run out like a mad-woman, without bothering to take her coat. Ever since the night she stayed at her father's, I have been extremely high-strung. I don't sleep well. I've completely lost my appetite. I'm constantly making plans to leave, though without much con-viction. Whenever I'm away from her, I start to worry that she'll meet another man. But when I'm near her, all I want is to escape. What to do? She is so disagreeable! With the excep-tion of the day the Borels came to visit, she has barely spoken to me. In the end, I snapped. This morning, when I told her what I wanted to do, she made this unfortunate reply: "You would think I'm standing in your way." At first I ignored what she'd said. I was filing papers. It's a task I enjoy, one that can make me forget the worst troubles. Then I went out for a walk. When I returned, I found Madeleine waiting to have lunch with me. I told her that it was a fine day, albeit cold. She made no reply. She stopped answering me so long ago that I ignored this minor point. We had lunch. While having our coffee in the living room, a ray of sun introduced a note so gay and yet so melancholy that I felt myself overcome by the urge to change surroundings for a few days. To avoid meeting with a disagreeable reply, however, I carefully avoided making any mention of this. I lit a cigar, and as Madeleine had just left the room, I sat and waited for her return, though for no good rea-son since I had nothing to say to her. I glanced through the morning papers and had a second cup of coffee. As our apart-ment faces south, the room was now being flooded with sun-light. Despite my melancholy, I was filled with a sense of phys-ical well-being. Still unable to explain why, I awaited Mad-eleine's return. That was when it suddenly occurred to me that she wasn't in the apartment at all, but had gone out. It would be impossible to relate how angry this made me. All at once, my pleasure vanished. I was enraged. I was about to get up and run through the apartment looking for her when she reappeared, idly, like a woman who left the room to go touch up her makeup and, to make her absence last longer, leafed through a book rather than returning immediately. Nothing more was needed to restore my equanimity. As Madeleine sat down, I got up and left the room unhurriedly, saying, "I'll be back." I didn't know what to do with myself. I went into my study and leafed mechanically through the papers I'd filed that morning. For a few seconds, I pulled back the curtains and watched the passersby below. I was in such good spirits that I caught myself thinking that, leaning on the windowsill, I looked a bit like one of those youths in romantic etchings who seem to be regretting their fiancée's departure. When the charm of that reflection had worn off, I returned to the living room. I'd noticed when leaving that Madeleine had sat down in such a way that her left hand, which dangled over the side of the armchair, was almost touching the floor. When I returned, the first thing to catch my eye was that her arm was still in the same place. Unreasonable as this may seem, I felt I was about to lose my temper yet again. I can't say why I found this immobility a provocation. Not moving a muscle like this seemed an unspoken challenge, as if by doing nothing Madeleine wanted to show me how little I mattered to her. Her eyes were closed. My exasperation as I scrutinized her was heightened by the fact that she seemed not to have heard the noise I made as I approached. If I had thrown a vase to the floor in the middle of the room, or, even better, into the big mirror above the mantelpiece, Madeleine would not have reacted any differently. It was only with the greatest of difficulty that I contained myself. My eyes were riveted on that inert arm. Then, suddenly, she opened her eyes and, in a supremely graceful gesture, raised the hand off the floor and carried it to her forehead. My peace of mind was restored. A movement of any kind was all I'd needed to enable me to resume adoring the body I'd despised a moment earlier. I sat down, and had just resumed reading the newspaper when Madeleine got up and went out. After reading for quite some time, I heard the front door close. This time, she really had gone. To assure myself of this, I went into our bedroom. She was gone. I have to say that, to my great surprise, her absence left me indifferent. Not for a moment did I think of getting angry. I now found it utterly natural that Madeleine had gone out, even without saying good-bye. I went back into my study, and stayed there until four o'clock. I then had tea brought in, after which, not knowing what to do, I decided to go see a friend. Upon reaching his house, however, I doubled back. This often happens to me. The fact is I need to have a goal in life, my day must have clearly defined objectives. I'll therefore plan to go see someone in perfect good faith, and leave the house as if I really intend to go there. Along the way, I'll even plan what I'm going to say. But once there, I'll abandon the idea. What I need is not so much to execute the plan as to be occupied by it. I therefore headed back the way I'd come. Passing by a florist, I thought of buying orchids to show Madeleine I held no grudge against her. But it struck me that this would be in bad taste, and that my wife would interpret it as a wicked or ironic gesture on my part. I'm like those people who, no matter how delicate their intentions, realize upon reflection that they may be mis-interpreted. This fear is partly responsible for the fact that I appear so cold, and loathe displays of friendship. When I got home, I found Madeleine deep in conversation with a fashion designer. Ordinarily, I avoid sitting in on such conversations. This time, however, to play the gallant young man and try to please Madeleine by appearing interested, I approached the two women and pretended to listen attentively. To my great surprise, Madeleine said, "Leave us, Louis . . . You know nothing about these matters . . . I'll be with you in a moment." Spoken with great amiability. Bursting with happiness, I went into my study. Was Madeleine going to return to the way she used to be? I was overjoyed by this change. But time passed. When I heard the front door close, I knew the designer had left, yet Madeleine still didn't come join me. All the same, I didn't want to force my presence on her. I resolved to wait a bit longer, but as time passed and she didn't come, I felt an increasingly violent rage building up within me. Finally, unable to hold myself back any longer, I went into our bedroom. Madeleine was there, and was now wearing a black dress. "You didn't come to me, then?" I asked. "Obviously not, since I'm here." "But you did say you would come?" "You say a great many things too, don't you?" These words filled me with joy. Had Madeleine decided to resume speaking to me? Had she forgotten everything? Happy as I was, I was careful not to let this show so as not to indispose my wife, whom it pleases to think that a man's contentment, however slight, is fatuous. "I was waiting for you, eagerly," I went on. "No doubt so you could say some more cruel things to me." There is one point on which Madeleine and I differ totally. After losing my temper, I feel deeply embarrassed if we return to the subject that provoked my ire. When Madeleine and I have patched things up in the past, what I've always found most distressing is the way she reviews every detail of our quarrel, albeit in a spirit of reconciliation. That was what she now began to do. My happiness vanished immediately, replaced by irritation. "No, Louis," she went on, "it's no use pretending the orchids were the only reason you lost your temper the way you did." "Let's drop the subject," I said, not even daring to utter the word "orchids." "What would you like us to talk about, then, if not that?" she asked coldly. Often, when a reconciliation is on the verge of being concluded and I'm looking forward to living again, to elevating myself, Madeleine will revert to the cutting tone of voice she used earlier. Although I know this about her, I was shocked by what she'd just said. "But there are a great many things we could talk about," I answered quickly. "Well then! If that's the way things are, let's not bother talking at all," she said even more harshly. Madeleine had put a pretty dress on to please me. She'd made an effort to put her resentments behind her. She'd been willing to slip back into the skin of the woman she used to be, and then, all of a sudden, she'd abandoned her resolutions. She is one of those women who never feels bound by her decisions or by the preparations she's made. At the last minute, and without the slightest regret, she can deprive herself of a pleasure she's been looking forward to for weeks. Anger filled me yet again. This time, however, its roots went far deeper: the bottomless abyss which separated us, her failure to understand me, and her inconsistency, which I didn't understand. "If that's the way it is," I said like a man who's lost his mind, "I'm leaving." "Go on, then, you might as well," she shot back. "Actually, no. I'm staying." I was all the more enraged because she now dominated the situation as a result of my awkwardness. Seeing her perfectly in control of herself while I choked with rage made me violent. I grabbed her hand and squeezed it with all my might. She cried out sharply, and as she did I suddenly saw in her eyes that she was the weaker. I squeezed even harder. When she fell to her knees in pain, I let her go. She ran off immediately, crying for help as though I were a criminal. Alone, I felt something like a sense of deliverance. Once again, I was the master. Hearing barely perceptible footsteps all around me, a silent scurrying, I stood motionless, drained, slightly troubled, not realizing exactly what had just happened and yet feeling an overwhelming sense of relief deep in my heart.

December 20th

A note arrived from Curti asking me to come see him immediately. Worried, I went off to the avenue de la Grande-Armée at once. Barely two weeks had gone by since I'd lunched with him, but he seemed completely changed. He received me in bed. His face looked rested, but there was something sad and distant in his expression. He was propped up on a pillow. A glass and a box of pills stood on a card table that had been set up at the head of his bed. "I was extremely unwell the day before yesterday," he told me wearily. "I had three attacks in succession, and they lasted much longer than usual. I thought the end had come. That night, my pulse was barely forty beats a minute. I'm feeling better now, but I have to face reality. The end isn't far off." I studied him more carefully. Even more so than when I'd arrived, I was struck by his eyes. Unlike the rest of his face, which was smooth, rejuvenated, even pinkish in spots, and seemed asleep rather than dead, as though resting after a massive effort, they darted anxiously from side to side, the pupils ringed by a colorless band. I can't explain why, but they made me think of two prisoners trying to escape. They no longer seemed connected to his face in any way. They were like the wildly spinning needle of a compass, terrified and power-less, desperate to escape from the surrounding flesh. As I looked at them, I realized Curti was right about his condition. I tried to reassure him, but he paid no attention to what I was saying. What I found particularly strange was that his eyes weren't appealing for help, nor did they attempt to latch onto anyone. They simply moved about, mysterious and astonished; one felt there was no sight on earth that would have affected their peculiar luster. They no longer wanted to be a part of Curti's body, and when they stared fixedly off to one side or another one could sense his fear. It was as though he was trying to see himself as he did this, to reassure himself he hadn't changed. As I sat down next to the bed, the nurse came in carrying an herbal infusion. At the sight of it, Curti made an indifferent gesture, as though he intended to refuse it, but at the same time he extended his hand to take the cup. When he'd finished drinking its contents (which he did with great care), he extended his hand to me in a very trusting, unguarded way. "My dear Grandeville, what do you think of my situation?" I replied that I thought he looked well enough, that his attacks had probably been brought on by overexertion of some kind, and that he needed only be more vigilant to ensure they didn't recur. He was deeply relieved by my words. "That's exactly what my doctor told me, in fact," he said. "And I've since remembered very clearly that the morning of my attacks, I was angry about something." "Come now, Monsieur Curti, you! Angry!" "Why certainly," he replied, with the merest hint of a smile. "You don't know everything about my life." I was astonished that he could say such a thing. To tell me that I didn't know everything about his life, when I thought I knew it so well, seemed insane. It was hardly to be believed. Nonetheless, I concealed my astonishment. "And I'm sure that fit of anger is what brought on the later attacks." Just then, the maid came in and, in hushed tones, told him Doctor Mariage was here to see him. It would be impossible to describe the burning intensity with which Curti's face lit up. His joy was painful to see. It revealed how desperately this sick man still clung to life. I got up to leave, but Curti insisted I stay, and I sensed this was because he thought the doctor wouldn't dare give him bad news in the presence of a third party. Looking slightly worried, Doctor Mariage entered the room. After taking Curti's pulse and listening to his heart, he seemed reassured. He was a large, ruddy man, with closely cropped blond hair. Every aspect of his appearance lent itself to creating an impression of sincerity. "I never hide anything from my patients," he seemed to say. Curti's eyes never left him, but the doctor pretended not to notice: not taking his patients' childish fears into account was one of the traits that added to his confident demeanor. Patients were made to think that they were insignificant; if their entreaties and apprehensions failed to attract the doctor's attention, it must be because he didn't find their condition particularly worrying. Doctor Mariage finally took his leave. As soon as he'd gone, Curti asked me, "Would you trust that doctor?" I answered that I would, which seemed to put his mind at ease. "What about Madeleine?" he then asked so abruptly that, for an instant, I thought he was asking whether she too would trust him. "I've never asked her about Doctor Mariage," I said. "That's not what I'm asking. I'd like to know how she is, whether she's happy. Above all, you mustn't tell her what's happened to me. It would cause her such anguish. There will be time enough to tell her when nothing more can be done." I told him that things were absolutely fine at home, then thought myself compelled to add it probably was best not to alarm Madeleine about her father's illness, which was sure to vanish as quickly as it had struck. In spite of this, Curti remained pensive. He knows perfectly well his daughter isn't happy with me. Until now, he's pretended to believe we're a happy couple. I now sensed, however, that he no longer thought it necessary to deceive me. Doubtless because he was aware of the seriousness of his ailment, he suddenly wanted to confide in me, and presumed I knew as well as he did that his daughter didn't love me. He wanted to talk to me about her, addressing me not as her husband but rather as the person who would replace him after he was gone. "She loves you as she loves me," he continued. "Less, certainly." I sensed him growing tense. "Why less? You mean a great deal to her." I couldn't understand where he was leading. My initial impression of him had been eradicated. Instead, I was now in the presence of a courageous man, who no longer feared death and was making a final attempt to put his affairs in order. "Louis, you mean a great deal to her. You're the first man she really loved. You've always guided her. Without your experience and your indulgence, what would she have become? Listen to me, Louis, I could disappear from one minute to the next. Promise me that, whatever happens, you'll always protect her. Promise me you'll never abandon her, never make her suffer, and that you'll forgive her for any pain she may cause you. Promise me that when I'm gone, you will take my place in her life. You will be her father. What I mean is that, no matter what she does, she will always be like a daughter to you. If need be, stop loving her as a husband. I love Madeleine so much, it would be terrible for me if I thought the day might come when you wouldn't be there for her, that there would be no one in the world to protect her as I would have done. Madeleine is a child. Listen, Louis, I want you to promise that on the day you stop being her husband, you will become her father." His words made it so plain Madeleine didn't love me that I was thunderstruck. "I promise," I replied with feeling. "I'm infinitely grateful to you.

I know how wounding my words must sound, but I can assure you that when your kidneys and heart and liver are old and worn out, and there is nothing young or healthy left in your body, it becomes much easier to say these things. Life isn't long. We're all going to disappear one day. I believe the strong have a duty to protect the weak, to defend them, even if they are shown no gratitude for that protection. Imagine what would become of Madeleine without you. Men would prey on her. She's eager to live. She doesn't know what love is. Only you can guide her, can gradually make her understand, day by day, without her even being aware of it, that she's making mistakes. I even believe that only you love her enough to make her give up her unrealistic illusions without making her suffer unnecessarily. I'm asking you to love her more than a wife or a mistress. If I hadn't foolishly lost the better part of my fortune, I would have been able to provide for my child. What I'm most afraid of, you see, is that one day she will yield to temptation and you'll abandon her, leaving her alone to face the world. Promise me that will never happen." I knew Madeleine didn't love me, but that this should be so obvious to others made me terribly unhappy. Listening to Curti's words made me feel as though some harsh, crude light had been trained on my soul. For a moment, I resented him for talking to me this way. But seeing him before me, my bitterness disappeared. His revelations had made it clear to me that he had only a few days left to live. My fear of losing Madeleine vanished. It had struck me that, like Curti, I too was going to die one day, and that nothing mattered in this life except powerful emotions. To avoid being caught unprepared by death, we had to live each day in the fullness of those emotions. I took Curti's hand in mine and clasped it tightly. "Have no fear," I said fervently, "your daughter will never be alone. Even were she to find me repulsive, I would continue protecting her as though she'd pledged her eternal love to me."

When I returned home, I was feeling very emotional because of the promise I'd made. Although my intention was to be especially nice to Madeleine, the memory of what had occurred two days ago stopped me. I was embarrassed to have lost my temper so violently with the very woman who now seemed so worthy of being loved. I was about to be reunited with her. There is nothing more moving than these reunions when, unbeknownst to our loved ones, our perception of them has been altered. Because they think we are still angry, their expressions haven't changed, whereas we now look at them with all the mischievousness of a father who hasn't yet showed his child the toy he's brought home. We put off the moment when we'll reveal that we've changed. We smile like someone planning a pleasant surprise, but say nothing and save the agreeable news for later, taking pleasure in their sulking now that we know ending it is entirely in our power. I was delighted that Madeleine had no idea of how happy I was going to make her. Haughty, sullen, she was so far from suspecting the immensity of my love for her! As soon as I began to speak, however, she would forget everything I'd ever done to her. Curti's words had so moved me that I wondered how it was I'd ever made Madeleine unhappy. I now saw her in an entirely new light: no longer the enemy, she was now a fragile creature in need of my protection. Knowing I wouldn't begrudge her that protection, knowing how much I was prepared to do for her—all of it unbeknownst to her—convinced me she would be mine forever, despite the malevolent expression she currently wore. Very sure of myself, I sat down near her and scrutinized her, saying nothing. "Why are you staring at me that way?" she asked after a moment. "No reason." "Are you mock-

ing me?" Without answering, I lit a cigarette, a glib orator
about to present arguments so irrefutable that, in the meantime, he can afford to create the impression that his is a lost
cause. I felt so superior to trivial, everyday quarrels that
Madeleine could have done just about anything without irritating me. I loved her in spite of herself, and was so sure I
understood her that I was prepared to forgive her anything.
"Look, Louis, there's no point in staying here like this. Please
leave me alone." Still I said nothing. "I'm asking you one last
time to leave me alone." I realized abruptly that the change in
me shouldn't be revealed when she was about to lose her temper. A different mood was needed. "If you don't leave right
now, I'll go," continued Madeleine. I nearly answered, "Who's
stopping you?" but checked myself. I was still far too happy to
allow myself to lose my temper. In any case, I had precious little time to think about it. Barely a second later, Madeleine put
down her book and, without saying a word, left the room. Left
alone, the strangest sensation came over me. Even as I drifted
above all worldly cares, a sort of discontent began to penetrate
my idyll. I saw very clearly that if I didn't do something, it
would take over entirely, and so I got up and went to find
Madeleine. "For heaven's sake, what's wrong with you today?"
she demanded angrily. This time, I understood that in spite of
my reticence to open my heart to her in these circumstances, I
had no choice, or it would be too late. "I love you, Madeleine,
that's what's wrong with me," I said with feeling. "I love you in
spite of yourself, and in spite of all the pain you may cause me.
No matter what you do, I will always love you. My love is
above everything. I know you so well that, even if you call me
the worst names, I know what you really think. That is all that
matters, you see. I know that you have a beautiful soul, that
you are a defenseless little girl, and that, without me, you

would be the loneliest woman on earth." Out of breath, I stopped, my hands trembling, transfigured as men are only when they admit wrongdoing, or speak with all the force of their innermost feelings. Madeleine was looking at me incredulously. Although I'd thought I was above everything, I found myself anxiously awaiting her reaction. She didn't move. "But I believe you, you poor thing," she said at last, as though I'd been trying to convince her against her better judgment. She had retained only one impression from my impassioned speech: that I'd been trying to convince her of something, whereas my only intention had been to declare my love for her.

December 23rd

Late this afternoon, the concierge called me over as I was coming in and handed me a note. I recognized the handwriting of Curti's maid, who said her master wanted to see me immediately. I hurried to the avenue de la Grande-Armée. Whereas everything had seemed normal when I was there yesterday, I sensed an atmosphere of distress upon arriving. Under the archway, I crossed a man who broke into a run. Although it was nearly the dinner hour, as I passed the concierge's loggia I saw she was deep in conversation with several people. On the second floor, where Curti lives, I found a note on his door, written in the same hand as the note I'd just received, which read: "Please come in, quietly." I was afraid Curti might already be dead. There was no one in the entrance hall. Three or four overcoats hung on the coat rack. Shadows moved beyond the glass doors of the living room. I could hear hushed voices conferring. I pushed open the door and saw a group of men, among whom I recognized Sospel. They all turned and looked at me, their faces grave. As soon as I'd slipped into the room, they resumed their conversation. I walked toward Sospel, who was the only person there I knew. When I was standing behind him, I touched his arm to attract his attention, for the men surrounding him made it impossible for me to stand either next to or across from him. He acted surprised, turned away immediately, and resumed talking to the man next to him. At the risk of seeming insensitive and preoccupied by my own concerns when a man's life was at stake, I must say that I found his attitude bizarre. I had the impression that, to add drama to the situation, Sospel had decided to be antagonistic toward me, without any reason. In other circumstances, he would never have behaved this way. Using the pretext of the events unfolding in another room, one could sense he was pretending to ignore my presence, either to add to his own importance or to show me how upset he was. Just then, a door opened and Doctor Mariage appeared. The youngest member of the group broke away and went to greet him. After exchanging a few words, they left the room together. I hastily took up the place that had been vacated, for fear the group would close ranks. It was only then that Sospel deigned speak to me. "Curti is lost," he said in a voice devoid of all emotion, while to my right, a short and badly dressed man, whose nose was adorned with a pince-nez, a little man whose presence I couldn't explain, nodded his head. Although I had anticipated the news, I was thunderstruck by what Sospel had just said. Making a second appearance, Doctor Mariage interrupted Sospel. Still speaking in hushed tones, he asked whether there was a Monsieur Grandeville among us (in other words me), in spite of the fact that he'd seen me and must have remembered that we'd been introduced the day before. I came forward. "I'd like to have a word with you," he said. I followed him. After crossing two rooms, which seemed enormous to me, we entered Curti's room. I saw him immediately. He seemed to be asleep. He was surrounded by indescribable disorder. The nurse was looking for a socket to plug in a diathermic machine. There were vials and bits of cloth everywhere. Just when I thought I'd taken in everything, I suddenly noticed a man writing near one of the windows, leaning on a portable heater. I was overwhelmed. In that aura of death, I felt like a mechanical, empty shell rather than a friend. This sensation always comes over me when I enter the room of a dying man. It brings a sort of relief. It's hard to resist the urge to reduce oneself to nothing when confronted with the dying. It's an animalistic urge to abandon the weak, the doomed. I chastised myself silently for thinking such base thoughts. Suddenly, I realized I was standing by the side of Curti's bed. Doctor Mariage, who wanted nothing to do with me, said curtly, "Tell him who you are." I said my name softly, but Curti didn't move. He was recovering from yet another attack, and had just begun drawing regular breaths. His suffering seemed to have been alleviated, and it seemed to me that if he wasn't opening his eyes, it was because he was feeling better. I didn't dare repeat my name. Doctor Mariage took his hand and, having finally remembered who I was, said, "Your friend Grandeville is here, the friend you saw yesterday . . . " Curti's eyes opened then, but instead of the familiar gaze I was expecting, I found myself looking at a stranger. It wasn't just his gaze, but his entire face, which had been transformed. It was thinner, and had none of his familiar expressions. Although they'd seemed dull and yellow yesterday, his eyes were full of extraordinary life, yet they didn't see me, in spite of which Curti looked at me, and murmured, "I'm happy you've come. Are you alone? Where is Madeleine? I want to see Madeleine, tell her to come, now . . . I want to see the two of you together. Promise me again that you will take care of her, that you will protect her. Very soon now I won't be able to look after her myself." He stopped abruptly, looked for the doctor, then asked with unforeseeable calm, "Isn't Alice here yet? Why is that?" His question surprised me. Who was Alice? I had no time to speculate further, for Curti had resumed speaking to me: "Louis, I beg of you, promise me you'll never abandon my daughter, that you'll always love her, that you'll take my place in her life. I'm asking you to love her more than her father loved her. I didn't do what I should have done. That's why she hasn't come, isn't it? She holds it against me." His mind was beginning to wander. "No, I didn't do everything I could have done. Rather than leading such a self-ish life, I should have thought of her, worked for her, planned for the day when I wouldn't be there to protect her. I let myself be happy that she'd married you, even though I knew the marriage was making her suffer. That's the sort of man I am." Although this confirmed my own misfortune, and the fact that Curti regretted his daughter had married me, the scene was so tragic that his words caused me no pain. In fact, I thought they had a noble quality, even if Curti was now reduced to placing all his hopes in the man he'd considered so unworthy of being his son-in-law. I excused myself to go call Madeleine. As I wait-ed for the call to go through, I could hear Curti, who was still talking to me as though I'd never left his bedside, while the doctor endeavored to calm him. "Madeleine will be here very soon," I said upon returning. He said nothing. It was as if he had mistaken my return for my departure. I kept on talking, so that there would be no silence, but Curti had dozed off again. I stepped away from the bed and began talking quietly with the doctor's assistant. News of Curti's illness had spread. Doors opened, then closed again. One sensed that the apartment, unvisited by friends or family in normal times, had now become a sort of public arena. Because Curti was resting, I had no reason to remain at his side and should have gone back into the living room. It occurred to me that the men I'd seen upon arriving must be eager for me to return so that they could take my place. But the thought that Madeleine and I were his closest relatives made me stay. In spite of all the people in the apartment, it was extremely quiet. Only muffled noises reached our ears. The doctor looked at his watch. Silently, with an upward nod, I asked him what the time was. "Seven o'clock," he replied in a normal tone of voice, as though the minutes no longer mattered. Just then a door opened and Sospel appeared. Without even glancing at the bed where his old friend dozed, he went directly over to the doctor. They exchanged a few words in hushed tones, after which Sospel left by another door, which opened onto a corridor that led directly to the front hall. I heard a door slam. As I wondered in amazement that Sospel could be thoughtless enough to make such a loud noise just when Curti was resting, a young woman came into the room, accompanied by the little man I mentioned seeing earlier. I examined the couple carefully. The man looked like an employee who's come to claim his rights. Upon entering the room, the newcomers scrutinized the sick man at length, and though I may be wrong, I had the impression they wanted to be sure Curti saw them. One sensed they apprehended a fatal outcome more than any of us, in the way the friends of a famous man or the lover of a young woman would have done. We stayed like this for several minutes, none of us saying a word. I kept hoping Madeleine would appear. Suddenly Curti opened his eyes, as calmly as someone waking late in the morning, only to close them immediately. He groaned loudly, then pushed himself up to a sitting position. The doctor tried to make him lie down again, but he refused.

"I'm feeling better. . . I think I'm going to be able to get up," he said all in one breath. Taking advantage of his protests, the woman, who must have answered to the name Alice, drew nearer the bed. She neither knelt nor sat down, but stood towering over the sick man, looking at him with an obvious effort to appear compassionate. In spite of her intention, however, her features remained graceless due to a combination of deep-seated repulsion and that unpleasant expression people sometimes have when, although they are silent, they seem to be saying "I'm here!" Curti studied her face assiduously, then suddenly remembered who she was. A tremor shook his hands. The nurse drew near and tried but failed to cover them. Pulling sharply away from her, the patient lifted his trembling hands toward the young woman, who remained motionless while her companion, protective yet clearly shaken, moved closer to her. "Alice, my darling Alice!" babbled Curti. As he did so, the friend or relation of this strange woman turned first to me and then to the doctor, visibly trying to convey the message that our presence was not wanted. "Alice, Alice . . . ," repeated Curti, still trying to hold the young woman's hands in his own, and failing repeatedly, for whenever he held them he would drop them and search for them elsewhere. The truth slowly dawned on me. Curti had a mistress. Finding out in this way, seeing the liaison that had been so carefully concealed suddenly out in the open and the lovers no longer caring about keeping it a secret, made the scene seem all the more tragic. The death of a man is terrifying enough. But when his death becomes the instrument by which mysteries of his past life are revealed, when a host of demands, threats, and entreaties circle around the dying man's bed, and he no longer has the strength to defend or answer for himself, it is then we realize how insignificant the elements are out of which we create our happiness and sorrow. Secrets disappear, and no one thinks of reproaching the departed one for anything he might have done. Nothing remains but the miserable frailty of our beings. A week ago I would have been stupefied to learn of his affair, but now it seemed utterly unimportant. I could have learned the most wonderful, or the most abominable, things about Curti's life, they would no longer have made any impression on me. "Alice, Alice . . . ," he continued babbling, his voice weakening. Whether from shyness, fear, or indifference, the young woman made no attempt to show any tenderness toward the dying man, who clung to her as though she were the most precious creature on earth. It was almost as though it wasn't life he was leaving, but Alice, this ordinary girl for whom being here at all seemed to be a chore. It broke my heart that this man had reached the end of his days with no other love than the one he felt for this unknown woman. Suddenly, his hands dropped back into his lap. He took a few labored breaths, while his mistress continued staring at him. Sitting up straighter, he looked at his surroundings for a long while, then called for me. As I came closer, something quite unbelievable happened. Rather than stepping aside to allow me to reach the patient, the young woman, who'd had neither a loving gesture nor a heartfelt word to say since her arrival, remained where she stood. "Louis," murmured Curti, "go into my study. There is a paper in one of the desk drawers. Bring it to me." I did as he asked. When I returned, Curti had sunk back down into the bed. The young woman and her companion stared at me unblinkingly. Their eyes were locked on my own; they didn't quite dare lower their gazes to the envelope I now held in my hand. The scene was so shabby, so undignified, that I put the envelope on the

bed without even waiting for Curti to awaken. As I did so, the
doctor left and Sospel came back in through the same door. He
had taken only a few steps into the room when Curti emerged
from his torpor. "Louis," he said immediately, without even
looking to see where I was. "The envelope is next to you," I
answered, my voice betraying the irritation I felt at the young
woman's attitude. "Give it to me," said Curti, who had it
beneath his fingers but was incapable of grasping anything. To
my surprise, Alice didn't move. As she was standing nearest the
sick man, I had thought she would hand him the envelope. By
remaining motionless, however, she wanted to show that she'd
done nothing to make him hand it to her. Before I could do as
he'd asked, the nurse slipped the envelope between her patient's
fingers. Transfigured, looking as though he were performing
the most important act of his life, he thrust it at Alice with a
jerking, unsteady hand. For a moment, she hesitated to extend
her own hand, then snatched the envelope, folded it, and
passed it to her companion, who immediately stuffed it into
one of his pockets. This scene had barely ended when Sospel
left the room yet again, making me think there was something
very bizarre about the way in which he constantly came and
went, without ever saying a word. "Be happy, Alice . . . ," Curti
said laboriously. "You have been my only happiness. I did all I
could for you. Louis, come here . . . Where is Madeleine? You'll
protect her, since I wasn't able to do anything for her? Where
is she?" I was astonished by the last words he'd spoken. "This
is what happens when death takes us by surprise, and we aren't
ready to die," I thought. Weak and on the brink of death, a
man who'd always struck me as being a model of scrupulous-
ness now seemed empty and spineless. As recently as yesterday,
I'd thought his only love in life was his daughter. Rather than

opening his heart to me, he'd chosen to conceal everything until the final hour. Because of his weakness, he'd been reduced to making a man he's never esteemed the guardian of that which he holds most dear: Madeleine. He was about to disappear forever, and the person for whom he felt the most contempt was the very one he was relying on to watch over his child. He'd never given a thought to securing his daughter's future, choosing instead to put his trust in me. He'd used me the way you might use a relative you despise, but from whom you have no scruples in extracting any possible advantage. In a sense, he'd made me his associate. He'd said to himself, "Louis will take care of Madeleine, and I will take care of Alice." It was only when Alice's presence at his bedside revealed his secret life that he understood how unworthy of a father his conduct had been. His only concern, then, was that I not fail him. He saw he was at my mercy: that is his punishment, and it is also what makes his end such a tragic one. Watching him slip away, it struck me that what makes dying particularly distressing is the legacy of hundreds of confused situations, the friends waiting for promises they think the dying man is going to keep. Happy are those who've thought about death, who've anticipated it, and whose only legacy is a blameless life! But what painful exits the others have, as they lie helpless on their deathbeds watching people gather round who loathe one another, people they've made no provisions for, people who suddenly learn they weren't alone in being loved! By then, they are beyond the stage of being able to provide explanations for these unexpected complications. As they grow progressively weaker, their machinations become apparent, the details of their intimate life are revealed for all to see, until all that is left of them is their corpse. After the scene that had just taken place, M. Curti seemed similarly naked to me. There was nothing left of the man who'd organized his life, kept parts of it secret. He was already dead.

As I stood looking down at him, filled with tremendous pity and sadness, Madeleine arrived. At the sight of all the people gathered around, she understood immediately what was happening, and flung herself on the foot of the bed, sobbing like a madwoman. Only then did M. Curti notice her. With a great effort, he lifted his hand and put it on his daughter's head. She looked up. She knew nothing; in her eyes, her father was still the only person alive who loved her more than anyone, the person she turned to for comfort when she found the future terrifying. Speaking in rapid-fire bursts, as though he could understand her, she asked, "What is it, Father? Answer me. Please, say something." Alice had moved aside and was observing the scene with obvious indifference. As for M. Curti, he had ceased recognizing anyone. Nonetheless, he was struggling to remain dignified, trying to maintain the customary distance between himself and the world around him by the only means still left to him.

December 27th

Since the death of her father, Madeleine has only spoken to me two or three times. She hasn't stopped crying, as it were. Today, for the first time, she seemed to understand what had happened. She asked me who the woman was who'd been at M. Curti's bedside. "A friend your father cared about a great deal," I replied. I dreaded having to tell her that her father had bequeathed this stranger everything the law allowed. And yet I did tell her, to avoid putting off the moment too long. To my great surprise, it didn't seem to sadden her.

January 1st

I spent a long time thinking about Madeleine. I really should be taking into account the fact that she's deprived of affection now. I alone can understand her, forgive her, protect her. Instead of doing so, I'm behaving as any man would with any woman. I hound her, knowing that she is defenseless, and that I am stronger. Although I sense that I'm behaving despicably, I can't control myself. I'm then filled with remorse. I want to ask her to forgive me, but she would be surprised rather than touched by such a departure from my usual behavior. And so I'm condemned to make her suffer, with no hope of acting otherwise. There are moments when I find myself casting about for a way to prove my love to her. Today, for instance, to try to comfort her a bit, I talked to her very confidently about the future. I told her that we were going through a difficult time, but that we were young and the day would come when we would both be happy. She looked at me with such genuine distaste that I was terribly hurt. Every fiber of her being cried out that I didn't know what I was talking about, that I was a poor fool who was incapable of being rational. She thinks some ulterior motive is at work when you talk to her about the future. For her, as for most young people, the future is something that will unfold outside of the world we know. It's an Elysium to which she alone will be granted entry, and she doubtless finds it presumptuous of me to have booked a place there. She must wonder if I need to be separated from her before I'll stop expecting more happiness in life than what I have now! And yet, what greater proof of my devotion could I give her? I decided never to discuss the future with her again, but what will become of her when she's lost me, when she has to face the world, alone and inexperienced, and defend herself against advances and propositions whose ulterior motives she'll never suspect, and in which she'll believe with all the fervor of her youth? The day she recognizes I was right and realizes how much I really loved her, it will be too late. She'll have given herself to countless men, and left behind a part of herself each time. I picture what her life will have become without affection, without a home, maybe even without money. My poor Madeleine, how she will suffer from being old, from not having the means to conceal her wrinkles with opulence, from being deprived of the witness to her beauty, so that she doesn't have to regret its loss alone! I picture her having become meticulous and orderly, qualities she scorns at present. I imagine her caring for all her possessions, not daring to wear a new dress for fear of damaging it. She will no longer tolerate any irritation. The tiny kitchen in which she prepares her meals herself will be spotless. She will have acquired the characteristics of those inconsequential women who have no one but themselves to think about. Until now, I've done everything in my power to combat this tendency, which always gets the upper hand in women whose lives aren't rounded out by the presence of a man. One day, when we were out with Hélène, she suddenly pointed a passerby out to us and said, "Look, do you see the man walking over there? He's a friend of mine." Filled with zeal, Madeleine took on the role of a counselor, "Go and say hello . . . go on, Hélène. Don't worry about us. We'll wait for you." Was this not an early sign? I am the only thing preventing her from developing that complicity women have among themselves, which is so unattractive, so unrefined. Although at the moment she doesn't worry about a thing, I can picture her, oh yes, ferreting out addresses, trying to keep up her wardrobe at a discount, haggling with shopgirls, leading a petty existence. Although she doesn't like women and feels no compunction to socialize with them, I can picture her controlling those tendencies, forcing herself to get along with them, trying to make herself like the rest of them. What will remain of the woman I knew? Her freshness, her innocence, her extraordinary qualities, they all will have disappeared. She'll have become a poor, bitter, unloved woman, her home filled with charming knickknacks. One will sense she was let down by life. And yet it's not too late. The blows to our marriage have been glancing ones. If she agrees to stay with me, none of those evils I foresee for her need ever come to pass. She is unaware they even exist, however. Were I to describe them to her, she wouldn't understand. In fact, she thinks I'm the reason she leads a petty existence. What can we do when the person we love refuses to recognize our greater experience? We are left with the hope that they will be patient, that they won't have the courage to leave us, that they will gradually grow fond of us. Better the tribulations, which are only illusory, than moral mediocrity. That is why I've avoided a discussion. Were I to say to Madeleine, "You're free. I'll provide for your expenses, and you can enjoy yourself and do as you please," she would accept happily, and even, I think, refuse my offer of material assistance. But I mustn't do that, even if it means she suffers from my inertia. After all, as long as she stays with me, she's protected. But what will happen when I cease watching over her? Her father clearly understood the danger when, just before he died, he begged me not to abandon her.

January 4th

Today was no better. Madeleine avoided every opportunity of talking to me. Even worse, Sospel came to see me. To hear him tell it, Curti was a horrible sight on his deathbed. There are some people who take pleasure in relating the most macabre details. They give us lengthy descriptions of corpses, taking care not to omit that the beard had grown, or that a rictus had pulled the face off-center. What interests them are the dying person's gestures, his grimaces, his agony. I thought of Spigelman, too, and considered going to see him to attenuate the bad impression Madeleine and I made when he came to see us. But then it struck me that rushing to see him would only aggravate this impression. Besides, I'm in such a state that it's better I not go anywhere.

January 6th

Whenever I've loved a woman, I've been tormented by the thought that she would belong to another man one day. As a result, anxiety ruled my love affairs. I never felt my love was strong enough to last a lifetime, and therefore knew from the start that I was going to be responsible for the inevitable breakup. Thus, I suffered in anticipation of an event I was going to precipitate myself, in spite of which I never considered putting an end to this dilemma by forcing myself to be faithful. I suffered, made women unhappy, picked quarrels with them and asked them to swear that, no matter what happened, they would always be mine. Although I knew at the outset these affairs were doomed, I abandoned myself as though they were going to last forever, and demanded to be loved in return with an intensity that matched the one I pretended to feel. Madeleine has been the only woman I've ever loved without thinking ahead to the day when another man would hold her in his arms. When I was with her, it was a great relief to know that I was the only man she would ever know, since I loved her so much that I'd given up my compulsive flirting for her. The possibility that the woman I truly loved could ever belong to another man never occurred to me. On that score, I was at ease. When I looked at Madeleine, I felt a pleasant sense of security, of complete possession. Since I'd decided to make this woman my companion for life, she was therefore going to be mine for all eternity. But now I'm more worried about Madeleine than ever before. In the past, despite my jealous tendencies, some remote voice told me that I was the architect of my own unhappiness, but now that voice has fallen silent. I have ceased being the instrument of my own misfortune, nor am I the master of my own happiness: my fate is in the hands of someone other than myself, and this has happened just as I'm starting to grow old. Is this an early warning of life's transience? In the heat of my wildest rages, I used to feel that I controlled their outcome, but now I realize that I'm just a plaything in the hands of another. I think this is a sure sign that age is creeping up on us. After a lifetime spent orchestrating our own joys and sorrows, it feels very strange to realize that this gift has been taken from us. Other people have become the masters of our destiny. In spite of our confidence, in spite of having chosen a companion when still young, we are forced to accept the fact that there is a sort of earthly justice. Although we entered into battle on equal terms, we've gradually grown weaker. Madeleine has just demonstrated this to me for the first time. If a woman hadn't loved me, if she'd made me suffer the way Madeleine is doing now, our liaison wouldn't have lasted. I would have broken it off very quickly. Now, however, I accept everything, I endure everything. The thought that Madeleine will belong to another man some day haunts me, invades my mind at the most unexpected moments. I know of no sensation more distressing. As recently as a few months ago, all I held against Madeleine were the innocent flirtations of her younger days. Despite everything she's put me through, that retrospective jealousy now seems a very childish torment, compared to what I'm apprehending!

January 7th

The days pass. An ever-growing sadness has taken hold of me. I feel as if every week is a week gained against some lurking unhappiness. How distressing it is to live the way we're living, Madeleine and I! We've reached the stage of engaging only in polite conversation, from fear of a terrible scene: in my case from fear of making it, in hers from fear of having to defend herself. She went out shopping this morning. I stayed at home alone. I realized then that nothing interested me anymore, that everything was foreign to me. In an attempt to recapture something of our intimacy, I went into our bedroom. The familiar surroundings of my married life suddenly seemed to exist independently of me. I wasn't the person who slept in this bed, nor was I the person who looked at himself in this mirror. I fled to another room, only to find the same sense of isolation. Everything had suddenly grown old; it all seemed destined to be cleared out one day. Someone else would make the necessary adjustments. All was desperately immobile, distant, hostile. Often, we can go on for years without being aware of our existence, and then suddenly some sign or event will make us aware of our mortality. These may be warnings from heaven, intended to make death seem less terrible. Although nothing had changed in our life, my surroundings were sounding a warning. A current seemed to be running between the rooms, repeating that the old era had ended and a new one was about to begin, which wouldn't be as glorious as the first. In that deserted apartment, I felt as if I had just concluded the ascent of some summit, and was resting there before beginning my descent. In spite of my despondency, an aura of great calm surrounded me. Madeleine and I still lived here; I was still in the space the two of us shared. There was no sign of evanescence, everything was there in front of me as if it would be there for all time, and this lulled me into a sense of serenity which, although sweet, was like the calm before the storm.

This painful impression lifted as soon as Madeleine returned. She immediately brought the house to life; she came and went, gave orders, asked if there had been telephone calls for her. Although she thinks she is exceptionally sensitive, the fact is Madeleine doesn't perceive impalpable things. She realizes the day is fast approaching when this apartment will be nothing more than a memory, yet she continues living just as before. Tomorrow, were she forced to leave this home forever, her mind would immediately be occupied with ensuring she didn't forget anything, that everything was left in order. And when she daydreams in the midst of this uncertain home, one senses she will have no regrets about leaving. Her imagination is so great, and makes what will come next seem so marvelous, that expecting her to have regrets about something would be like asking her to prefer a single rose to an entire bed of flowers. Some people are attached to objects, even when these are quite ordinary. A trinket, a book, or an armchair will be far more precious to them than costlier replacements, because they have been their companions for years, spectators to their lives. Madeleine isn't attached to possessions for such reasons. What matters to her is their rarity, their exquisiteness, their price. Given the opportunity to exchange a ring she'd received as a child, and which she'd never taken off, for another ring, which happened to be a grander one, she wouldn't hesitate for a second. It would never occur to her that the ring which had been in contact with her flesh for all those years might be more precious than the other.

January 11th

A particularly unattractive feature of our nature is that, even in times of extreme distress, we can weigh the disadvantages of a separation with icy detachment. This may simply be because, regardless of how deep their attachment, couples nonetheless remain distinct entities. At the end of the day, certain things belong to us alone. There is our health. There are the thousands of little differences of opinion which arise at any given moment and which, in spite of our efforts to be as one with the person we love, maintain the illusion—unbeknownst to us—that we are in fact alone. In the throes of the most acute despair, the deepest sorrow, I can light a cigarette, think ahead to an appointment, consider the state of my business dealings, or remember the hour of a dinner engagement. That is the real me, the one I've been neglecting, and which is reminding me it exists. A surprising thing sometimes happens: it will abruptly supplant the other me, the one whose existence was entirely focused on another person. It happened today. As though I was going to feel no pain at losing Madeleine, I began to think very calmly about the future. My wife was no longer the center of my thoughts, which turned instead to what I would become without her. Before marrying, I led an unsettled life, and chance encounters sometimes ended with my bringing strange women home. I couldn't help myself, and yet I was always panic-stricken the next morning. Doctors are well aware that there is one disease in particular about which men are prone to the most extreme phobias. How many times have I heard them say they'd seen perfectly healthy patients who were terribly alarmed because of an imaginary or "insignificant sore" (as they put it). I was like those patients. Throughout the incubation period, and God willed that it be a long one, I trembled at the thought that I might have contracted the disease. But as soon as I was out of danger, some uncontrollable impulse would compel me to expose myself again, after which the same fear would possess me anew. I must say that, by freeing me from this phobia, married life has been a great relief. I thanked God for having preserved me intact until I met Madeleine, and throughout the years we spent together, if I happened to think back on my youthful follies, I would smile at the thought that they were dead and gone, never to return. Today, however, it dawned on me that were Madeleine to leave me, I was going to be exposed to those risks all over again. I was going to resume my acquaintance with those forgotten horrors. That nightmarish distress—which comes when, thinking we have escaped some evil, we suddenly realize we are still at its mercy—filled me. No longer thinking of Madeleine, or of the sorrow I'll feel when she's gone, I began to consider what sort of life I would have to lead to ensure I didn't become prey to the fears that haunted my past. I did this coldly, as though I'd never loved Madeleine. I promised myself to have physical relations only with women I knew, women I could be sure of, and not behave as unthinkingly as I had in my youth. An even baser thought occurred to me, which was that I could use this self-serving sacrifice to tell Madeleine that, even if she left me, my love for her would make it impossible for me to return to the life I'd led as a young man. Had she told me at that moment that she was leaving me, I would have forgotten the real reasons for my abstinence on the spot, and told her with utter sincerity that I was forsaking all others because of her. No woman would ever tempt me again, now that I had lost the one I loved.

I decided today not to let myself be caught unprepared, therefore, and to start sketching a rough outline of my life without Madeleine. I imagined myself in dignified solitude. I wondered briefly whether I ought to keep my servants, or whether it might not be better to hire new ones, who wouldn't have been witnesses to my unhappiness. I even dreamed up a new demeanor. I would lunch alone, never speak harshly to the maid, rarely go out, and always have a slightly distant look on my face. What I find strange is that picturing this new attitude cheered me up greatly. It seemed to me that it didn't lack dignity, and I found myself beginning to embellish the melancholy freedom which lay ahead, to ennoble it so that it shone in comparison with the present. When I realize I spent an hour doing this, I blush with shame, but given the scant notice I paid these reflections when Madeleine came home, I can be forgiven for having indulged in them. When I saw her, my ridiculous plans evaporated; I suddenly realized how much I loved her and how ludicrous my plans for the future seemed when compared to the happiness she brought me. I find solitude horrifying. I need to have someone near me at all times. I need to devote myself, and please forgive me if what I'm about to say seems grotesque, but seeing her, so beautiful and so familiar, it occurred to me that if she'd demanded I brave the dangers I spoke of earlier to prove my devotion to her, I would have done so. I was captivated all over again. I'd forgotten everything I'd been thinking about earlier; nothing leaves my mind faster than the fruit of solitary reflections.

January 22nd

What's become of the time when Madeleine used to be jealous, or at least touchy? I vividly recall an incident that took place about three years ago. We were in a restaurant when, with no untoward intentions, I happened to look at a young woman Madeleine couldn't see from where she sat. A few seconds later, when the stranger crossed Madeleine's field of vision, she said abruptly, "You can do what you like when you're alone, but please don't make me look ridiculous when I'm with you." Madeleine is sometimes guided by a sort of sixth sense. Certain things exist for her, even if she hasn't actually seen them. She was absolutely convinced that I'd noticed the young woman; in fact, her certainty was greater than if she'd actually caught me looking at her. Taking no account of her lack of proof, she reproached me for my behavior as though I'd been caught in flagrante and gave me no chance to defend myself, so that I capitulated with the same contrite expression I would have worn if truly guilty. As it happens, I found myself in a similar situation today. We happened to cross paths with an attractive woman, one I'd stopped looking at by the time Madeleine noticed her. Trembling hopefully, I waited for her reproach. She said nothing, however, and seemed never to have noticed what had just occurred.

January 23rd

When meeting people for the first time, Madeleine is always somewhat cold and aloof. I like this about her. Today, however, a friend of Sospel's came to see me and I had the impression that Madeleine was being more amiable than usual. On the subject of Madeleine, I've noticed she isn't as generous as she used to be. She no longer feels the need to extend invitations, to provide. It's almost as if she's suddenly realized the value of money. Her perception seems to have deepened. She doesn't want to give orders anymore, nor be yielded to, nor even loved for her beauty. She is preoccupied. She no longer loses her temper when forced to change her plans by someone who means nothing to her. She has grown more patient with the petty tribulations of daily life, whereas in the past the slightest contretemps would exasperate her. She has stopped claiming that she is wasting the best years of her life, stopped saying that the women she knows are all schemers. She always used to crave expensive gifts, and before even receiving them, would want other, more expensive ones. Now a trifle satisfies her.

January 24th

When I'm feeling discouraged, it dawns on me that nothing matters in life, that all our feelings, be they grand or vile, will end up being swept away in a similar fashion. In the past, when I felt this way I would tell myself, "One day, all this will change." I thought that again today, but rather than seeming a distant promise, it struck me that it could become a reality right then and there, if I wanted. "In order to be happy, I have to make myself happy now," I thought. It couldn't be put off any longer; my happiness had to begin immediately. I used to be blissfully happy for a few hours because of some resolution I'd made, but now I find that's not enough anymore. No matter how grandiose my resolutions, something is lacking. That is why I wanted today to be the day I've been anticipating for so long. I've been so agitated that I wake up at the slightest hint of something unexpected. I could have reasoned this way long ago and done what I did today, for it's a trifling thing to tell yourself that from now on you're going to be happy. Yet thanks to this simple decision I'd made, I suddenly felt a tremendous sense of relief, as though I'd finally found the key to happiness. Today I was going to be happy! Until now I'd done nothing but wait, but at long last I'd understood that I shouldn't wait any longer, that if I wanted to be happy I had to be happy right now. "I'm happy, I'm happy," I repeated several times. Almost immediately, however, something cast a doubt in my mind: the nature of the life I was leading. No matter how I tried to keep telling myself I was happy, I couldn't stop thinking about my many problems, about Madeleine, about the world I find so irritating and yet can't ignore, about my capital, which diminishes every year, about my health, about everything I wanted to do and never did, and which others did instead. In spite of my best efforts, I began to think the moment was badly chosen. But then, carrying my reflections further, I convinced myself that happiness had to be attainable even in the midst of over-whelming problems. There was no reason to think these would disappear in time; just as a lazy person will always find some excuse for his inaction, so there would always be a reason for my failure to act if I didn't do so immediately. I therefore told myself that I had to be happy with my lot in life, no matter what; otherwise, I would suffer till my dying day.

This commendable resolution only lasted out the morning. After having been distracted by a trifling matter, I was unable to recover the initial force of my resolutions. Anger filled me, bred of disgust. I was incapable of adhering to my own rules! I was at the mercy of my own spiritual disorder. I found myself wishing for a catastrophe, which would have hurled me into the thick of life and made me forget all my preoccupations. I was so horrified by my own weakness that I would have wel-comed fire, bankruptcy, wealth, anything at all as long as it dis-tracted me from myself. I was nothing more than a pinwheel, and the slightest change in mood was enough to set me spin-ning wildly. Could it really be that a day, or even a few hours, was all it took to annihilate a careful, well-thought out, important decision, one whose necessity was so clear to me that I'd been prepared to upset everything just to see it through? No, this couldn't be. This simply couldn't go on. I needed willpower. My future, my happiness, my very being depended upon it. How I suffer when, deprived of all willpower, the will to act is the very thing I most desire! As the minutes tick by, a crushing sense of defeat overwhelms me, and what is most terrifying is that, rather than being moved to action by this sense of worthlessness, it paralyzes me further. I've observed that, for many people, these moments of despair actually provide the impetus they were lacking. With me, it's the opposite. They bring me further down. Everything I've been longing for strikes me as utterly insane. I no longer have the courage to move, even less to defend myself. I become a miserable wreck of a human being.

Such was my state of mind, if you can call it that, when Madeleine came into my study. Gloomy disgust with life had made me stupid. I felt I was of no interest to anyone. The feeblest of men could have taken me by the hand and led me into a murky swamp crawling with frogs; I wouldn't have put up a fight. I found myself unable to speak, or use my hands, or touch my face, in spite of the fact that barely an hour earlier I'd been pacing up and down, full of life and light of heart at the thought that I'd finally discovered how to be happy, and had managed to accomplish this without being troubled by the doubts which past experience usually planted in my mind. For a brief moment, it really had felt as if something had begun which nothing in the world could destroy. But now, alone with Madeleine again, everything was gone, vaporized. All that remained was my usual self, as if those wild orgies of the will had never taken place. I no longer knew what to say. Given my exuberance a few moments earlier, I was astonished that

Madeleine didn't notice anything. The fact that she suspected nothing of my private torments, that I was always and forever the same man in her eyes, whether I happened to be filled with self-love or self-loathing, made me realize that the man she thought I was didn't deserve to be loved. I had that man before me, and was thinking about him when, hearing her say she was going out, I answered, "If you want, you don't need to come back, you need never come back. If you want, you're free . . . free." Madeleine looked dumbfounded by what I'd just said. "But what's come over you?" "Nothing. I only wanted to tell you that, if you want your freedom, you can have it." As I said this, I felt I was defeating myself, exacting revenge on myself, crushing myself beneath the weight of my own self-disgust and yet, rather strangely, I also had a confused sense that my attitude was noble, somehow. "Are you speaking seriously?" asked Madeleine. Her question threw me for a moment. So there were two ways of speaking—seriously, or not—and I had chosen the former. Although I can't explain why, it struck me all at once that everything I'd just said had lost its impact. Like a dream in which our fate hangs on a single answer we give, I grew wary, for no reason. For the next few seconds, I was silent. Then I said, "I was being dead serious." "Really! You're truly serious?" she asked again. "I am speaking seriously," I repeated, prey now to that apprehension we feel when the person we're speaking to asks, "Is it true? Is it really true? You claim that's true? For the last time, you swear what you're saying is true?" and we continue saying yes, while vaguely dreading that these affirmations are going to have unspecified consequences. I suddenly sensed that merely answering her questions wasn't enough, and that by limiting myself to that it might seem I was being capricious, so I added, "I'll say it again, my dear Madeleine: you're free to go, if that's what you want. I can see

you're not happy with me, that you find my presence unbearable. I realize you were made for something other than this.
I've made a decision; I no longer want to be an obstacle to your
happiness. I'll say it again: you're free to go, and if you want to
make your own plans for the future, I won't stand in your
way." I was convinced that Madeleine was thrilled by what I'd
just said, and continued talking. Imagine my shock when I saw
how sad my words had made her! Although I'd always thought
that regaining her freedom was the only thing she wanted, she
now seemed terrified this might really happen. The more insistent I became (in the course of a discussion, I constantly retract
what I've just said, and end up affirming things which I began
by only insinuating), the more authority I spoke with.
Although I'd begun in a pleading tone of voice, when I saw
how upset she was becoming I found myself ordering her to
leave, telling her my mind was made up and it was impossible
for me to go back on my decision. I pretended not to notice
the effect my words were having on her. Madeleine had
stopped asking if I was speaking seriously. Her expression
made it clear she was afraid of the unknown, and that she was
suffering terribly at the thought that I no longer wanted her
and she was about to find herself all alone in the world.
Nonetheless I went on, feeling no remorse. I was relieved that
she was suffering because of me. As I looked at her, I realized
just how weak she was. The fear of losing me wasn't what had
put her into this state, no, not at all: it was the fear of being
alone, defenseless, short of money. You can scarcely imagine
how afraid Madeleine is of the unknown, the unpredictable.
The idea of being with another man is intolerable to her.
Although she doesn't love me, she's incapable of being unfaithful to me, and yet I mercilessly continued telling her over and
over again that we had to part. As I spoke, Madeleine made no

reply, and didn't even seem to hear what I was saying. Her features, however, were slowly growing taut. Her face revealed everything that was going through her mind. As terrified as a child abandoned in the dead of night, the poor thing was thinking there was no one left to protect her, that men were going to hunt her from all sides, forcing her to flee, and she was imagining herself at their mercy when, exhausted, she fell to the ground. I sensed her turning to me in despair. Her eyes were pleading. She is so delicate, so refined, that she loses her composure at the thought of having to confront the unknown, the larger world. How many times have I heard her express her distaste for strangers, even when they're young and handsome! Madeleine has no friends, and to lose me would be to lose everything that connects her to life. Nonetheless, I cruelly continued urging her to leave me and start a new life, full of the confidence which comes when we know we won't be taken up on what we're saying. As I went on, Madeleine suddenly dropped into an armchair, murmuring, "You're so unkind! . . . You're so very unkind!" When reviewing our behavior after the fact, it's always easy to say, "I should have done this or that." But at the time, without the benefit of hindsight, we saw nothing. I've often noticed this at the theater. If there is a scene in which a man behaves brutally, I'll be genuinely repelled. Right now, however, I was even guiltier than that character, for even as I was being cruel, I was thinking that, in my place, another man wouldn't have behaved this way. I did, however, have an excuse known only to me, an excuse the audience couldn't know, one that would have allowed me to be a hundred times more cruel: the knowledge that my cruelty disappears in the face of genuine distress. I knew that I could end Madeleine's distress from one minute to the next. Today, however, doubtless provoked by my deep disgust with myself, it seemed to me that the moment hadn't arrived, that Madeleine hadn't suffered enough yet, that there would be time enough to change my tactics in a few minutes. In spite of this, for the first time ever I felt terribly afraid I'd overstepped the mark. This has never happened to me before. I can picture how dreadful it must be for a man who torments his wife, then fails to recognize the moment when he should stop, only to have her jump out of the window and kill herself. He was making her suffer with the calm certitude that he would know when to stop, that she would then forgive him and he would go on to make her happy. Now, because of his misjudgment, he would never be able to make it up to her. For the rest of his life, he'll carry the guilt of having caused the death of the one person he most loved in the world. Don't ask me why, but today I didn't think that moment had come. In spite of the fact that Madeleine was crushed, terrified at the idea that she was going to lose me, I didn't feel any need to reassure her. Instead, I continued to harangue her, going so far as to say that it was all over between us, that I had put up with enough, that I would never go back on my word, that I would rather die. Then all at once Madeleine burst into tears. For a moment, I thought that my excuse had lost its validity and the time had come for my customary about-face. But something wicked in me prevented me from acting. It seemed to me that I hadn't gone far enough, that I had to continue, especially as the windows were closed and I was standing close enough to Madeleine to catch hold of her in an instant. Although she was crying, she wasn't asking me to forgive her. Her pride irritated me intensely. "I'll continue," I thought, "until you beg me not to let you go." Just then, Madeleine looked at me between two sobs with such a humbled expression that I sensed she was begging me to leave her in peace. I wasn't moved, however. In fact, I had the distinct impression that no matter what happened, I wouldn't be able to stop myself. The basest, vilest aspects of my nature now had the upper hand. I was so angry with myself that I probably even took some comfort in my despicable behavior. Although I ran the risk of losing everything, I wanted to go to the limit, just to see what would happen. My will was urging me to plumb the depths of my wickedness. Earlier in the day, that same will had allowed me to feel happy, but now it was keeping me a prisoner of my own rage. I had abdicated too often in the past. I no longer wanted to. Abandoning myself to my instincts this way was deeply satisfying. If I could muster the strength to persevere, to crave one thing alone—albeit vile—without faltering, it seemed to me that a new life would begin, that I would emerge from myself and become another.

January 25th

I had a bed made up in my study, and slept there last night. For the first time ever, I kept to my resolutions. At the end of yesterday's scene, just as I was beginning to wonder whether I hadn't gone too far, Madeleine suddenly pulled herself together. One minute she was sobbing, the next she'd stopped. I've often noticed this ability my wife has to stop crying all of a sudden. She got up, her face serene beneath its tears, and passed in front of me, looking neither proud nor vengeful, but rather as if I'd had no part to play in her distress, and everything was finished between us. She went into her bathroom, and from the sounds I heard of objects being replaced on the glass shelf above the basin I deduced she was freshening her makeup. This only made me angrier. Furious, I retired to my study. I no longer wanted to see her, and took great pains to avoid her. That night, however, as I lay half-asleep on my sofa, it suddenly struck me that I'd been unfair. I was filled with remorse. For a second, I considered going to her and asking her to forgive me, but my sense that she would react angrily kept me from going to her. If you don't ask Madeleine to forgive you on the spot, you later find yourself facing a woman who seems unaware of the pain you caused her, a woman made of stone, indifferent to everything around her. These silent wars are so distressing to me, however, that when morning came I made up my mind to go knock at her door. Once in her room, I asked, "Madeleine, have you forgotten?" To my great surprise, she spoke sadly rather than bitterly, "I thought all night long, Louis. Now I understand that you're right. No matter what, we would have come to this point. We might as well get it over with now. We'll get a divorce. You'll have your freedom, and I'll have mine." Her words, spoken softly, as after a long period of reflection, made me tremble. Madeleine may be afraid of me when I'm angry, but I'm afraid of her when she's composed. "You mean to say you didn't understand that this was all a joke?" I asked. "Perhaps it was, but nonetheless it's true." What I found extraordinary about Madeleine just then was that she didn't seem at all surprised by my claim that yesterday's scene had been a joke. As I've said before, she doesn't take anything I say seriously. It didn't occur to her to reproach me for my unkindness. What matters to her are the consequences of events rather than the reasons for them. What did my explanations matter to her, since everything had now been decided! "Louis, we must part. It's the most sensible solution for us." She didn't make the slightest allusion to what had happened. It had already ceased to exist for her, and I sensed this so clearly that I lost all desire to ask her to forgive me. She wouldn't have understood why, and would have thought I was just acting. Yet I'm one of those men who likes to regret his mistakes and atone for them, in order to live again afterward. Whenever I've tried to follow that course of action with Madeleine, however, I've been stopped cold by her stony demeanor. She doesn't understand the nature of the happiness I aspire to in those moments. The mere fact of trying to make amends terrifies her, as though I were some monster. What I now found most frightening was that I had no means left with which to keep her: my heart was powerless. All I could do was ignore what she'd said and try to keep her by force, but you can imagine the astonishment with which she would have looked at a man who ordered her to leave one day, then begged her to stay the next! I have no doubt she would have told me I was insane. Prepared to brave even that, I said, "I don't want you to leave. I love you too much to let you go." Contrary to what I'd been expecting, she didn't seem surprised. "But it's what you wanted!" Madeleine couldn't fathom the idea that I no longer wanted what I'd claimed to want earlier. The moment had come when she was going to look at me with stupefaction. "But I changed my mind!" I hadn't been mistaken. As soon as I'd said this, Madeleine's expression turned to one of astonishment, though not as pronounced as I'd been expecting. It was apparent that she'd decided to play the game of pretending not to understand me, and that in the course of her nocturnal reflections, she'd decided to do what she thought best, without taking me into account. It's always distressing, in these situations, when your adversary fails to respond to your generous impulses merely out of a desire not to be hindered by any scruples. I was free to say or think what I wanted. Nothing mattered anymore. A decision had been made, and no matter what I did, it would stand. Madeleine was probably thinking that if she listened to me, we would never reach a conclusion; ending everything now precluded any discussion of my capriciousness. I was tense, and didn't know how to make myself seem believable. "It's better," she went on, "to end it all now, which is what you want." "But I don't want that anymore." I no longer knew what argument would make her yield. Until now, whenever I changed my mind about something I'd said, I did so in the manner of a young man who brings such grace to his about-faces that he can do what he pleases. But I sensed that such childishness wouldn't pass this time; out of the blue, I said harshly, "You'll do as I say. If I don't want you to leave, you won't leave." These words made no impression on Madeleine. "Don't get angry," she replied simply. "After all, you're the one who wanted it." Although she usually takes very little notice of what I say, it seemed that this time she'd taken my words to be final. I pointed this out to her with some irritation, "Not at all." A lengthy discussion ensued, in the course of which I tried to make her admit that she had never taken my threats seriously, and that if she was doing so now, it was because, at heart, she wanted to leave me. Upon hearing that insinuation, she, in turn, got angry. "Was it you or me who first spoke of this separation?" she asked curtly. As insane as it might seem, I answered that it was her. I have a peculiar trait: whenever I feel I'm gaining the upper hand with a woman, I refuse to acknowledge the truth. "What do you mean, it was me?" she asked, astounded. "Yes, indeed—it was you." I was also hoping to force a smile out of her, to make her say, as she usually did: "You're monstrously dishonest!"—which would have been a relief, because of the loving undertone in that sort of remark. I have often disarmed Madeleine this way: when I'm being so blatantly unfair, she realizes she's weaker than I am, because she hasn't the power to reason with me, and that is usually enough to restore the bond between us. But this time my dishonesty occasioned no reflection on her part which might have reunited us. And yet I sensed there was something on the tip of her tongue that she was deliberately holding back, precisely because we seemed on the verge of moving closer. Just as she doesn't let herself call me "darling" when she's sulking, she now was refusing to let herself call me a monster. "What next!" she cried. "You actually have the audacity to claim that I was the first to bring up leaving this marriage?" I think that dishonesty may well be the one form of injustice she finds most wounding. As obvious as it is, Madeleine reacts to it as though she alone had noticed it. But whereas before she would break into a quick smile at her own ardor in defending the truth, she now wanted to discuss the matter in detail. "You dare to claim such a thing?" "Yes, I do," I replied, in hopes that the unlikeliness of such an affirmation would disarm her. It was then that she showed me just how mistaken I'd been. "Well, my dear, this is the last time you'll ever amuse yourself at my expense like this." Her words made my blood run cold. The fact that my deliberate dishonesty was failing to produce the desired results enlightened me. The decisions Madeleine had made during the night had stood the test of the long day that followed. I was silent for a moment. Then, as if admitting I'd been wrong, I said, "You're quite right, Madeleine. I was the one who first mentioned it. Forgive me. It was a sort of trap I laid for you. I wanted to know what you would say if I made you such an offer." She looked at me with surprise for a second, then blurted out, "You're nothing but a vile actor, then!" As soon as she'd uttered this awkward insult, I felt myself filled with tenderness. I knew that it wouldn't be long now before her exasperation with me evaporated entirely. In spite of this, I couldn't resist provoking her a bit further. "No! I'm not a vile actor." "You're worse than that. I don't think any woman would put up with a man like you." I concealed my joy beneath a contrite air. I had a vague sense that I was regaining the upper hand. My hope now was that she would insult me, lose her temper, become increasingly violent and angry. It was fulfilled. The more she berated me for having dared to put on such an act, the less capable she became of ever considering a divorce. What I'm most afraid of is her iciness, which usually conceals carefully pondered decisions. But this animation, this excitement, filled me with joy, not because I took it to be a sign of love, but rather because the more carried away Madeleine gets, the weaker she becomes. She raises her voice, grows tense, and it all ends in tears. As I was expecting, she suddenly began to cry. I approached her softly. She pushed me away listlessly. Her sobs never lead to a desire for revenge. A sort of willingness to submit to the man for whom she's made a spectacle of herself comes over her. Although she is terribly proud, and would be incapable of crying in the presence of a brother, she seems to think that losing her composure in my presence signifies I mean something special to her. I had suddenly become her husband again. The day she leaves me will certainly be the day when she doesn't shed a tear, when she has stayed calm and in control to the very end.

January 26th

Madeleine has barely spoken to me since yesterday. It isn't that she holds anything against me, but rather—and I can feel this—that she feels no need to say anything. Immediately after lunch, she goes out and doesn't come back again until the evening. Something strange has happened to me, too, which is that I no longer feel the need to make the first move as I used to. I'm waiting for her to change, while doing nothing to make this happen. And yet I'm entirely in the wrong. I remember what happened very clearly. I'm responsible for everything, and I hold this against her. Such duplicity is normal for me. My pride has always made it impossible for me to admit my mistakes. Rather than admitting to feeling guilty, I will doggedly try to find worse faults in someone else. I was utterly indifferent to the fact that Madeleine might be right on a few points; for me, she was in the wrong. Many a time, faced with the facts, I've been on the verge of admitting my imagination had misled me, only to suddenly advance another argument, neglecting all the previous ones in favor of the newest! In those instances, Madeleine never noticed that I was merely casting about for a pretext to stay angry, and defended herself just as vehemently against the new charges. When these would collapse and I would produce yet others, it never occurred to her to scream at me, as I would have done: "But what on earth do you want with me?" She spent entire evenings listening to my extravagant accusations and disputing the merits of each one until, worn out, I would admit to her that she was, in fact, perfect. After I'd reproached her for twenty distinct faults, the inanity of which she would point out to me in succession, she would still answer, "No, no, I'm not perfect at all, you're mistaken." She admitted she wasn't perfect, but I was always in the wrong.

It suddenly struck me that the cause of my irritation these past few days was the fact that Madeleine actually toyed with the idea of leaving, that rather than giving her something to think about, my declarations made her realize that a separation was possible. That is what's been troubling me for the past week, without my realizing it or being able to admit it. I'm speechless with anger at the thought that she never said no to my generous offer. And yet I'm being unfair, for at heart she was right. How can a man who's thought out the consequences of his decision implore his wife (in her own best interests) to leave him, tremble at the thought that she might refuse, so convinced is he that she will only be happy without him, only to hold it against her when she yields to his wishes? My ardor, my tense supplications, had made her accept, and yet I was now holding it against her that she'd agreed to everything my love demanded I ask of her. A man like me was made to live alone, with neither friends nor affection. Yet God knows how fervently my heart wants to love. I'm unfair. The fact is I don't know what I want. I want her happiness with all my heart, even if it means she isn't with me, yet even as I yearn for that with every fiber of my being and every ounce of strength I have, I can't forgive her for having accepted.

I decided today that Madeleine should do what she wants. I don't want to be a ball and chain. Let her be happy! Whatever it costs me to lose her, I'll put her happiness first. Since she doesn't love me, since it makes her suffer to be with me, well, then let her go make a new life somewhere else. This time my selfish feelings won't come as a surprise. I'll protect myself, I'll organize my life. I'll find new strength in solitude and renunciation. At lunch, I told Madeleine my plans. I told her that, having thought about it, it would be for the best if we parted. I said this with some awkwardness, for the memory of what followed a similar announcement a few days ago suggested she might burst out laughing. Nothing of the sort happened. Madeleine pays no attention whatsoever to the most flagrant contradictions. I could tell her that I hate oysters and then go out and order a dozen shortly afterward: she wouldn't notice. Last week, I criticized her for wanting to leave me after having urged her to do just that, and here I was starting all over again.

But for Madeleine, life starts all over again every day. The past doesn't exist. I might as well have been setting her free for the very first time. And yet, I got the feeling that she was wary, not out of mistrust, but instinctively so. Although she wasn't calling up any particular memories, the impression the last scene had made on her was sounding an alarm. Something, but not experience, was preventing her from taking me seriously. When she went out after lunch, I felt a certain pleasure—I'm being unfair again—at seeing how much I dominate her. When I'd mentioned a separation a few days ago, a dramatic scene had ensued, but now it seemed the most natural thing in the world, an idea one no longer pays any attention to. I've noticed that all of my ideas seem destined to end this way. At first, they upset everything; later on, Madeleine discusses them as though they were utterly insignificant. If I repeat myself, she seems to think it's just a peculiar mania of mine. What made her cry the first time leaves her indifferent the second. I found myself casting about for some other way of affecting her. The ease with which she dismisses me as a maniac is actually a consequence of the power I have over her, and of which she is unaware. As soon as she was gone, therefore, I turned my attention to finding a new strategy. Setting her free was no longer making any impression on her. It suddenly dawned on me that I had grown more distant from her than ever, that the more I spoke, contradicted myself and behaved irresponsibly, the more she thought I was unbalanced. I understood I was losing her, that the key to my happiness was in her hands now, that all of my efforts were in vain. I no longer had any influence on her: I felt utterly destroyed. Every one of my thoughts seemed ridiculous to me. I had no idea how to make her stay with me. What I'd said at lunch had confirmed her in the certitude that I was impossible to live with. I should have been

sweet and kind to make her forget all of this. But that takes
time; being forgiven takes time. My heart was overflowing with
tenderness, and I hadn't time enough to express it. An overly
abrupt change in me would have been counterproductive. I
needed to win back the lost ground bit by bit, without her
noticing. The thought that there might not be time enough
made me terribly afraid. What I needed was a slow, gradual
progression. If there is one thing that always trips me up, it's
the undue haste with which I express my feelings, my eagerness
to please, to love, and be loved in return. I want to do it all
immediately. Today, however, was a day that called for a great
deal of tenderness, and circumspection.

January 29th

Have you ever noticed the extent to which good news can distance you from the person you were a short while earlier? In
my current anxious state, I have been hoping with all my heart
for some happy event that would annihilate the troubled man
I've become. It would be an event I'd been awaiting for
months, and today it would come to pass. What a relief!

February 1st

As I've been doing for several days now, this morning I bad-
gered Madeleine at length, insisting she leave me, speaking at
times like a martyr, at others in authoritarian tones, but always
with a menacing expression that made it clear I would lose my
temper if she dared take me at my word. Like those jealous
men who reproach their wives for some innocent flirtation
years after the fact, I belabored the point endlessly. All at once
Madeleine drew herself up, and looking me straight in the eye,

spoke unflinchingly, "Listen, Louis, there's something I want
to confess to you. What I'm about to tell you has nothing to
do with your constant threats. Don't think that I've made this
decision because of the pain you inflict upon me day after day.
I forget everything you do to me, and you should forget it too.
What I want to tell you has to be said out of the context of our
shabby little marital scenes. I'm in love with someone. Until
now, I've been wondering whether I should start a new life
with this other person. Having thought about it, and without
being influenced at all by your behavior, I decided to ask you
today to let me go." In a flash, what had been our life together evaporated. The things I'd been repeating to her day after
day now seemed childish, as inhuman as only unjustified accusations can be. I no longer thought I was cruel; Madeleine was
the cruel one, now. I stared at her hard, in an effort to make
her grasp the seriousness of what she was planning to do, my
expression at once supplicating, incredulous, and questioning.
"This can't be," I said with difficulty. "But it is, my poor
friend." She uttered no reproach, nor any of the excuses which
my previous behavior could have supplied her. A moment earlier I'd still been harrassing her. She made no mention of it. I
could have been the most affectionate and devoted of husbands, she wouldn't have treated me any differently. I understood that, in her mind, what she had just announced had
nothing to do with what had been going on between the two
of us. She was much too honest to lay the blame on my maliciousness. Because she had to answer to herself, she was speaking just as she would have if there had never been any quarrel
between us. She felt sorry for me, and therefore called me her
"poor friend." She felt sorry for me, and that showed me just
how impervious she'd been to everything I'd said. The pain I
felt was compounded by disgust with myself at the memory of

the way I'd behaved. I'd been violent without encountering any resistance. If there is one thing I've always cherished, it's my influence. I've always dreamed of having people trust me. I've always dreamed of leading such a blameless life that, whenever I spoke, my words would be important, as would my actions. But in fact, because of my stupidity, because of some unidentifiable gap in my intelligence, I've always undermined that influence. Regardless of how fervently I express an opinion, no one believes me anymore; no matter how ardently I swear to something, it's all over, no one trusts me. I'm left standing there, with my sincere heart and my inability to make myself understood. By calling me her poor friend, Madeleine had unwittingly shown me just how impossible it would be to make her stay. My tenderness, my love: they had lost their influence. I could have thrown myself at her feet; there was too much in my past which spoke against me. Yes, Madeleine felt sorry for me. She pitied me. While I'd been tormenting her, arguing with her, she'd been living another life, never bothering to hold my unfairness and maliciousness against me. For months, then, I'd been addressing someone who hadn't even been listening to me. My rages must have seemed all the more ridiculous if they weren't even being taken seriously. I'd lost my self-control, while she'd always remained calm. My disgust with myself deepened. I was unable to keep from asking, "But who is it you love?" "Someone you don't know." "And does this someone love you?" She looked at me without answering. I guessed then, by her ardor, that she would have gone so far as to say no just to please me, so certain was she of his love. For a moment I thought of insinuating that this man must not amount to much, the way Madeleine does about women she doesn't know. But a sort of modesty held me back. Knowing neither who he was nor what he looked like made me seem like a child in comparison. I felt achingly inferior. Without having ever seen him, I imagined him tall, strong, honest, and had the impression that, next to him, I was a worm. It also struck me that Madeleine was now in a position to judge me, that she had elements to compare, and that this was all to my disadvantage. All I could do now was try to exploit that female tendency, because of the maternal instinct, to be drawn to the weak and suffering. Never did it occur to me for a moment that my rival might be far worthier of her protection than I was; I looked at her imploringly in an attempt to convey the magnitude of my distress, the misery of my fate, and how much more I deserved her pity than that potent man who was replacing me. "For heaven's sake, Madeleine, you can't expect to keep this man's identity from me." "He has nothing to do with this," she answered in a sort of ecstasy. As she said this, I sensed that she loved him just for that reason, that he was superior because he wasn't involved in the misery of our conjugal life. And yet I still couldn't believe any of this was true. It distressed me deeply to know that Madeleine was no longer dependent upon me and that she could nonetheless be happy. I made an attempt to address her own best interests, as though not thinking of myself at all. "But are you certain, at least, that he loves you?" The smile with which she answered was full of self-confidence; it was a smile that said if there was one thing in the world she was sure of, that was it. My distress gave way to rage. "So you've been unfaithful to me, then?" Madeleine looked at me with amazement. "You really don't know me," she said simply, "if you can even think such a thing. I haven't been unfaithful to you. Nothing has happened between this man and me. I wouldn't have done that without telling you. I've thought long and hard. Now my mind is made up." My anger subsided. The fact that she had just accused me of not really knowing her had suddenly made me realize that, no matter what I did, she would always think this. She was so convinced of it, in fact, that it would have been sheer madness to try to change her mind.

Me! Not know her! Why, there isn't a thought that crosses her mind which I don't divine. And she accuses me of incomprehension! "Do what you like," I said sadly. "You'll probably be happier with another man than with me. But maybe one day you'll remember me and regret I'm no longer around. You'll understand, then, how great my love for you was, how superior to everything else it was." As I spoke those words, I had to make an effort not to cry. I was speaking from the heart to the only person I had ever loved, and whom I was about to lose. I had put aside my wickedness, my unfairness, all those things which had nothing to do with the essence of my nature, the better to extricate the pureness of my soul from that confused mass. Madeleine replied, "I understand that you're hurt, but I beg you, please don't talk of love." I realized then just how distant from her I'd become. She had never been with me. And today, when I would have laid down my life to keep her, she continued to believe that I didn't love her. "But how old is he?" I asked. "How is that of any interest to you? You've never asked me so many questions." In spite of the pain I was feeling, I was calm. Some mysterious authority was preventing me from losing my temper. For a brief moment the thought crossed my mind of trying to keep her by force, but it vanished just as quickly. I pictured myself as one of those tyrants who terrorizes his family, but grows fearful when stronger people join his household, and then becomes docile and accommodating. This humiliated me. Although I'm capable of great violence, I'm such a coward that when I sense I'm beaten I find it impossible to get angry. I wasn't even trying to win back

Madeleine; if I had any hope at all, it was in the pity I might inspire in her. "Look at me, Madeleine, you can't leave me," I said, looking her straight in the eyes for as long as I could. "Please," she answered, "for once in your life, try to be sincere."

February 2nd

Yesterday evening, I stayed in my study. After her confession, Madeleine underwent a complete change, and in the most natural way possible. For the first time since we've been married, she went out. Once things have been said, she considers it perfectly fine to act upon the consequences immediately, and feels no need to wait a few days out of delicacy, as I've always done. Left alone, an immense sadness came over me. I reflected upon my life, my past, and suddenly pictured myself abandoned by everyone. I was overcome with such lassitude that I cast about for something to distract me, and what came to mind was the way Madeleine had broken the news to me that she loved another man. "I'm in love with someone," she'd said. I can't explain it, but those trivial words suddenly made me feel great pity for her. I don't know why that manner of imparting such an important piece of news made me realize Madeleine was defenseless. I had the presentiment she was going to be dominated, that she was going to suffer even more, because I wouldn't be there to understand her. That last thought suddenly revealed a reality I hadn't even considered before. The deepest understanding, that understanding which I'd always considered as the very foundation of love, is useless. There's nothing to be gained from understanding people. Understanding, no matter how profound, adds nothing to love. The weariness weighing upon me has a terrifying quality. I've passed my fortieth year, and here I am, having to start life all over again. If I do start life all over again, I'll do so very cautiously, but will I even start? Caution, understanding, it's all useless. There is weariness, and nothing more. What will become of me? She loves "someone." And I'd always thought that she could never be happy, elevated, loved, without me. Well! It would appear I was wrong. Noble sentiments count for nothing. Nothing matters, neither caution, nor understanding, nor love. What more did she want? She wanted an ideal love. But he's not going to teach her that it's ugly to say you're in love with "someone." No one will ever tell her that. Happy as she thinks she is, her happiness will never be great. No matter that she loves, and is loved; she will have lost me. She will become a different woman, less beautiful than the woman who belonged to me. People she knows will fail to recognize her. New friends will have replaced them. Her qualities and her defects will have been transformed, and she will be loved for the new ones as much as I once loved her. She won't even spare a thought for the man who was once her companion, for how can you ask a woman who's forgotten who she was to remember the friend she had back then? And why hold it against her? Time passes. Who will ever know that she once walked away from the life she had, because she was in love with "someone"? No one, except me.

Afterword

Emmanuel Bove (1898–1945)

I

On the "Disappeared" in General

The oblivion into which some artists fall is an interesting sub-ject in itself: at least as interesting as how a literary canon comes to be established. What is the difference between the canonized author and his forgotten rival? Celebrity during his lifetime is a help, but no guarantee—just where are Franz Werfel or Sigrid Unstetter today? Each literature bears its freight of the eclipsed; each generation shows us writers in the process of disappearing. Gide, Faulkner, and Hemingway are currently *chefs d'école* getting themselves "disappeared." Many factors weigh into literary slaughter: malice and envy are for-midable opponents; self-promotion is only of temporary assis-tance. Innovators have a good rate of survival: Borges and Kafka have made it, but then Robert Walser and Marinetti haven't, and imitators or followers sometimes succeed where the originators fail to last—thus Gabriel García Marquez, author of one remarkable novel, is at the apogee of his fame, but where is *his* literary father, the once-celebrated Alejo Carpentier?

What happens to those who dwell in the Land of the Memory Hole? No decade goes by that does not see a reevalu-ation—under the pressure of art critics and historians, but more transparently by the owners of their works or galleries with stock—of a half-dozen "new" painters few in previous generations thought much of. The record industry, its army of performers, its intricate ties to festivals and such, has achieved miracles of recuperation. Fashions in the arts do change, but in literature, works written for another time seem much harder to recover than music or painting.

It may be that literature involves a much more personal relationship between writer and reader. Paintings and scores, painters and composers, disappear too, but it requires a minimum investment to restore them to life: a performance, an astute critic, an exhibition can do it. In a publishing industry that has lost its collective mind, its taste, and its generous patrons, the outlook for revival is dim: not least because the act of reading requires something more than an open eye or ear. Writers evoke periods and societies in very particular ways, and these are not always recuperable once the habit of open-minded reading has gone and been replaced by best-sellerism and the quick fix.

Emmanuel Bove is an excellent example of the "eclipsed" writer, but far from unique. Writers fall out of favor from the political correctness of the day, from the sluggishness and overheads of publishers, from not being kept in print, from the primacy of critics and lazy academics; a single bad book can do them in as much as death.

But after that fatal point, there remains the risk of the eager or necessitous widow. No writer should ever trust his immortal remains to his wife or family. The result is sure to be bowdlerization, suppression, or commercial disaster, for wives (and children) like to think they know their man, and who knows that he may not be more profitable dead than alive?

Bove has had, in this regard, some exceptional bad luck. His whole period—the Jazz Age (only enjoyable and jazzy if you had access to the high jinks, which Bove emphatically did not), the Depression (universal access, but to be forgotten, if possible—too painful), and the unsavory 1940s (in France especially, to be obliterated)—is in disrepute. Mind you, he is in good company as he lurches from publisher to publisher and hand to mouth. Well outside the pantheon of the accepted, which runs from Proust and Gide to Montherlant, Mauriac, Giono, Cocteau, and such, he inhabits a world into which few still dip: with Eugène Dabit, Pierre Bost, Paul Garenne, and many others, nearly all of them entirely unavailable. The literature of 1919–39, apart from its "masters," in whom publishers have a vested interest, is little studied and less read.

Then Bove's career, after the success of his first book, *Mes amis*, was always a creaky and unpatrician affair. Not for him Marcel's *rentes;* Emmanuel was a prole, a Grub Street man. He had a family to support. If he had made it, he could have afforded to make his older brother and his mother shut up; since he didn't, he lived at daily risk of their importunings. Thus, though one might say that between 1924 and 1935 he was—in terms of literary visibility—a successful author, he was seldom a regarded one. He didn't move in the circles of the successful, but rather in that French demi-monde that lies between the fat cats of the maison Gallimard—all mutual log-rolling, long-term contracts, the support of the *Nouvelle Revue Française*—and the popular press, to which he was compelled, by nature and by need, to contribute.

Being a Jew (his real name is Bobovnikoff) didn't help. He is not the Jew of the Agonized Conscience; he had nothing whatever to say about the Holocaust (though he must have known about it); he is barely a "Jewish" writer in any recognizable sense. But during the war years, Bobovnikoff can hard-

ly be published—the house of Gallimard, a Jewish house, only
barely squeezes by, and that by playing the Occupier's game.
Even an arch-anti-Semite like Céline does not fare that much
better at the *Nouvelle Revue:* Pierre Drieu de Rochelle edits the
house magazine, with extreme difficulty, but Céline is no star
in his firmament; he is something both less and more than an
inconvenient, noisy ally. As for Bove, he does not exist: only by
the merest coincidence (Marcel Aymé's goodwill) do the two
men share a literary executor.

We have to face the fact that Bove had almost no visible
life—he was a subterranean writer, a mole working in the dark
of poverty and urgent need—and that can by no feat of the
imagination be everyone's cup of tea. He belongs to that class
of writers with a rigorously circumscribed invention, whose
universe is banal because quotidian, which is unmythic
because it does not reach for any dimension beyond itself.
Fernand Vandérem, an early supporter, pointed out in 1928
why even Bove's most popular book, *Mes amis*, met with critical silence: "Not the shadow of a thesis or an idea. A volume
without ideas to agree with or argue over, critics find difficult;
they don't know how to deal with it, what to write about it."[1]
What he means is, the critic can't shine talking about Bove. As
Bove leaves his characters to their own fate, so critics left Bove
to his. Only a very few grasped the essence of his art.

The point about critical failure is important. Now, too. For
as critics have gained power, they seem to have lost the faculty
of impartial reading. Satisfies only the writer who can serve as
a structure on which critics can elaborate their own claims to
be central, rather than parasitical, to literature. Céline, yes, an
inexhaustible mine! Proust? To be quarried forever. Bove?
Nothing useful there. Bove just represents the world: a man
without theories.

In this neglect, too, the academy plays no small part. It may be that, somewhere, a department of French literature might include Bove in its curriculum, at least in France, and possibly in Germany. I can find no trace of any learned articles on Bove among those who profess the métier of instructing the young in French literature. No theses![2] *The Reader's Guide to Periodical Literature* remains silent! Only in the last few years have a few English translations begun to appear, and not always in translations that are particularly *soignées*.

Bove was self-effacing to an astonishing degree. Which allows him to be effaced. No notoriety (that great savior of artistic reputation) attaches to him. He did not write in a cork-lined room, was not homosexual, not a communist (though his wife hawked the party newspaper at metro entrances), not a gossip, did not keep a journal—indeed did his best to obliterate his own life—was only once, so far as I can ascertain, translated during his lifetime.[3] He failed to cultivate critics, did not seek election to the Academy, did not frequent other artists.

His timing continues to be rotten. His last prewar novel (not a success), *Adieu Frombonne*, his second with Gallimard, is published in 1937. When he resurfaces in 1945–46 with four remarkable novels, he is not present for interviews, being dead. Another literature, other reputations, are being made. A Jean-Paul Sartre, to Bove's credit, is another sort of literary animal. Albert Camus, who recommended Bove, was not long for this world either. And everyone wanted to forget the years before the war; they became, like the Occupation, discreditable. Bove is vaguely a resistant, certainly aligned with De Gaulle, but, being a Jew and in danger, he sits the war out in Algeria and is dead before he can claim his place in the myth-making of the Resistance.

Then, when enlightened publishers and critics—or real

readers with long memories—sought to exhume Bove, they ran into his wife. She had unrealistic views about her dead husband's value on the market and kept the flame of his reputation burning too close to her breast. As a result, projected reissues of his books fail: Louise wants too much money, times are hard.

It is not a pretty picture. Bove is a case study in *l'Oubli*. Would Bove have survived at all were it not for the fact that, like the few Just Men, there are also some writers and readers of extreme generosity? Though these are far fewer than writers avaricious of their own reputations? The painter Bram van Velde inquires of Samuel Beckett in the early 1950s whom he should read. Beckett says: "Emmanuel Bove. No one else has his sense of the moving detail" (quoted in *EB*, 239–40). Revealing, for Bove is an avatar of Godot. Who else? The Swiss publishers Rencontre exhume Bove in 1964: with this very novel, this bleakest, most devastatingly Bovian of all his works. Had it not been for Raymond Cousse, an actor and fine playwright who killed himself in 1991, and to a much lesser extent the enthusiasm of a few others—Samuel Beckett, Peter Handke, Valéry Giscard d'Estaing—what would have happened?

Think of the places where he is missing. As Cousse and Jean-Luc Bitton note in their admirable biography,[4] in the major standard histories of French literature, Bove gets short shrift. Bove is mentioned in Lalou's immediate postwar (1946) history of French literature; in 1949 he gets a page in Clouard's history, but only three lines when it is refurbished in 1962. He is cited in that standard work Bédier and Hazard (1949), but not at all in the Larousse (either the Twentieth Century or the New Grand Larousse.) He is missing from the Pléiade literary encyclopedia, and so on and on. Belgium to the rescue! In 1948, the Belgian poet and late surrealist Christian Dotremont, then twenty-five, takes up Bove's case in 1971. He writes a remarkably perceptive letter to the widow:

> Bove has invented a new way to see the real. His genius is to show us what is evident but which we do not see just because it is evident . . . He went beyond that: he accounted for the logic of the real, which seems absurd to most human beings, because their logic is not realistic. I think he took pleasure in showing how the logic of the real and Cartesian logic are in opposition to each other. (quoted in *EB*, 242)

After Dotremont, the cinematographer François Beloux, in 1971 (he was then also twenty-five), began to unravel the Bove life in long, invaluable interviews.[5] Like Cousse, who did the hardest work of all (because he was the first), he, too, would take his own life. In 1972, a publisher of art books, Yves Rivière, proposes to reissue Bove in limited editions (only one, in an edition of 108 copies appears).

I myself come to him purely by accident.[6] The name Bove is being bandied about; I stop by a bookshop below the Place Pigalle; I buy a slender volume, *Afthalion Alexandre* (which has obvious elements of Bove's father's life); beguiled, I translate it, immensely conscious of the difficulty involved in conveying a style at once so flat and "evident," to use Dotremont's word, and so nuanced, flexible, complex, and even mannered (has anyone but Proust played so originally with the many repetitious, insistent, subtle variations of the subjunctive mood? Or, since the great moralists, offered the reader so many bleak maxims about the human condition? Maxims, of course, in the Bovian style, expressing formulaic characterizations.[7]), and publish it in *Bostonia*.[8]

II
Evasion by Choice, Life, and Work

Who was Emmanuel Bove? His father (by no means the lesser figure in Bove's life, despite the fact that paternity runs much less strongly through the writer's work than maternity, or near-maternity), Emmanuel Bobovnikoff, was born in the Kiev ghetto in 1867, and showed up in France toward 1897 after having walked through Germany with stops in Berlin and Strasbourg.[9] He is generally known as *le Prusco*, a generic name applied to Germans of the old federated armies who settled in France or along its borders;[10] and indeed, German seems to have been, for many years, his first language. There are other paternal relatives: a grandfather who also walks to Paris, with fleas, and an aunt who is described by Bove's younger brother, Léon, as so deadened that "one knew she came from a faraway land and had been drowned in misery" (quoted in *EB*, 26).

Bobovnikoff *pére* is listed on his passport as *sans profession*, which suggests, in those far-off days, either wealth or unemployment: in his case, the latter. At least nothing regular, unless you want to consider the state of marriage as employment, though he did set himself up as writer, publisher, printer, and vendor of a dictionary for Russians visiting the 1900 Exposition. What father contributes to son—alongside poverty, an often reused model of optimistic inventiveness and fantasy, a world of Defoe-like "projects," and a mother fecundated almost in desperation—is a spectacular vision of repeated failure and, ensuing from that, the dreadful fear of falling that haunts those who aspire to the middle classes and see themselves forever in danger of slipping, forever, into the proletariat. This living on the edge of the abyss is a reiterative theme in the son.

Bobovnikoff also clearly had charm, was a ladies' man and

rarely without a mistress. He offered a high brow, a well-trimmed beard, narrow shoulders, and much wistful yearning. In Léon's words, he is a dreamer: "His main idea was that as there were people with too much money, one might as well take advantage of the fact."

Bove's mother, a lifelong problem to him—along with his beloved, richer stepmother, *the* problem (guilt, incest, envy, Oedipus flourishing)—was born Henriette Michels in 1874 in Luxembourg. Her father was a decent farmer who ran a logging business and owned lime kilns. He also drank to excess and died at fifty-four, propertyless, his body turning violet in death, as if pickled. Henriette was the sixth of twelve children, all of them educated by nuns, and none of them feeling much affection for each other.

It is likely that Henriette was slightly mentally retarded: "At seventeen," Léon reports, "not having had her period, she was convinced she was pregnant, though she had no idea how this might have happened." She was a victim born. In Cousse's description, "a rather simpleminded woman, strictly brought up, and hardened by circumstances."

A little before seventeen, her father dead a bankrupt, Henriette is in Paris, where she lodges with a brother. The only employment available is as a maid of all work, a skivvy: an occupation she pursues with diligence, abused and half-starved, in Paris, Orléans, and Marseilles. It is during her second job in Paris that she succumbs to Bobovnikoff senior. This sordid, utterly Bovian scene is described by her son Léon as follows:

> When around ten at night Henriette, worn out by her work, returned to her garret, almost nightly she would stumble across a sort of student who lived in another attic room on the same stairwell. The "student" was a thirty-year-old Russian in frayed, dirty clothes. He had a little pointed beard . . . and lived a life of

> Bohemian destitution, surviving by expedients amidst constant
> rows . . . Every night he would slip little notes under [Henriette's]
> door . . . Then one night, Henriette having left her door open to
> talk to other servants who shared the floor, he managed to slip into
> her room and hide under her bed. When she had finished undress-
> ing and was about to fall into bed, the Russian quit his hiding place.
> She shouted . . . and the Russian fled to his room, pursued by one
> of the maids who threw water on him . . . Though constantly
> rebuffed, and thanks to a misplaced insistence that combined cheek
> and unbelievable candor, he succeeded in his purpose. With a sort
> of presentiment, however, standing on the balcony beating a carpet
> and spying that thin and bearded Russian . . . Henriette said to her-
> self: "Any man but that one." (*EB*, 31)

Thus, appropriately, like a scene in one of his own novels, was
Emmanuel Bove conceived. The Prusco confined her, two
months before delivery, to the French state's equivalent of a
home for wayward girls, from which she promptly walked out.
The couple then set up house in one room on the top floor of
a building overlooking the Montparnasse cemetery, and there
Emmanuel was born. He can see it from his grave.

Henriette's hatred of the men who betrayed her
(Bobovnikoff senior certainly, and Emmanuel probably), and
of the woman who was to come between herself and a "decent
life," later became engraved on her soul, which was always an
unforgiving one. She wanted marriage, and failing that—the
Prusco ironized about the prospect: "Sure," he said, "let's take
the twopenny bus and go off to the Mairie"—she insisted on
respectability. The Prusco's soul was of the more sentimental
and would-be conscientious sort. He did what he could for
her, and certainly for his children (for Léon was to follow short
of three years later.) He did not want to live with her, certainly; nor, however, did he wish to abandon her heartlessly. He
felt more pity for Henriette than affection, which carried over

to his oldest son, and perhaps even, had Léon been more self-aware, to his second.

The breach between them came in 1899, when Bobovnikoff met Emily Overweg, who was three years older than he was, ten years older than Henriette (she was then twenty-five), English (by nationality and birth, in Roehampton, if not by blood), and rich and artistic. Though she was a plain woman, and half a hand taller than Bobovnikoff, Emily was everything that Henriette was not: she didn't scrub floors, she played Chopin and painted; she wasn't inflexible, but understanding—in Victor's words (Victor was the third Bobovnikoff, and Emmanuel's stepbrother), "charming and very tolerant"(*EB*, 37).

This family background is important to understanding Bove in that, first, he never discussed it, save in fiction; and second, the obvious culpability Bove felt at his imaginary near-incest. There is a photograph of Emily, Bobovnikoff-as-swell, and young Victor in costume (together with a nanny) strolling in 1914 in Menton that tells a story. Bobovnikoff's beard is fuller; Emily's fur wrap is in the height of fashion; Victor, the result of this mutually profitable union, is clearly *safe*, and everyone in the picture knows it.

Somewhere in the space that separates Bobovnikoff's two liaisons, there is a writer in formation, yearning toward Emily's world, dreading that which contains his mother and younger brother. Yet, despite the fact that Bove effectively commuted between his two families, as for that matter did his father, only a few, very rare stories (and *Le Beau-Fils*) touch on the world which Emily represents. Henriette and the world of the poor is Bove's sheet anchor, his drag, the fate he has to live with. He is too fine a realist to mistake that fact.

Missing fathers are the secret gardens of writers: they are such an elementary fact for many children. Bove's missing father—he is missing in most of Bove's novels as well—is both there and not there: perhaps least there when needed, as when Henriette and her children are thrown out of apartment after apartment, and there when least desired, bringing with him the fragrance of that other life on which his first family depends. To grow up in the complex geography of Bove's two families must have been like going with a compass to the Pole, a place in which all directions are equivalent. Bove's heroes, almost all men, resemble the Prusco, and Bove's writing is that of the itinerant and intermittent schoolboy that he was: bereft of a controlling, reassuring worldview, desperate for a salvation that was ever just in the offing, and circumscribed by a dismal reality.

To read Léon (a reliable though resentful witness, at the rudimentary level as much a writer as his older brother, but without genius), life—between evictions, importunings, and unexpected salvations—sounds like hell. They were lodged in San Remo while the Prusco was in Menton, for so Bobovnikoff had decreed, and Henriette knew no better than to obey. She was a woman entirely without inner autonomy. Between absent father and incompetent mother, literature became, for the young Emmanuel, a means of survival.

The explanation may seem rudimentary (if common enough), but it has ample evidence to support it. Bove himself dates his writing vocation from about his fourteenth year. But is it need, or more simply an excess of sensibility, a genuine neurosis, a need for guilt? There are clues, after all. First there is Bove's own mirrored description of himself as an adolescent in *Monsieur Thorpe,* a miniature *Bildungsroman* of adolescence, "discovered" in his own life and experience:

> If I remember well, I was then visibly terribly shy . . . The slight-
> est reproach threw me into turmoil; I blushed at the slightest thing.
> Nonetheless . . . I was forever committing indelicacies. I constantly
> found myself in disagreeable situations, particularly when I had to
> justify myself for having done something I knew was ugly but had,
> however, done, and had to defend myself against people who were
> certainly right. Bit by bit, for those around me, this gave me a rep-
> utation for falsehood.[11]

Falsehood, of course, is what fiction is. Recently I ran
across a French definition of sexual perversion which strikes
me as particularly apt for that form of perversion we call "writing":

> Putting into play a partial pleasure or an aspect of pleasure which
> seems sufficient unto itself; having recourse to associated ele-
> ments—ritual, scenarios, place, specific object; the irresistible side
> of such a desire or momentary impulse; its personal, confidential
> character, which makes of it a mystique for whoever lives it, and
> excludes a partner.[12]

Put together this prevailing guilt, this culpable habit, and
the extremity of Bove's solitude, his habit of detaching himself
and observing—

> One of my most ardent desires was to feel safe, in a place to which
> I alone could have access, a desire to retreat within myself which I
> can only compare to another desire, that to possess a piece of land,
> however tiny still so huge, since it would belong to me, deeply and
> forever, in whose basement I would have dug out a palace, to the
> point of encroaching on my neighbors' properties, since no one
> would ever have known.[13]

—and I think it becomes plain where this "writing by seeing"
(*écrit avec le regard*),[14] as Jean-Yves Reuzeau writes, originates.
Bove's fiction is first lived, and then *occurs*, as fiction. And,
despite the strong autobiographical content of his work,
should we not take it as significant that he was never tempted
to the journal form? That his correspondence does not seem to

have been, as it was to most writers of his period, an important exploration of themes? That he barely survives, as a person, in the memory of others? That he inexplicably misses all the great controversies and events of his time?

Whatever the prime cause, Bove's intent, or his acquiescence to his fate as writer, almost certainly takes form in adolescence, and that adolescence is marked by a significant event: he divorces his mother and for the next six years dwells in the paradise (so erotically potent in *Le Beau fils*) represented by his father's new wife, Emily. For ten years he had lived more or less exclusively with his mother; but from the age of ten to sixteen, when he returns from England, he lived with Emily. It was a radical change of environment, if not any more stable. In Emily's house he received the rudiments of a "proper education"; he rode, learned to play golf and tennis; and, as his stepbrother Victor says, "he heard intellectual and artistic talk about him; in another milieu he might never have become a writer."

I don't think much of this argument. Bove confounds the whole heredity-versus-environment debate; both condemn him to be the man he is, as they condemn his characters. They are innumerable in his works—these men who live on the marches of life and slowly, almost insidiously, become aware that they can't escape themselves. Among the extraordinarily ordinary characters who collect for *Un soir chez Blutel* is Demongeot:

> At thirty, he had noticed that all the things he had hoped for in his youth would not come about, that his status in the world was already fixed, his path laid down, and that the best he could do would be to live tranquilly exercising his profession as a dentist . . . The passage from a youth full of dreams to adulthood took place without his knowledge. Just what he regretted was not clear . . . At forty he lived in the same decor as when he was young. Now he took care not to be overcome by bitterness.[15]

Some writers are indeed formed by their education; others by their experience. Bove obviously read, but, despite attestations to his large library and his prizing rare first editions, it is singular that I can think of not a single reference to another writer in his work, nor did he ever, to my knowledge, publish any critical articles.[16] He himself says he reads little:

> . . . and even when I force myself to read, I am often bored. No sooner have I opened a book than I want to write . . . The book [before me]—good or bad, that's not the question—I would like to rewrite in my own way. Ideas, memories, and objections surface, so many of them that I have to stop. (quoted in *EB*, 111)[17]

The few notes and fragments we possess consist exclusively of observations and analyses. He may, therefore, have turned to writing as a form of salvation, as a way of distancing himself from his "situation," not to "be overcome by bitterness," but my guess is that this is not, for him, therapy, but rather the central perversion.

The Prusco was to die in 1915 in a Leysin (Switzerland) sanatorium: once he was dead, Bove, who had always feared this loss, at last felt he possessed him entirely. Now he could turn him into fiction. And that meant facing the real world, in the form of Henriette and Léon, who feel as if Bobovnikoff had died just to spite them, to deprive them still further. From that moment on, mother and son badger: persistently, tenaciously, vilely, unashamedly. Badger Emmanuel, badger Emily, who herself has lost all her fortune in the postwar inflation. This pursuit of the unattainable, this sense of terrible injustice, is to provide the narrative strength of Bove's fiction. High drama is counted in a very few francs due, in a switch of affections, in the changing tone of a voice: in all those things, in fact, which make up daily life. Notably missing in his work—for any form of politics is absent until after 1940—is the Great War (he wasn't mobilized until April 1918), the Bolshevik

Revolution. Much more important is his separation, which is going to last twelve years, from Emily (she remarries a Mr. Lamont, who has many children of his own, but it would also appear that he stole her valuable Bible and she threw him out of the house). Much more important is the fact of poverty.

This poverty, which the modern reader can scarcely conceive, is very real. It doesn't consist of living less well, of deprivation; it is a matter of having *nothing*, of not knowing how one is going to make it to tomorrow. Bove works in a Marseilles restaurant, he hides on a train to Paris, he travels on used trolley tickets; worst of all, he is condemned to living with Henriette and his brother in a furnished room in Versailles. He survives this by what he calls his "somnambulism"; he is simply absent; in the eyes of his family, he is irresponsible; he is an actor. From a restaurant to a hotel (porter); from hotel to prison as a drifter; conscripted at twenty, serving a long and boring occupation, he marries for the first time in December 1921.

It seems not to have been a happy marriage. Suzanne Vallois was a striking-looking woman, full in face, with short, dark hair; she looks Spanish and practical. But her background is rural and narrow-minded. Demobilized, Bove and Suzanne left for Austria: a defeated country has the virtue of being cheap, and Bove wanted to write.

For in the meantime, mysteriously, he has become, leaving little trace of creation, a writer. It is as though his two earliest books (by date of writing), *Le Crime d'une nuit* and *Mes amis*, had long been written in his mind, and all that was required was that they should be set down.

A stroke of good fortune (one of the few) was that the reader of *Le Crime d'une nuit* was Colette, then in charge of fiction at *Le Matin*. Drafted in Vienna, it was probably written for the paper's Christmas edition (it was too long), which probably accounts for its lyrical, parablelike language. Henri Duchemin is a typical Bovian down-and-out. Sitting in a café on Christmas Eve, he recounts his misery to a woman. "Don't be ridiculous," she says. "If you're as unhappy as you say, you can kill yourself." In fact, he kills a banker, shares out the proceeds, and has a mystical encounter with a white-bearded man in a park. It turns out to be all a dream.

This tale, however slight and philosophizing, however much the work of a young man at his beginnings, nonetheless strikes the true Bovian note: "He remembered his dream somewhat; and also, a little, the white-bearded man who said that, to redeem himself, he should suffer. But none of this concerned him, for he had never harmed anyone." What marks it as true Bove is the enormous distance between event and description, the indefiniteness until—and this is the Bovian way of rendering reality, true prose, no ambiguity, a flat, declarative sentence—he reaches his encapsulating conclusion: "None of this concerned him." In between are all the hedges and twists and qualifications, the "somewhat" and "a little" that are woven seamlessly into his mature style, not to be discarded until his last two novels.

It was Colette who encouraged him—she directed a fiction collection for the publisher Ferenczi—to write his first full novel, which he did, locked away in a hotel room, in a remarkably short time. This novel, *Mes amis*—no more than a series of short stories, aperçus of life among the falling and fallen, truly those he knew best, though the title is ironical, in that the thread that keeps the novel together is his hero's search for friendship—made his reputation and remains the one book discerning readers may know. It was also a resounding success. Edmond Jaloux, who had befriended Proust in his later years, caught the resonances—and the differences—right away:

> *Mes amis* is the confession of a poor man with feeling. He seeks to attach himself to others; he ends up alone. No events, nothing novelistic, just everyday, lacerating, wretched meetings. This simple story is woven through with a fantasy that is ingenuous and melancholy, a truthfulness that extends to the comic, and a trembling pain. (quoted in *EB*, 93)[18]

As Bove's biographers point out, *Mes amis* is a book against the grain. Bove is immediately marginal. The Jazz Age is about to begin: without Bove. Peter Handke, who is more than just an admirer, who indeed has used many Bovian disguises himself, has noted the freshness of the young writer, not yet twenty-five: "The writing is so clear, so modest, and yet not at all modest. It's a form of writing that doesn't exist before him, nor since. It's like drawing with very clear lines" (quoted in *EB*, 94). Philippe Soupault, the surrealist (and communist) was present at a dinner that Colette gave for her new authors. He recalls that

> Bove did not say a word, save to say "thank you" when his wine was poured . . . He preferred writing to speaking . . . He never criticized others. I've never heard him speak ill of anyone. His few friends thought he sought to be forgotten, as others sought to be known. He always preferred silence to publicity . . . He never spoke of his childhood, his adolescence, or his family. (quoted in *EB*, 96)

Like his contemporary, Georges Simenon (they are very likely to have read each other), Bove did not have access to the sinecures by which most French writers survive. Instead, like Simenon, he worked as a free-lance in the newspapers of the day. Both writers were most attracted to crime and the *faits divers*, the strange little news items ("Cow stops Express," Louis Guilloux, another underestimated writer would declaim at the breakfast table) which tie reader to reality. Indeed, the list of Bove's published writing is extended by such *faits divers* as: *Le pigeon mécanique . . . , Jean Taris est vainqueur de la traversée de Paris à la nage*, and *Un drame de vanité*.[19] And there are other affinities: in style, subject, perversity, and sympathy for the downtrodden, the anonymous mass. Like another contemporary, L.-F. Céline, both men are close students of the *banlieu*, the dreadful 'burbs that housed those who could not afford the center.

A most interesting study could be made of the relationship between many writers' fictions and their journalism, which in their minds lie in two different worlds: that of the imagination and that of the real. Practical journalism is part of the writer's life, all the way back to the founding of the periodical press. And why not? It offers the writer a way to hone his writing skills, to compress, to speak to a guaranteed audience, to respond to a deadline, to desacralize his language, to speak directly to an avid readership. And it offers (relatively) easy money; it consumes text. After all, *Le rouge et le noir* began its fictional life as a *fait divers*.

As you will find out in reading this novel, or if you so much as set foot in Bove's world, the autism of his characters, their ineffectuality, is disturbing by its curious calm. You may not know what to make of a girl like Louise, for instance, in *Une fugue* (1929). Louise has a crisis on her hands: she's been caught stealing a fur coat. Louise is one of a gallery of Bovian women who are both victims and savages: that is, they give as good as they get—to be sure, in their own passive way. As she relates her story to the lawyer she wishes to engage, we find out that she suffers from being unloved. Holed up in a hotel room—much of Bove takes place in the anonymity of a hotel bedroom or a *meublé*—she is discovered inert with a phial by her bedside. A suicide? Not at all. It is just water. Her perplexed parents bring her home. They ask her what's wrong with her. "Nothing," she answers.

I can't remember if Louise's purloined coat is returned, but that doesn't matter. The question is, what's the matter with these people? Where is will? Free will?

I take my text here from Bove's own life. The year is 1925. Suzanne and their daughter, Nora, go off for the summer holidays. Emmanuel is busy: he stays behind in Paris. In September, mother and daughter come back and find the concierge at the foot of the stairs. "Don't go up," he says. "M. Bove has given up his lease." Where is he? They don't know, we don't know. When Bove seeks divorce, which required proof of adultery, Bove says he would rather jump into the Seine than cohabit again. And Suzanne later confides to her daughter that she had divorced him (in 1930) "without ever having a marital quarrel with him. His humor was absolutely constant" (*EB*, 110–11).

Louis Martin-Chauffier points out the ties that bind the guilty to their victims in the Bovian oeuvre:

> Bove's world is a refuge for the victims of society, or rather for those unable to live in society: unprotected against the blows of society, they show all their scars, and how they got them. Even if they don't complain, just looking at them one is horrified by a world that refuses shelter to those whose only crime, an unwilling one, is that they are simultaneously devoid of both virtues and vices, therefore literally defenseless. Without showing his colors, Bove's major books show him to be an enemy to the social fabric. Not by principle, but by temperament.[20]

The divorce from Suzanne—unstated because, as Nora points out, "my father was incapable of saying anything unpleasant or wounding"—is a symptom, not an illness. Bovian inaction shows how Russian he is. His illness is a form of *Oblomov-schina*, a profound moral sloth that precludes both judgment and act.

Take the story "Est-ce un mensonge," in which the wife, devoutly independent, is regularly missing every afternoon (Bove's women, largely proletarian, share a distaste for possession) until she stays out one whole night. On her return, she tells her husband a cock-and-bull story about old friends:

> He didn't believe her. He was profoundly convinced that she had lied. But it suddenly struck him that he was approaching old age, and rather than lose everything, it was better to suffer silently, so as to go on enjoying living with the woman he loved, and who had enough respect and friendship for him to have taken the trouble to lie.[21]

All this may make it seem that Bove was a melancholic, passive, the author of his own unhappy life. This is not quite true. At the time that he separates from Suzanne, for instance, he is having a two-year affair with Henriette de Swetschine, about whom we know little, apart from Léon's testimony that she "passed herself off as a lady of some style . . . [and had] a rather disagreeable nature. A woman of the world. She claimed to be related to the noble Galitzin family in Russia" (*EB*, 112).[22] This relationship, dwindling thanks to periods of enforced cohabitation with Bove's mother and brother, vanishes as effectively as Suzanne by 1928, apart from a typically mysterious Bovian *Nachlass*, dated October 21, 1936: "A visit today from Henriette. Her friend, M.R., is dying in Colmar" (*EB*, 310).[23]

If one had to venture a guess, on the basis of very few facts, Henriette (his mother's name! Germanic!) represented a higher station for Bove. Possessing a mistress indicated, in Bove's mind at least, a certain financial independence; it also gave him a public stance as an author (for most writers felt a mistress was necessary), and Henriette's companionship allowed him (as his father had with Emily) to show off someone better placed in society than himself. That it did not last, I divine, may have had something to do with boredom and poverty on his part, and infidelity on hers.

All in all, life between 1925 and the mid-1930s is not unpleasant. He is a published author with a resounding success to his name; he works hard—a succession of books, four and a reprint in a limited, illustrated edition of *Mes amis*, appear in 1927, eight books in 1928, three more in 1929, and, in fact, until 1935 he publishes constantly—and in nice places like Bandol, where the jacketed, waistcoated, bow-tied Bove gives way to the *sportif* who indulges his passion for golf. In 1928, Bove meets his second wife, Louise Ottensooser, from a family of bankers (shades of his father, again!), with whom he amicably shared the remainder of his life, the only shadow being the stillbirth of their only child in London, and in the same year wins the Prix Figuière (50,000 francs, and among his rivals were André Malraux and Pierre Drieu la Rochelle!).

To this fertile and happy period belong some of Bove's most emotionally deprived novels, including *Un père et sa fille* (1928), *La Coalition* (1928), and the present book, *Journal écrit en hiver* (1931). All three are in some way despairing works, thus proving that life and art do not always coincide perfectly in time.

Of the first of these, Max Jacob, the poet, was to write (to Bove, of whom he was a fervent admirer): "*Un père et sa fille* is one of the most beautiful books I know. It could be by any great master: it is yours" (quoted in *EB*, 135). But the critics did not all agree. John Charpentier asked: "Will M. Bove ever escape his nightmare? . . . [This is] a lamentable story. It is about a mediocre man who, realizing that he cannot live up to his ambitions, having been deceived and left by his wife, and abandoned by his daughter, gives in to a complete abjectness."[24] That encapsulates the plot, but does not convey the perverse eroticism that runs through the short novel. It would be fairer to sum up the book as a tale of casting one's affections on the wrong women. Bove, who was able to say that though he had been with many women, he could "not remember one who could be called beautiful," had a double difficulty in dealing with his female characters: first there was his fixation with his mother, and his guilt at having no feeling for her, and second, a deep, underlying misogyny.

Jean-Antoine About is sixty-four, a fleshly, vigorous man become a recluse in a state of advanced self-destruction. The objects of his life are three: his maid, Nathalie; Marthe, the headstrong country girl he had selected to be his wife; and their daughter, Edmonde. The nicety of the argument, which unusually for Bove is told in retrospect, is that it is double-edged: either About is a sonofabitch with whom no woman could possibly live, or all women are simply whores. The maid refuses his attentions ("Fear or weakness made his attempts quite without risk").[25] In marrying him, Marthe knew "that the man she was marrying would appear ridiculous to her, and full of defects which she would seem to ignore . . . This character did not displease About."[26] About's "situation" doesn't change with his daughter: "Her coldness wounded him. She didn't want to fall at his feet. She had no intention of taking pity on her father. Nothing, he thought, not even the most extreme act, could touch her."[27]

About, like many of Bove's antiheroes, is afflicted with accidie and rue: like a number of Gogol's wounded clerks, he is "convinced he was condemned to mediocrity." What is the reader to make of this? That, deprived of love, a man will seek to create it where it cannot flourish? The novel ends with About grappling, still unsuccessfully, with his maid Nathalie.

It is not just that Bove's relicts are ridiculous, but that they are ridiculous in their own eyes. They have no safety net, social or psychological. Take away the props they erect (respectability, the esteem of others, a brief fling at sex or marriage, a job) and they have nothing left. There is in Bove no blood, no sweat, few tears, and much inevitability. His people suffer from a *class* disaster: that of those who have known better things. His *nouveaux-pauvres*, marginals all, are so much flotsam; they drift in a sea whose strong currents and depths somehow—and inexplicably to them—sustain others without effort. Where one might, in the nineteenth century, have expected social anger at such an outrage, Bove's characters are internalized, self-condemning. They live in Incognito, whose capital is Mea Culpa. But even here they are not welcome, for their ills are all the fault of others, of circumstance. Bove's characters do not see themselves clearly. It's as though they didn't speak the local language (they don't understand paying their bills, telling the truth, earning a living).

This *dépaysement* is a major theme in Bove, but seldom as clearly dissected as in *La Coalition*.[28] Paul Léataud, whose *Journal littéraire* faithfully, if unkindly, registers all the shifts in French intellectual life over seven decades, sums this novel up as "the story of a woman come to Paris with her son, still very young, to find him a job. Both of them slide steadily into the worst sort of poverty and downfall, the mother nearly going mad in her hotel room and the son drowning himself. It would occur to no one to write such books." Léautaud thus unconsciously echoes the remark made about Rossini (that his works shouldn't be composed) by noting that these are books one would be well-advised not to read.[29]

Peter Handke hesitated to translate the book into German. As he wrote Cousse, "It would take a lot of courage to translate it. I couldn't write such a book. That [Bove] was able to write such books, so black and so right, is a mystery." Biographically, *La Coalition* is no mystery. As Léon notes, "It is us [my mother and myself] he has set down, at the heart of our lives." This is the obsessive Léon speaking, whose entire world is himself and his mother (Louise and Nicholas in the novel), but in fact the presiding ghost in *La Coalition* is the father, M. Aphtalion. It is he who made social immigrants of his wife and son. It is his dreams, his fecklessness, which paralyze them. It is his "foreignness" which renders them incapable in a real world, one whose language of obligations they do not understand. Seeking to borrow money (yet again!) from his Uncle Charles, young Nicholas, who no longer even thinks of getting a job, is told firmly that life is not a matter of luck: "You have to want, you hear me, young man? But not want just like that, up in the air, but really want something. Take me. When I want something, I can't sleep, I can't eat. No matter what happens, I still want . . . What do you think of that, eh? That would amaze the people in your country." Well, Nicholas's country, like Bove's, happens to be France. But everyone spots how mother and son don't seem to belong where they are. The hotel treats them like "dirty foreigners," Nicholas's girl feels there's something "alien" about him. It is a status that will weigh on Bove, too: the Bobovnikoff status.

Now, despite being successfully launched on a literary career, despite his happy marriage to Louise, disaster is lurking in the wings. It comes in a context that radiates contentment and a certain illusory well-being. Bove's life seems quite normal. Bove's son, Michel (born in 1924, and like Nora from Bove's first marriage, to Suzanne), asked if he would rather stay with his mother or come and live with him, relates that the question was "hardly honest. He talked about horses, golf, a life of ease . . . I felt he was a *grand seigneur*, without realizing he didn't have the money to keep it up."

The question indeed wasn't honest, but it's one that belongs to normal life, and would not be unfamiliar to a child of our own times. Similarly, when we read Louise on their life at the time, it carries no omen of disaster. On the contrary:

> Mornings, he would play golf. The afternoon he worked in the study he had designed. He hated noise, the comings and goings in the house. He built a library with his own hands. It had more than 3,000 books. Rare editions were his pride and joy. At five, after tea, we would go out together. We never went out without our dog, a Brie, and cat, a Persian Chinchilla. We always took a box at the movies, because the dog didn't like staying home alone. (*EB*, 186–87)

The condition of a gentleman of leisure, indeed. Or is this public relations?

Whatever, on September 6, 1936, the couple is forced to leave Compiègne. Bove has had a flu, he hasn't looked after it properly, and now he comes down with pleurisy. As Cousse puts it bluntly, "this respiratory illness marks the beginning of a phsyical and psychological etiolation" (*EB*, 193).

Bove lives by his pen; now he can't work, or only intermittently. Louise's mother dies, as does Bove's own mother (of breast cancer). Now Léon, orphaned, redoubles his demands for money; Louise has to put him off, for they haven't much themselves. The novel written in Compiègne, *Adieu Frombonne*, sells only 1,300 of its run of 3,000; it gets little or no attention. Bove is forty; there are clouds on the horizon; Bove senses the slipping away of his powers. In a notebook, he writes:

I am alone in a hotel room . . . I look back, for now that's the most considerable part of my life . . . Nothing great, nothing noble, nothing worth mentioning. Nothing in life is more tragic than this sort of cut-off against which, as one ages, one approaches. What is provisional becomes doubly definitive. The sort of gesture by which one might free oneself becomes daily more difficult to perform. One makes it anyway, but it weighs, it's embarrassed. (*EB*, 196)

Weakened by a long convalescence, depressed, he jots down what could be a note toward a future novel: "As I reach my middle age, I realize I have nothing, that I've always been wrong, that I've always acted like someone who thinks he's on the right path when in fact I was on the wrong one. Everything breaks up, and that's how I am today. I have no friends, no money, no job." Then, switching to his potential fictional character, he goes on: "He saw everything as black, and odd as it may seem, he felt a certain relief. Having admitted that he had nothing . . . he felt a bitter pleasure in being free" (*EB*, 196–97).

In March 1939, he published a collection of such tales, *La Dernière nuit*. The title story, wrote Edmond Jaloux, is that of a "Bovian man, alone in a run-down hotel room, who tries to measure the insanity of his life." Jaloux goes on to mark what I think to be a central issue in the Bove oeuvre: "He is a writer of the twilight zone, one of the sharpest explorers and analysts of those ill-lit fringes that surround and sometimes obscure the very core of our life. When our times are past . . . his greatness will consist . . . in the way he shed light on these so far ignored intermediary states."[30]

His next novel, *Mémoires d'un homme singulier*, is refused by Gallimard ("It's about Bove's usual hero," the reader reports, "and his usual story"). In the original draft, which differs somewhat, especially in its ending, from the published version,[31]

Bove seems to establish, in the words of his hero, his own balance sheet:

> I no longer want to live this way. I am so disgusted with the life I've led, I want to make a clear break with it. Is the war going to do this for me? . . . If a new war breaks out, this time I'll be a hero or I'll be killed. But there'll be no war. I won't be killed. What shall I do? I'm forty-one . . . I have to risk my life if I want happiness. Unless I write some more books. If I can't tell stories, I at least can tell the truth. Perhaps that's my destiny. (quoted in *EB*, 200)

The war came, as Bove knew it would. He was a Jew, so was his wife, who was also a communist. Mobilized, he is assigned as a "military worker" to a steel mill in the Cher, then as secretary to his local commanding officer; when France is defeated, he demobilizes the local farmers, then himself.

Like a true Bovian character, France becomes a twilight zone. No posturing from Bove. He understands what is going on around him: "If every Frenchman were to examine his heart . . . he would realize the immense relief he felt when the armistice was signed." This is the territory Bove explores in the first of his last two novels, *Le Piège*. Vichy *is* Bove. It's as though all the most marked characteristics of his nature (given the heavily autobiographical nature of most of his writing, that also means all those traits portrayed in his novels—susceptibility, fear of failure, indirection, silence, fantasy, doubts about others, inability to connect, fatalism, ambiguity) had been applied to Vichy and France during the Occupation. With his usual gift for picking the right, defining text, Cousse picks out Bove's essence of Vichy:

> With the crush of people who had invaded the town, with all the difficulties that each of them faced, amongst all those whom one might have known in Paris, but didn't frequent, there was no room for any sort of solidarity. One shook hands, one forced oneself to look as happy on the tenth time one met as on the first; one felt the

sympathy one feels in an immense catastrophe, pretending to believe that misfortune unites rather than divides, but as soon as one stopped talking of the general wretchedness and tried to interest someone is one's own petty problem, it was like running into a wall.[32]

Like his hero, Bridet, Bove was in Vichy (he and Louise were living in Lyon) to find a way out of France. What is wonderful about this most Kafka-like of his novels is Bove's total detachment. Though Bove had refused to allow his novels to be published during the Occupation (and was thus, unlike many French writers, on the "right" side, something which the Gallimard family could not say), Bove maintains his unjudgmental stance: things *are*, and life is hard enough without subjecting human frailty to condemnation. Though the man from whom Bridet sought help, Paul Basson, is a thinly disguised portrait of Jean Giraudoux, not a word of reproach was ever heard from Bove.

Nonetheless, the times were dangerous. Vichy was creating its own anti-Semitic legislation, and the "France and the Jew" exhibition had opened in Paris (December 1940), with Céline sitting, half-smirking, in the back row. Salvation was not a fiction for a Jewish writer who was refusing to publish and whose wife was a vociferous communist. Like a good number of other artists, Bove and Louise first sought refuge in Dieulefit, a Protestant stronghold and a refugee center since the aftermath of the Spanish Civil War, a remote village, charitable and possibly (the question is controversial) "tolerated" by the Vichy government. Whence we have a remarkably accurate picture of Bove and Louise in the last years they shared:

> He went about like a shadow, slightly bent-over. He looked almost-ill. He was sweet, very gentle. Though a handsome man, one hardly noticed him. He was convinced by what he wrote; he wrote for nothing; nobody would ever read him. His wife was an extro-

vert. On the outside, she was what he was inside . . . He wanted to leave no traces of his passage.[33]

From Dieulefit, they moved to Cheylard in the Ardèche to await a way into Spain. By the summer of 1942, the anti-Semitic laws were beginning to press, and a few weeks before the Germans took over southern France, the pair of them undertook the long and hazardous journey out of France, through Spain and into Africa, via Gibraltar—all of which is described in his last novel, *Non-Lieu* (*Charge Dismissed*). Bove carries with him a novel written in the last two years, *Un homme qui savait*, which is a species of summation of the pre-war Bove, his attributes and interests, that secret part of his characters which he alone perceives.

It is the story of Maurice Lesca, a doctor struck off the register, and his sister Emilie, raped by a farmworker on her parents' property. As age creeps up on them, they unite their "poverty, inaction, and even their mutual scorn in the attempt to survive" (*EB*, 210). A brief anthology of Lescaisms will, I think, show how compelling is Bove's analysis of character, his quite certainly morbid, even pathological, study of failure:

> Now I understand why I failed in everything I've ever undertaken. I understand why I'm poor, why I have no friends, no wife, no child . . . I please only those who suffer, those whom life has already eliminated, only in places where nothing happy could ever happen to me.
>
> I was speaking like a reasonable man. But I'm not reasonable. I've never been. You know that. Things have to be left as they are. One must live. One must love. One mustn't dwell on one's wretched mistakes . . . there are times when I become like a real Don Quixote. I can't bear attacks on those I love. And then, day after day, I'm far too much alone . . . I think too much, and I realize I've always been fooled, that all the good I ever wanted to do was ridiculed . . . so I revolt.

Nothing terrible had happened to him, he no longer wanted to think. His face hadn't changed . . . When people asked him something too precise, the middle of his face trembled, as a precision instrument might on a table when someone walked by it . . . He knew nothing. He didn't want to know anything. Why did people ask questions? Couldn't he be left alone?

I am becoming someone else. Suddenly I feel I'm about to be in great pain . . . and I feel nothing at all . . . In my panic I am quite incapable of maintaining my relationship with the few people who feel sympathy for me. I want to do all sorts of things and can do nothing.[34]

This collective *cri de coeur* is pure Bove: the flat, declarative sentences that succeed each other, imperceptibly widening misery with knowledge; the purported neutrality of a camera that knows of no psychology, that never *explains*. This is what The Man Who Knows knows. All Bove's people do is continue to survive. As Bove and his wife must.

Though Bove is by now terminally ill (my view is that this publicly unacknowledged fact is the determinant of his later fiction), Algiers, where he and his wife arrive, a week after the Allied invasion of North Africa, on November 1, 1942, is nonetheless something of a respite for Bove. He rents a room where he can work, and once again we have a memorable portrait of the man: "He walked about with his hands behind his back, bent over, pale as a cave-dweller . . . His voice was muffled, always very calm. His way of speaking, the sobriety of his gestures, impressed me. He often smiled, and he had good eyes, kind eyes."[35]

In October 1944 Bove and Louise (she has to pawn her jewels to pay their passage) finally receive permission to return to Paris. Isolated, his books largely forgotten, his last two novels in limbo, he died (of "heart failure after a series of acute malarial attacks") during the night of July 12–13, the day before the fall of the Bastille. Perhaps in order not to be noticed. His brother Léon has the apartment disinfected, as his mother had done on the death of Bobovnikoff. Why not? Father and son were intimately interconnected; they died at the same age and in the same conditions. For which we have the testimony of Bove's son, Michel: "I got a call saying, 'Your father is dead.' I rushed over. The bathtub was full of dirty dishes. It was terribly hot, and we couldn't open the windows because of the oompah-oompah of the balls for the Fourteenth of July" (*EB*, 238).

III
Journal écrit en hiver, A Brief Exploration

Bove is a writer for true readers. Though he is still startlingly effective with nonliterary readers, of whom there used to be more than there are now, and though his work shares more than a little, in both style and theme, with what used to be known as "shop-girl" literature—that is, stories with recognizable characters written directly and realistically—this novel is far from a quick fix, even for those who have read a good deal of Bove.

In the first place, it is much closer to mainstream French writing. It has overtones from a number of other writers, including especially Paul Morand and Bove's close friend Pierre Bost (another remarkable writer to be rescued from the memory-hole.) Second, it strays from those themes which give Bove such an individual voice. The hero of the *Journal*, Louis Grandeville, lives in a recognizable Bovian nowhere-land, but he at least has a home, a wife, a servant, and a large circle of decently placed friends. Neither he nor anyone else in the novel actually works for a living. We are told he has lost

100,000 francs in a recent transaction; he doesn't bear his broker much malice. Another peculiarity is the lack of specificity as to place and milieu. Normally addresses and districts in Paris mean a lot to Bove—he is as admirable a cartographer or topographer as Léautaud—but this novel smacks of a one-set stage: the home of Louis and Madeleine, with occasional forays to mundane events such as dinners and "at homes." In short, it is a novel of bourgeois manners, with a close relationship to some, though not all, of *Le Beau-Fils*, which follows it three years later.

It is not a book that immediately yields up its treasures. The journal, even of so acutely self-conscious a character as the narrator, lends itself better to analysis and reflection than to narrative action. As is true of most journal-writers. The opening chapter, for instance, shows us a writer in search of his subject. The quasi-anatomical or entomological style does not help the reader get into the narrative, to become interested in its hero and his relations with Madeleine. It is not until the entry for October 20 that we become directly engaged in the novel's subject: whether a "life devoid of any affection, of any goal, a life one fills with a thousand trifles intended to relieve its monotony, populated with human beings one seeks out in order not to be alone and whom one flees to avoid being bored by them, whether such a life isn't ridiculous, whether anything whatsoever wouldn't be preferable."

The implication is to do something *else;* but of course the Bove hero is condemned to be himself, and this fact alone makes the *Journal* one of the most unsparing novels on the self-destructive impulse in all marriages ever written. At the same time—because its subject, jealousy and the harm two human beings can do to each other, is so universal—it is thoroughly accessible to the modern reader. The manner of sexual attachment, of the commerce of marriage, may have changed, but the fact that a stable relationship between two persons of the opposite sex is one of the riskiest of all human transactions is unalterable. The wary reader will simply ask himself, have I behaved like Louis? or ask herself, am I a Madeleine?

Not, of course, that we enter into Madeleine's mind. It is Louis's *image* of Madeleine that affects him. He owns that image as he thinks he owns Madeleine, and one of the many mysteries in this extraordinary novel is that one has no idea how or why they have ever got together to practice their mutual auto-da-fé. An auto-da-fé is two things: the judicial act or sentence of an ecclesiastical court (the Inquisition, or marriage) and the execution of the sentence (burn, baby, burn.)

The reason for Madeleine's sentence is set out in the first entry:

> She accuses me of being jealous, of thinking that the world is wicked, never for a second perceiving the truth in my observations, nor the profound love which is at the heart of my desire that she not be the laughingstock of our friends. She doesn't understand I'm only trying to protect her. Instead, she thinks that I go out of my way to discover faults in her which no one has noticed.

To summarize a Bove novel is always hazardous. In fact, it is very likely (this is one of the many seductive aspects of the *Journal*) that three different readers would come up with three very different definitions of the central subject. The translator has her view, which is judicious and exact:

> Louis is a man obsessed by the nagging reality that he never has and never will amount to anything. The "winter" of the title is in fact a period of four months during which, every few days, Louis commits to paper the minute details of his unhappy marriage. Although his wife, Madeleine, is the focal point of his journal, and his obsession with the minutiae of her life, mind, and body, is dangerously so, his painstakingly rendered analyses of her behavior tell us far more about him than about her. The book's incongruity lies

in the contrast between the unsavory traits Louis reveals about himself and the innocent candor with which he does so—he is a sort of idiot sadist.[36]

In abeyance here are the classical loci of fiction: class, milieu, description. Dialogue is minimal. Instead of a setting, we have cardboard props, a minimalist scenario. In *La Coalition*, we have Mme Aphtalion's beloved objects, which she transports down the hotels of her decline; here we are in the heartbreaking domain of memory:

> There is a certain sadness, when abandoning one home for another, in watching rooms being stripped bare, furniture from different parts of the house assembled haphazardly, an object we hold dear slipped hurriedly, for want of space, into an indifferent trunk. A distressing sense of being out of one's element is born of all the commotion, of the suddenly deserted apartment with the next one yet to be occupied. But when everything is staying behind and we alone are leaving, when our possessions are being gathered from various parts of the house where, once they've been removed, their absence won't be felt, and we sense that as soon as we're far away life will go on without us just as it did in the past, that feeling of sadness is even greater.

How often this happened to Bove! How often the apparently settled turned out to be unsettled, and unsettling! Like Bove, deprived of an ordinary life, Louis recognizes that he is "not a man like other men . . . I seem somewhat backward . . . I'm like a child." As for Madeleine, she is a prisoner of his mind. Louis notes with surprise that when she is angry, she "always starts by pretending not to care about anything other than some vague notion of freedom." The key word here is "pretend," for this is a misunderstanding of Louis's, and it is going to provide him with as much tragedy as his limited life can comprehend. The denouement begins early with the return of Roger: girl (Madeleine) meets old flame (Roger). "I'm certain that when Madeleine saw him again," Louis writes, "it must have dawned on her that she could love him." In Louis's eyes, this is true of every man she meets; the reader will not be slow to discover in the narrator a splendidly obsessive, Othello-like form of jealousy, a jealousy all the more potent for the purported rival being always an invention of Louis—yet something that is doomed to happen. *Tu l'as voulu, Louis!*

If the reader wants to grasp the quintessential flavor of Bove, the basic scaffolding, in all its labyrinthine detail and speculation, on which Bove has constructed the archetypical marital spat, I suggest he look at the entry for December 8. As he will see, it is genuinely insane: in the root meaning of the word, *un*-healthy.

Of what is this scene constructed? It turns on a basket of orchids Louis finds on the mantelpiece. Would they be there if they "compromised" his wife? He both wants and does not want his wife to have been unfaithful. First he wants her to know he's seen the florist's delivery note, then he doesn't. She foils him by coming into the room too quickly, and refuses to say who sent them. Of course, if she were innocent, Louis reflects—though of course she isn't—she wouldn't have dreamed he would ask her who sent the fatal orchids. Perverse as ever, this finding gives Louis a feeling of her "beauty." She is like a child, denying the obvious; she thinks no explanations are needed, for she has done no wrong. On the other hand, she is acting *as if* she'd done wrong. This reinforces Louis's position, for he can now play "the role of the husband who's sure of his facts and finally has proof of his wife's infidelity." When Madeleine finally admits the flowers came from the Count Belange, an anodyne suitor whose seductions are routine, universal, and incessant, this does not appease Louis. All his marriage he has been waiting for this moment: when "the truth burst out into the open." Since she prefers another to him, he says, "Have it your way! You'll be happy, that's all I want."

Having made his putative move, a whole set of contradictory emotions now assail Louis. First, he may regret his decision; he may suffer remorse. Rage overtakes him. "Is that right,
you don't love me?" he says to her. She refuses to answer, and
now he fears his anger is cooling, so he starts packing. Now, it
is Madeleine's turn to cling to him tearfully. Briefly, he relents:
"Madeleine's choking sobs made me realize she was no longer
herself, but a creature in pain"; but her tears "stripped her of
her personality." Nonetheless, he again relents: he's only going
to Versailles for a few days, he'll be back. This makes him realize that "you have to make a start. . . . After that, she'll be much
nicer . . . suddenly . . . I was free; nothing was holding me
back." He is "crushed by her renunciation. . . . She seemed
indifferent to anything I might do." This makes him feel "a
deep disgust with myself," and the scene ends with his kneel-
ing and begging her forgiveness.

All this takes place in a little over a thousand words! The
reader will be aware that the scene is *constructed*, and with great
care. There is crisis, argument, doubt, divided feeling, and
catharsis. Anyone who has been through such a scene will recognize the comings and goings of violent, contradictory, and
often purely artificial emotions. The whole book is a little mas-
terpiece of such paradoxes, and has to be read, listened to, and
seen in the round. One may be irritated with the self-destructive
Louis, as one is with the complacent Madeleine, but without
care, the denouement, the absolutely logical end of this discon-
solate tale, will be missed. It is an experience in mental claustro-
phobia. If you like, it is not so very different from certain Gothic
forebears, such as Wilkie Collins's *Woman in White*.

The reader is invited to see that for all the flatness of his
diction, the absolute nakedness of Bove's language, his deliberate eschewal of "effect," it is *style* that makes this novel work.
The narration, or argument, is itself subjunctive and condi-

tional. Each action depends on a previous life-clause, from some distant, neutral verb. *Journal*, like Bove's other autobiographical novels, is a novel of dependence; Louis's and Madeleine's relations are those of subordination. Read a passage of Homer and you will quickly recognize what has happened, in twenty-six centuries, to the concept of narration and the idea of the hero. Homer offers the intoxication of glue-sniffing; his fix is, what happens next? In Bove, the next defeats the previous. The scene is not Circe's island of swine, but a furnished room; all his voyages take place in a melancholy landscape consisting of table, chair, and bed.

Journal is a pivotal work for Bove. Before, he explored the world with which he was familiar: the suburbs of the human condition. He himself often noted ("How hard it is to come up with a subject!") how he was forced back onto people, onto ordinary human situations, those he could recognize from his own experience. With success—not unlike his three literary gods, Dickens, Balzac, and Dostoevsky—he sought to expand his repertory, to widen the scope of his vision. *Journal* and *Le Beau-Fils* are exceptions. Bove cannot escape his fate. He returns to his sources: to his own life and condition. This novel states the Bovian dilemma perfectly: "I rage; I have a soul; but I am ineffective. Indeed, I do not exist; you would have to turn me inside out for me to come into being."

IV
How Important Is Bove?

It certainly is not a matter of ranking, for Bove is very much *sui generis*. Like all good writers, he carved out a niche that is all his own. He is original not in language but in perception. A species of reductionism operates in Bove that makes his books particularly redolent of his period—what one might call the aftermath of capitalism in the volatile, would-be parliamentary nations of Europe.

As our century will, I am convinced, come to be seen as the century not, as America proclaims, of democracy, but of fascisms, Bove's novels, like those of many of his equally unread contemporaries from between the wars (and not just in France),[37] will come to be seen as fundamental to an understanding of the twentieth century. This may be a large claim, but I think that the very fact that Bove, the writer, was *not* consciously dealing with political and social matters makes him a more perfect, if latent, mirror of that period in which fascism most prospered.

It may be difficult for the modern, especially the modern American, reader to get into the psychopathology of a period in which fascism was defined, but Bove offers a perception that no other writer does, for his characters are the very people for whom fascism was created, and their milieu—the marginal, the fearful, the indecisive, the new pre-proletariat of a middle class about to lose its respectability—is that from which fascism recruited. Had Bove's people any political vitality, were they truly on the middle-class ladder of rising and falling, they would have welcomed it, for fascism provided action to counteract their inertia; it understood their grievances; it would have subsumed them into something larger than themselves. Their failure to grasp this, to move either right or left, is Bove's legacy, and I find it truer than that offered by countless "political" writers with causes: whether of the left or right.

The very stasis, the immobility, of the Bovian world expresses those preconditions from which fascism—all movement, all rhetoric, all vectors and teleology—derives. In this he reminds me powerfully of another contemporary, Theodore

Dreiser, whose *American Tragedy* (which again few now read) is the ultimate expression of a failure to cope.

In the context of the French novel—which can hardly be said to have neglected social issues—Bove occupies a curious place. Where Balzac, Maupassant, and Zola (not to mention Bloy) saw a "class" poverty, a relentless Darwinian war of selection and destruction, Bove sees the struggle for existence as mental and internal, and by so doing left out of "his" France almost all its major external markers: for instance, the great gulf between rural and urban poverty, or the exploitation of the industrial proletariat. After all, those who worked machines were poor in a way that none was poor who handled a tool of his own making, and industrial workers were as invisible to Bove as they had been flagrant instances of abuse to writers before him. It is as though Bove had no sense of social injustice—so evident in Céline with his lacemaker mother, steamed noodles every meal (they were the only food one could cook over the shop that didn't spread its smell to the lace of the rich), and his surly remarks about *Das Kapital*—only of the forfeitures of justice inherent in the families of the deprived and the marginal.

Or consider how different Bove is from the Anglo-Saxon literature of the interwar years. No fizz. France has been bled. The chief (acknowledged) French literature of Bove's period is either severely classical (Gide, Giono, Mauriac) or nostalgic (Proust, Martin du Gard). To be sure there are jokers (Allais, Queneau starting out), but on the whole they are a sober lot. The sensibility of the period also runs *contra*. Consider only Carné's *Hotel du Nord*. Bove is *film noir* without murder or suspense.

It is curious that a Jew, a Russian Jew at that, should have been so sensitive to the (unstated) political climate of the

Crash and the Depression of the 1930s, have understood his raw material so well, yet never stated it in political terms. Like Alfred Döblin in Germany, Bove is the recorder of a petty bourgeoisie in disintegration. The portrait is all the more convincing for not being dressed up in ideological clothing. But then Bove lacks any form of redeeming spirituality; he is a secularized and would-be assimilated Jew, for whom, as for so many of his kind, there was nothing beyond the disasters of the day.

His is the chronicle of appearances that cannot be kept up; of the importunate, the whiners, of those who they think deserved (and had been born to—hence his adoration of his stepmother) a better fate. His is the poverty of accidie, a note totally alien to the class struggle represented by the mainstream of French social fiction. A Bove hero (or antihero, for one can see why Beckett admired him) does not make even a gesture of protest against the rock that is rolling down on him. It strikes a new note because it is so all-embracing, so mechanical, so intricately linked, fetter by fetter, so logical, so merited, that it comes to seem a perfectly apt description of the human condition: one to which God had originally offered some consolation. Nor is there in him the relief of even a single pleasure. Neither religion, nor talent, not art, nor sex comes to relieve that poverty of spirit.

This neutrality, I think, leads the reader into difficult, infrequently accessed parts of mass psychology; Bove's very refusals engender a near-hypnotic state. While fascism (and communism) extolled a romanticized Nature, alp and forest, and the power of a new technology and speed, with the exception of its train journeys Bove's is a world without movement, landscape, or even season. So stripped down is his oeuvre to the city (particularly its fringes) that such elements of ordinary life as storms, leaves falling, spring and hope, extremes of heat and cold, are foresworn as though they were just cheap effects. His is not a painter's eye—color is rare—but a photographer's: that of a photographer when Bove was young, who recorded shop windows, midinettes, surgical appliances, or the defiant expressions of the insane with equal objectivity, as though all aspects of the real world were equivalent. This is a truly modern sensibility, and utterly secular, for God, who sustained Dostoevsky, plays no part whatever (again, rare in a Jew) in Bove's world, where He has long been dead.

Had he been a painter, Bove would have created still lifes with the realism of an urban Courbet: because they were *there* to be seen and depicted. Reading him, I am reminded of the painter Felix Valloton, whose mournful, gray interiors depict a Bovian world. His own life, Valloton once said, had been "extremely solitary and disenchanted" and this "no doubt explains the acerbity and lack of joy in my painting."[38]

The writer with whom he has most in common, and with whom he is most often connected (not just because both were Jewish writers) is Proust. Bove is the Proust of the other end of the bourgeosie. But unresolved, one might say, lacking in general conclusions, occluded by his characters' own confusions, their lack of precise self-definition, their acceptance of their miserable fates. Proustian in the insistence on motivation, the why of behavior, but without the satisfactions of Proust's useful aperçus, the fixative of Proust's mind. But isn't that precisely the satisfaction Bove offers? Is he not in tune with the new post-psychological era, in which what counts is presentation, the "whole" image minus explanation: the "image" offered by film, television, advertising, photography, pop culture in general, which exclude the inner minds of its men and women?

In psychotherapeutic terms, Bove's characters "present." They offer the reader a version of themselves, complete with an explanation. They come bubbling to the couch, saying, "Listen, Doc, it's all the fault of my mother." But it's child's play for the reader-shrink to see that Bove's whole oeuvre is socially and class-determined, that there are explanations for their condition that they do not see and that Bove declines to define. Bove is the very opposite of "J'accuse!" Nor is there a trace of "Je m'accuse!" Instead, there is an integrity, a consistency, and a hermetic self-containedness to Bove's world that is fairly unique, at least in French literature. One understands the lament of the critic saying (of *Adieu Frombonne*) that it's just another Bove story, another slice of a world definably "Bovian." There is such a world because Bove has a remarkable sense of the collective unconscious of his class and period. When Maxime, in *Un soir chez Blutel* (that "novel of inaction"), returns from Vienna with eight people in his third-class compartment, this is how they react to their arrival:

> All these people with—as with roads on an isthmus—their briefly common destinies, all of them thinking they had done well to choose this particular compartment, for otherwise they would not have had these particular traveling companions, simultaneously understood they were about to arrive.

It is an unconscious, unthinking process. Because they are alike, a temporary lumpen proletariat, they arrive at the same conclusions.

Reading Bove is like watching something happen that is by nature inexplicable, and no explanation beyond the personal is proffered. To offer a reason why these people should be as they are would be a betrayal. This *refus* is of the most striking elements in Bove. Cousse calls it a form of auto-destruction, and I think he's right. It comes down to this: that there is no paraphrasing Bove. That is, you can explain the externals (to the degree that Bove offers them) of his characters, but not why they are as they are. The auto-destructiveness comes in the way all the intermediary "explanations" of the traditional novel are simply suppressed. This "making it impossible" to describe the novel in anything but its own terms strikes me as ultra-modern, very much part of our sensibility.

Characteristically, it shows up in Bove's peculiar obliteration of Jews. I cannot recall a passage in which Bove so much as mentions Jewish matters. It is not even a subtext. One may assume the "Jewishness" of an Apthalion, but it is never made explicit. Was this deliberate or unconscious? It might well be that Bove, as part of his denial, his self-suppression ("That is not me! That is not my real mother!") never thought of himself as a brief generation away from the Kiev ghetto. Both he and Proust understood social dynamics in another fashion: as rise and fall. Both are tempted by their own versions of the beau monde: Proust by aristos, Bove by *his* aristocrats—anyone with more than a sufficiency of money.

The refusals are constant. For instance, one of the ways in which writers interest us is by their domain, what they explore. Given something so drab as poverty (which is not merely financial, but poverty of ideas, poverty of language and feeling), the writer (e.g., Dickens) may seek to redeem poverty by a heightened style, a hyperbole of language. Bove's abdication here is even more remarkable. "There are," he seems to be saying, "*no* devices or artifices by means of which we may escape our condition; *I'm* certainly not going to provide any."

Rank (is Bove better, less good than X or Y?) is simply not a question; he is *hors concours*, he never went to the starting line. The man who wrote *Brecon* is simply the medium by which we become aware of this intolerable suburb—the physical existence of these so *other* people, those who are indeed as invisible as a suburb seen from a train.

To say that a writer is simply a medium is not to deny the artistry of the communication. Every sentence can be written in another way. Perhaps we should not forget that Bove is half-Russian. The Russia to which Bove speaks is not that detached, liberal Russia, subtle and painful, of Chekhov; it isn't the lofty, peasant wisdom of Tolstoy; and least of all is it the visionary Russia of Leskov and Gogol. The Dostoevsky in Bove is not that of *The Brothers Karamazov*, but of the early realist, the gambler, the man barely reprieved from death, the Dostoevsky who would have understood Bobovnikoff *père*. He shares with Dostoevsky that renunciation of a language appropriate to the condition of his characters. Bove's capacity was not such as to bring him to invent a twentieth-century version of *Oblomov-shschina*, but as Léautaud pointed out, there is in some people a force of inertia.[39] In the physical universe inertia is as much a force as energy, the two existing in a delicate balance; without inertia, we would have no need for energy. That may be why, raising these two forces to virtue and vice, the medieval church considered accidie—principally despair of salvation—chiefest of the mortal sins.

There is, in *Blutel*, a remarkable piece of Bovian analysis which I think brings all this out. Here is Maxime on himelf and his father:

> His memories were ageless. Some from his infancy were clearer than those from his youth. To work out how he was at seven or fourteen he had to find a starting point in the apartments his family had occupied. He knew their order and how many years had been spent in each . . . He barely remembered his parents, though they did not die until he was a young man . . . He had never found anyone who

could describe his childhood gestures. No one who had known him then had survived. His name and photograph would have had to appear in the newspaper for the last members of his dispersed family to have written him a letter. And even then, he would have had to receive the letters, doubtless sent to various prefectures in the hope of finding him.[40]

This prompts Maxime into precisely the sort of apparently normal, but in fact internally distorted, "explanation" to which I have been referring:

> His father sometimes came into his room to beg him to work. Maxime already had a confused sense that his father had suffered, that his life had been difficult. Though unconscious, Maxime's wish was also to suffer, to live to become a man. He said to himself, "I want to grow up by my own means" . . . He believed in just one thing: to create himself. When added to his laziness, this ambition led him to abandon his studies—they were so dry alongside the sufferings he was ready to endure. And when, later, circumstances forced him to live in third-rate hotels, it always seemed to him that the misery he could see about him was small beer compared to that which he had imagined. The closer he got to it, the lesser it seemed. He wanted to enter the suffering of the world. But each time it disappointed him. He thought it would be deeper . . . Having arrived in Paris at the age of fourteen and penniless, his only thought was to become a scholar. Alone and without the slightest help from anyone, he shut himself up in a room in the Latin Quarter with dictionaries, books as incomprehensible as those used in more advanced classes, and nourishing himself on bread and butter, tried to learn everything by heart . . . But he had a joker's heart which prevented his succeeding. Everything he tried failed. It was then, discouraged, that he separated from his first wife, remarried, and left Paris. All the things he hadn't been able to do, he wanted his son to do . . . Left out of his calculations was the fact that his son admired him, and that he too wanted to suffer.

As Cousse says, "Bove spent his life seeking a doubly impossible integration. On the one hand, the literary milieu of his time was powerfully anchored to the bourgeosie. To be admitted, one must belong to it or be godfathered into it . . .

But while Bove is being refused integration, such an integration would also be unacceptable to him; it would imply a denial of himself. [His whole career] is a double contradiction: the desire to be recognized and his inability to create the conditions necessary for such recognition."[41]

The internally *dépaysé*, the "un-countried," the internal exiles, have their particular problems with language, which was not made for their particular situations, their lack of status. The strategy adopted by most "alien" writers (whether foreigners or internal exiles) is either by the creation of a separate language, one particular to them, or, as with Dostoevsky or Simenon, by refusing language altogether, by neutralizing its inventiveness, its allusions, its "idea" content. Bove was not especially attuned to a language at which he did not excel at school; hence the embarrassing "incorrections" of Bove's style noted by some French critics. Bove's characters speak the generic language of their generic milieu; it is barely specific to character and it does not change according to condition or class. To this sort of quotidian language, French is ideally adapted: by minimizing its difficulties, avoiding them, one arrives at the flat language of description—prose in its very essence. Human society and human feelings thus take on mechanical properties: like the very workings of capitalism.

What is dull and gray in him is deliberate, conscious, a property of the times, of what Cousse once called "the constitutional infirmity . . of a society of war widows and orphans," of "poverty, unemployment, financial indelicacies, all the stigmata of a society in crisis." When Joubert calls ignorance *"un lien entre les hommes,"*[42] he might have been describing the intense commonality of Bove's multiple versions of himself and his immigrated-emigrated family.

This rootlessness arises in Bove's narration and plotting.

Much in Bove's skeletal plots is a bedroom farce inverted. People hop in and out of situations as they would onstage through doors and cupboards. The difference is that there is exhilaration, satisfaction, catharsis (of a comic sort) in farce; the viewer (reader) knows there is a resolution coming. The Bovian farce centers on what the reader knows will not happen. Nothing is going to work out. The doors, the cupboards, and the beds (the beds above all) are going to remain just that—doors, cupboards, and beds. They are not devices, they are the whole world.

At the same time there is in him an acute sense of injustice, a deep sensibility to slight, an identification with the humble and despised. In exile, there is always the possibility that it is not simply temporary, but that it is permanent, that it is forever. Bove's family, his nature, his marriages, his life belong to that sort of exile. He and they are *unspeakably* poor and respectable and deprived. This is, I believe, a new note in literature. In Zola as in Dickens, the poor struggle; they are picturesque in their misery, in their self-exaggeration. Bove might be writing about a duchess and the result would be identically neutral. But duchesses have many writers to speak for them (Balzac was as charmed by them as Proust), where the new-found land of the poor has no spokesman. The poor neither read nor write, and certainly they do not listen.

How very difficult it was for Bove, with no handle of any sort on the Christian tradition, to deal with this subject except in exactly the way he did: as a phenomenon observed and worthy of description! This is not merely un-Christian (God transfigures the poor, as in Bloy or Bernanos), it is also un-Jewish (for charity is there for the Chosen.) I think Bove is the most profoundly *secular* writer I know. There is nothing before his characters (no genealogy, no historicity) and nothing after.

Indeed, there is nothing outside. Nothing transcends, and this, I believe, is the source of his importance to us; it makes him our contemporary.

Léautaud quotes Stendhal talking to Mérimée who, already an old man, but still believing in a future, continued to lay foundations for his work to come. "What's the point of continuing to take aim?" Stendhal asks. "You're on a battlefield, you have to fire."[43] Well, Stendhal was an optimist. Bove belongs to those artists for whom silence, even in words, was a deliberate choice. His books will reproduce *"les conditions d'échec de son père, que, seule une disparition prématurée soustrait à la dépréciation inévitable, propre à tout les personnages de Bove."*[44] That is, they reproduce everything that stymied his father; only a premature death could subtract him from the inevitable depreciation which is the fate of all Bove's characters. His bathtub will always have been full of dirty dishes. While the July 14 balls, and the firing, go on elsewhere, in the last of his many, temporary, ill-furnished rooms, he'll have done what he's done all along, coughed his life out.

Keith Botsford

Notes

1. *Le Figaro*, 10 November 1928, quoted in Raymond Cousse and Jean-Luc Bitton, *Emmanuel Bove, La vie comme une ombre* (Bordeaux: Le Castor Austral, 1994), 51; hereafter abbreviated *EB* and cited parenthetically in the text. Short unattributed quotes in this afterword appear in *EB* as well.

2. Sorry, one. Thomas Laux, *Kompensation und Theatralik: Eine Studie su Emmanuel Boves frühen Romanen (1924–1928)* (Frankfurt and New York: P. Lang, 1989).

3. This is a detective novel published in Boston in the early 1930s.

4. Cousse first published a brief pamphlet, *Emmanuel Bove* (Paris: Flammarion, 1983), and his major biography was completed by Jean-Luc Bitton, another cinematographer. This book, besides being unique and a labor of love, is invaluable in countless ways, not least for the patient tenacity with which many obscure details of Bove's life have been tracked down and recorded. I, no less than anyone reading Bove or working on him, could not have done without it. As translations of Bove's novels succeed one another, this biography will no doubt someday appear in English.

5. *Emmanuel Bove, ou l'Absolu dans le dérisoire* (Emmanuel Bove, or the Absolute in the derisory). I have been unable to locate this book.

6. I missed Jane Kramer in the *New Yorker*, 20 May 1985.

7. A pair of examples will have to suffice: "This is what happens when one is not ready to die, and death takes us by surprise"; "The expression in his eyes was that of a father whose child has just committed a crime."

8. See the Spring 1992 issue of *Bostonia*. Other Bove translations include, in order of publication: *My Friends* (*Mes amis*), trans. Janet Louth (London: Carcanet, 1986); *Armand*, trans. Janet Louth (London: Carcanet, 1987); *Quicksand* (*Le Piège*), trans. Dominic Di Bernardi (Marlboro, Vt.: The Marlboro Press, 1991); *Memoirs of a Singular Man* (*Mémoires d'un homme singulier*), trans. Dominic Di Bernardi (Marlboro, Vt.: The Marlboro Press, 1993); *The Stepson* (*Le Beau-Fils*), trans. Nathalie Favre-Gilly (Marlboro, Vt.: The Marlboro Press, 1994).

Two more novels, *Départ dans la nuit* and *Non-Lieu*, are to appear under the Marlboro Press imprint from the Northwestern University Press.

9. It is this journey, I believe, that is celebrated in Bove's usual underemphatic way in *Afthalion Alexandre*. However, in Bove, all journeys, especially the most banal train journeys, play a major role; they mark the rare, genuine displacements in Bove. They have fixed starts and arrival times; they offer a chance, through their windows, to glimpse the lives of others. Only in the two novels written at the end of his life does movement take on some urgency; from Vichy to Algiers via Spain is a matter of survival; so are the hallucinatory scenes in *Départ dans la nuit*.

10. Cousse (*EB*, 24) explains a more specific use of the word *Prusco:* "Prussian vagabonds who went from village to village begging and were taunted thus:

> *De Ache fol fle*
> *De Bockel fol leiss*
> *Knachtig Preiss."*

Or: Arse thick with fleas / Back scratchy with lice / filthy Prussians. Needless to say, it is the poverty of Bobovnikoff *père* that is being thrown at him.

11. *Monsieur Thorpe*, (Paris: Le Castor Austral, 1988), 22.

12. *Synapse* (March 1993).

13. *Monsieur Thorpe*, 21.

14. Preface to *Monsieur Thorpe*, 12. *Monsieur Thorpe* is a great favorite among true Bove admirers. *Mes amis* is where most readers, including, for chronological reasons, his first readers, start, but *Monsieur Thorpe* and *Le Beau-Fils* are where Bovians, fascinated with his life, so inextricably mixed with his fiction, search for clues as to his true nature. It has to be remembered that until the Cousse-Bitton biography, next to nothing was known about Bove.

15. *Un soir chez Blutel*, (Paris: Flammarion, 1927), 61–63.

16. One exception is noted in *EB*, 109, but it is more a portrait of the writer (Maurice Bertz) than a piece of literary criticism.

17. In an interview (in *Candide*, 9 February 1928) he acknowledges Dickens, Balzac, and Dostoevsky as his masters ("These men are not *littérateurs*. They are men who write. Life is not literary.").

18. Jaloux is to further Bove's career when, a few months later, he is appointed literary editor at Émile-Paul Frères.

19. The last in *Regards*, 13 August 1936; the first two in *Le Journal*,

31 August 1935 and 2 September 1935, respectively. Not the least reason for gratitude to Cousse and Bitton is a reasonably complete bibliography.

20. In the *Nouvelle Revue Française*, 1 December, 1928.

21. "Est-ce un mensonge," reprinted together with six other short stories in *Henri Duchemin et ses ombres* (Paris: Flammarion, 1983), 232–33.

22. To be noted here is another similarity between Bove and Céline: what one might call the "German connection." Both have their Austrian periods; both cross over the racial barriers, Bove among the Gentiles, Céline among a series of Jewish mistresses.

23. This is the only published version of a "journal" Bove kept intermittently between 1936 and 1939. Bove's papers are to be found at the Institut Mémoires de l'Édition Contemporaine, 25 rue de Lille, Paris 75007.

24. *Mercure de France*, 15 November 1928.

25. *Un père et sa fille* (Paris: Au Sans Pareil, 1928), 171.

26. Ibid., 165.

27. Ibid., 209.

28. This is also the title of a separate short story. Bove was finicky about his (deadpan) titles. *La Coalition*, the novel, became (in a 1934 edition) *Histoire d'un suicide*. The story, first published in 1928, is reprinted in 1991 as *Aftalion Alexandre*. The story is an *Ur-Coalition*, and despite Le Dilettante's publisher's note disclaiming any relationship between the two works, written within a few years of each other, it offers an almost unique opportunity to study Bove's technique in the construction of a novel. It is also revealing for its use of the theme of immigration, of the displaced person (Bobovnikoff senior) in Paris.

29. Paul Léautaud, *Journal littéraire*, 24 January and 17 February 1928 (Paris: Mercure de France, 1986), 1:2158, 2186. Otherwise, Léautaud's judgment, debating against Yves Gandon, a convinced admirer, is wholly negative: "It is a novel entirely without originality or personality. It is work well done, that's all." While this is true, and while *La Coalition* is, as Léautaud says, "an invention," the suppression of "originality" and writerly "personality" is, in Bove, entirely deliberate, part of the world as Fact.

30. *Les nouvelles littéraires*, 20 March 1939, quoted in *EB*, 197.

31. Published by Calmann-Lévy in 1987.

32. *Le Piège* (*The Trap*) (Paris: Gallimard, 1991), 7. This novel, pub-

lished almost posthumously by Pierre Trémois in April 1945, met with total neglect and indifference. Understandably. Bove's main character is an antihero in a country looking for men who behaved honorably; the Sartre-Camus-Aragon axis wields all power; no one wished to be reminded of the recent past—so much so that it took over forty years for the beginning of a reevalutaion of the Occupation to take place in France. *Le Piège* appears, translated by Dominic di Bernardi, under the title *Quicksand*, in the Marlboro Press edition of 1991. As with all the translations in this afterword—except for those from *The Stepson* and *A Winter's Journal*—I am responsible for the English.

33. Simone Monnier, quoted in *EB*, 210.

34. *Un homme qui savait* (Paris: La Table Ronde, 1985), 24, 50, 74, 102.

35. Emmanuel Roblès, quoted in *EB*, 215.

36. Personal communication from Nathalie Favre-Gilly.

37. The neglected writers come, not coincidentally, from the "right" and fell into disfavor with a critical world largely oriented—after the distresses inflicted by fascism—to the left. Few of them were active "collaborators"; indeed, most were neutral and apolitical. It remains that by, say, preferring Pavese to Fenoglio or Bassani to Arturo Loria or Sartre to Morand, our picture is distorted.

38. Quoted in the *TLS*, 9 October 1992, 27.

39. Léautaud, *Journal littéraire*, 1:1281.

40. *Un soir chez Blutel*, 119ff.

41. Cousse, introduction to *Un soir chez Blutel*.

42. Cited in the *TLS*, 12 June 1992.

43. Léautaud, *Journal littéraire*, 1:1276.

44. This epitaph I noted in a margin. Alas, without a reference.